Say You Love Me

Johanna

Lindsey

G.K. Hall & Co.
Thorndike, Maine

Published in 1997 by arrangement with William Morrow & Co., Inc.

G.K. Hall Large Print Core Collection.

The text of this Large Print edition is unabridged.
Other aspects of the book may vary from the original edition.

Set in 16 pt. Bookman Old Style by Al Chase.

Printed in the United States on permanent paper.

Library of Congress Cataloging in Publication Data

Lindsey, Johanna.
    Say you love me / by Johanna Lindsey.
       p.   cm.
    ISBN 0-7838-1928-5 (lg. print : hc)
    ISBN 0-7838-1927-7 (lg. print : sc)
    1. Large type books. I. Title.
  [PS3562.I5123S3 1997]
  813'.54—dc20   96-42002

Say You Love Me

Say You Love Me

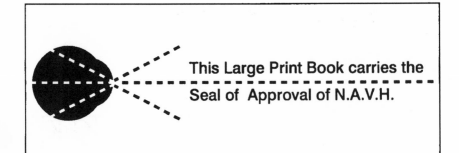

This Large Print Book carries the
Seal of Approval of N.A.V.H.

1

It wasn't such a bad place, this place that was going to witness her sale to the highest bidder. It was clean. Its decor was quite elegant. The parlor she had first been shown to could have belonged in the home of any one of her family's friends. It was an expensive house in one of the better sections of London. It was politely referred to as a House of Eros. It was a place of sin.

Kelsey Langton still couldn't believe that she was there. Ever since she had walked in the door she had been sick to her stomach with fear and dread. Yet she had come here willingly. No one had carried her inside kicking and screaming.

What was so incredible was she hadn't been forced to come here, she had agreed to — at least she had agreed that it was the only option available. Her family needed money — and a lot of it — to keep them from being thrown into the streets.

If only there had been more time to make plans. Even marriage to someone she didn't know would have been preferable. But her Uncle Elliott was likely right. He had pointed out that no gentleman with the wherewithal to help would consider marriage in a matter of days, even if a special license could be obtained. Marriage was simply too permanent to be jumped into without careful consideration.

But this . . . well, gentlemen *did* frequently acquire new mistresses on the spur of the moment, knowing full well that those mistresses would be every bit as costly as a wife, if not more so. The great difference was that a mistress, though easy to acquire, could also be easily disposed of, without the lengthy legalities and subsequent scandal.

She was to be someone's mistress. Not a wife. Not that Kelsey knew any gentlemen personally she could have married, at least none who could afford to settle Uncle Elliott's debts. She had had several young beaux courting her in Kettering, where she had grown up, before The Tragedy, but the only one with a large income had married some distant cousin.

Everything had happened so swiftly. Last night she came down to the kitchen as she did each night before retiring, to heat a bit of milk to help her sleep. Sleep was something she'd had difficulty with ever since she and her sister Jean had come to live with their Aunt Elizabeth.

Her insomnia had nothing to do with living in a new house and town, nor with Aunt Elizabeth. Her aunt was a dear woman, their mother's only sister, and she loved both her nieces as if they were her own daughters, had welcomed them with open arms and all the sympathy they had desperately needed after The Tragedy. No, it was the nightmares that disturbed Kelsey's sleep, and the vivid recollections, and the ever-recurring thought that she could have prevented The Tragedy.

Aunt Elizabeth had suggested the warm milk all those months ago when she had finally noticed the dark smudges beneath Kelsey's gray eyes and had gently prodded for the reason. And the milk did help — most nights. It had become a nightly ritual, and she usually disturbed no one, the kitchen being empty that time of night. Except last night . . .

Last night, Uncle Elliott had been there, sitting at one of the worktables, not with a late repast before him, but a single, rather large bottle of strong spirits. Kelsey had never seen him drink more than the one glass of wine Aunt Elizabeth allowed with dinner.

Elizabeth frowned on drinking, and so naturally didn't keep strong spirits in her house. But wherever Elliott had obtained that bottle, he was more than halfway finished. And the effect it had had on him was quite appalling. He was crying. Quiet, silent sobs, with his head in his raised hands, tears dripping down onto the table, and his shoulders shaking pitifully. Kelsey had thought it was no wonder Elizabeth didn't want strong drink in her house. . . .

But it wasn't the drink that was causing Elliott such distress, as she was to discover. No, he'd been sitting there, with his back to the door, assuming he wouldn't be disturbed while he contemplated killing himself.

Kelsey had wondered several times since if he would have had the courage to actually go through with it if she had quietly left. He'd never struck her as being an overly brave man, just a gregarious, usually jovial one. And it was her presence, after all, that had presented him with a solution to his troubles, one that he might not have considered otherwise, one that *she* certainly would never have thought of.

And all she'd done was ask him, "Uncle Elliott, what's wrong?"

He'd swung around to see her standing behind him in her high-necked nightgown and robe, carrying the lamp she always brought downstairs with her. For a moment he'd appeared shocked. But then his head had dropped back into his hands and he'd mumbled something she couldn't quite make out, so she'd had to ask him to repeat himself.

He'd raised his head enough to say, "Go

10

away, Kelsey, you shouldn't see me like this."

"It's all right, really," she'd told him gently. "But perhaps I should fetch Aunt Elizabeth?"

"No!" had come out with enough force to make her start, then more calmly, if still quite agitated, he added, "She doesn't approve of my drinking . . . and . . . and she doesn't know."

"Doesn't know that you drink?"

He didn't answer immediately, but she had already assumed that was what he meant. The family had always known that he would go to extremes to keep Elizabeth from unpleasantness, apparently even those of his own making.

Elliott was a large man with blunt features and hair that had gone mostly gray now that he was approaching fifty. He'd never been very handsome, even when he was younger, but Elizabeth, the prettier of the two sisters, and still beautiful today at forty-two, had married him anyway. As far as Kelsey knew she loved him still.

They'd never had any children of their own in the twenty-four years of their marriage, and that was possibly why Elizabeth loved her nieces so dearly. Mama had mentioned once to Father that it was through no fault of their not trying, that it simply was not meant to be.

Of course, Kelsey shouldn't have heard that. Mama hadn't realized that she had been within earshot at the time. And Kelsey had overheard other things over the years, of how confounded Mama was as to *why* Elizabeth had married Elliott, who was frankly homely and had had no money to speak of, when she'd had so many other handsome, wealthy suitors to choose from instead. And besides, Elliott was in trade.

But that was Elizabeth's business, and the fact that she'd always been a champion of the less fortunate might have had a great deal to do with her choice — or not. Mama had also been known to say that there was no accounting for love and its strange workings, that it wasn't, nor ever would be, governed by logic or even one's own will.

"Doesn't know that we're ruined."

Kelsey blinked, so much time had passed since she had asked her question. And that wasn't the answer she'd anticipated. In fact, she could barely give it credit. His drinking could hardly be cause for social ruin, when so many gentlemen — and ladies, for that matter — drank to excess at the many gatherings they frequented. So she'd decided to humor him.

"So you've created a bit of a scandal, have you?" Kelsey had chided.

"A scandal?" He'd seemed confused then. "Oh, yes, it will be, indeed it will. And

Elizabeth will never forgive me when they take this house away."

Kelsey had gasped, but once again, she'd drawn the wrong conclusion. "You've gambled it away?"

"Now, why would I do a fool thing like that? Think I want to end up like your father? Or perhaps I should have. At least then there would have been a slim chance for salvation, when now there is none."

She'd been utterly confused herself by that point, not to mention thoroughly embarrassed. Her father's past sins, with the accompanying reminder of what those sins had wrought, shamed her.

So with high color in her cheeks that he probably didn't notice, she'd said, "I don't understand, Uncle Elliott. Who, then, is going to take this house away? And why?"

He'd dropped his head back onto his hands again, unable to face her in his shame, and mumbled out the story. She'd had to lean close to catch most of what he was saying, suffering the fumes of sour whiskey to do so. And by the time he'd finished she'd been shocked into silence.

It was much, much worse than she'd thought, and it really was so reminiscent of her own parents' tragedy, though they'd handled the situation quite differently. But in Elliott's case, he hadn't had the strength of character to accept a failure, buckle up, and go on from there.

When Kelsey and Jean had come to live with Aunt Elizabeth eight months before, Kelsey had been too much in mourning over the deaths of her parents to notice anything amiss. She hadn't even thought to wonder why Uncle Elliott was home more often than not.

She supposed it wasn't something they thought it necessary to tell their nieces, that Elliott had lost his job of twenty-two years and was so distraught that he hadn't been able to hold another position for very long since. And yet they had continued to live as if nothing had changed. They'd even taken in two more mouths to feed when they could hardly afford to feed themselves.

Kelsey wondered if Aunt Elizabeth even knew the extent of their debt. Elliott had been living on credit, which was a standard practice for the gentry, but it was also standard to pay those creditors before they took matters to the courts. But with no money coming in, Elliott had already borrowed all he could from his friends to keep the creditors at bay. He had no one left to turn to. And the situation was out of control.

He was going to lose Aunt Elizabeth's house, the house that had been in Kelsey's family for generations. Aunt Elizabeth had inherited it, being the older sister. And the creditors were threatening to take it away. In three days' time.

And that was why Elliott was drinking himself sick, hoping to find some courage in that bottle to end his own life, because he didn't have the courage to face what was going to happen in the next few days. It was his duty to provide for them — for his wife, anyway — and he'd failed miserably.

Of course, killing himself wasn't an option. She'd pointed out how much worse it would be for Elizabeth if she had to face eviction and a funeral as well. For Kelsey and Jean, well, they'd already faced one eviction. Yet they'd had somewhere to go that time. This time . . . Kelsey simply couldn't let it happen. Her sister was *her* responsibility now. It was up to her to see to it that Jean was raised properly, with a proper roof over her head. And if that meant that she had to . . .

She wasn't quite sure how it had come up, the selling of her. Elliott had first mentioned that he'd already thought of marrying her to the best offer, but he'd put off broaching the subject with her for so long that now it was too late for that, and he'd explained why it was too late, the need for serious deliberation for something that important that couldn't be done in just a few days.

Perhaps it was the drink that had loosened his tongue, but he'd gone on to relate how the same thing had happened to a friend of his many years ago, how he'd lost everything, but his daughter had saved the family by selling herself to an old reprobate who prized virginity and had been willing to pay extremely well for it.

Then, in almost the same breath, he told of approaching one gentleman he knew fairly well to find out if he'd be interested in a young wife. The reply had been, "Won't marry the gel, but I'm in need of a new mistress. Pay you a few pounds if she'd be willing . . ."

Which was how the talk of mistresses in relation to wives had arisen, how some rich lords would pay very handsomely for a fresh young mistress they could show off to their friends, especially a girl who hadn't already made the rounds of those friends, and pay even more if she happened to be an innocent in the bargain.

He'd planted the seeds well, showing her the solution without actually asking her to sacrifice herself. She'd already been shocked by the talk of mistresses and heartsick over the situation and how it would affect them all, but mostly she'd been desperately worried about Jean, and how this could ruin her chances for a decent marriage one day.

Kelsey could find a job, possibly, but

hardly one that would keep them much above the level of poverty, especially if she took on the responsibility of supporting them all. She couldn't imagine Aunt Elizabeth working, and Elliott, well, he'd already proven pathetically that he couldn't be depended on to hold a job anymore, not for very long.

It was visions of her young sister resorting to begging on the streets to help out that had prompted Kelsey to ask, albeit in a mortified whisper, "Do you know of some man who would be willing to — to pay enough if I — if I agreed to become his mistress?"

Elliott had looked so hopeful, and so damn relieved, even as he'd replied, "No, I don't know a single one. But I know of a place in London that the rich lords frequent, a place where you can be presented to receive an excellent offer."

She'd stood there, silent for a long while, still so hesitant about such a monumental decision and so sick to her stomach that this did, in fact, seem to be their only option. Elliott actually broke out in a sweat before she finally nodded her consent.

And then he'd tried to console her, as if anything could just then. "It won't be so bad, Kelsey, really it won't. A woman can make a great deal of money for herself this way if she's smart, enough to become independent — even marry later, if she chooses."

That wasn't a bit true, and they both knew it. Her own chances for a good marriage would be gone forever. The stigma that would be hers when she went through with this would follow her for the rest of her days. She'd never be welcomed in polite society again. But that was her cross to bear. At least her sister would still have the future she deserved.

Still in a state of shock over what she'd agreed to, she'd suggested, "I will leave it to you to tell Aunt Elizabeth of this."

"No! No, she mustn't know. She'd never permit it. But I'm sure you will think of something reasonable to tell her to excuse your absence."

She had to do this, too? When it was doubtful that she'd be able to think of anything other than the appalling truth of what she'd agreed to?

She'd been ready to finish off that bottle of spirits herself by the time she left him. But she had come up with a weak excuse to tell the others. She'd told Aunt Elizabeth that Anne, one of her friends from Kettering, had written that she was seriously ill, the doctors not offering much hope. Kelsey had to visit, of course, and give what comfort she could. And Uncle Elliott had offered to escort her.

Elizabeth hadn't noticed anything amiss. Kelsey's pallor could be credited to worry over her friend. And Jean, bless her, didn't badger her with her usual hundreds of questions simply because she didn't recognize the name of this particular friend. But, then, Jean had matured a great deal during the past year. A tragedy in the family had a way of interrupting childhood, sometimes permanently. Kelsey would almost have preferred the hundreds of questions from her twelve-year-old sister that used to test her patience. But Jean was still mourning.

And when Kelsey didn't return home from the visit to Kettering? Well, she would have to worry about that later. Would she ever even see her sister or Aunt Elizabeth again? Did she dare, when they might discover the truth? She didn't know. Right then, she only knew that nothing would ever be the same for her again.

2

"Come on, dearie, it's time."

Kelsey stared at the tall, thin man standing in the open doorway. She'd been told to call him Lonny, the only name given when she was turned over to him yesterday. He was the owner of the house — the person about to sell her to the highest bidder.

There was nothing about him to suggest that he was a purveyor of vice and flesh. He dressed like any lord. He was pleasant-looking. He spoke in cultured tones — at least while Uncle Elliott had still been there. As soon as her uncle left, however, Lonny's speech slipped occasionally into the not so refined, indicating his true background. Yet he'd continued to be kind.

He had explained to her, very carefully, that because such a large sum of money was going to be paid for her, she wouldn't have the option of ending the arrangement as a normal mistress would. The gentleman who bought her would have to be guaranteed that he would be getting his money's worth for as long as he wanted it.

She'd had to agree to that, which in her mind seemed just short of slavery. She'd have to stay with the man whether she liked him or not, whether he treated her well or not, until he no longer cared to support her.

"And if I don't?" she'd dared to ask.

"Well, dearie, you really don't want to find out what would happen in that case," he'd told her, and in such a tone that she'd felt her very life threatened. But then he'd gone on to further explain, in a more chiding voice, as if she should know all this already, "The arrangements I make, I guarantee personally. I can't have my reputation ruined on the whims of a girl who decides later that she doesn't like the bargain she's made. No one would participate in these sales if that were the case, now, would they?"

"You have many sales like this?"

"This will be the fourth one that I have held here, though the first from your background. Most of the gentry who find themselves in your predicament manage to marry their daughters off to rich husbands to settle their difficulties. A shame your uncle didn't try to make a match for you. You don't strike me as the mistress sort."

She hadn't known whether to be insulted or pleased by that, had said merely, "There wasn't enough time to arrange a marriage, as my uncle told you."

"Yes, but still, a pity. Now, shall we get you settled in for the night? You will be presented tomorrow night, after I've had time to send out the word to those gentlemen I feel might be interested. Hopefully, one of my girls will have something appropriate for you to wear for the presentation. A mistress must look like a mistress, if you get my meaning, not one's sister." And he'd given her a critical once-over. "While your ensemble might be lovely, dearie, it's more appropriate for a garden tea. Unless you've brought something suitable . . . ?"

She'd had to shake her head, actually embarrassed to be looking so . . . ladylike.

He'd sighed. "Well, we'll find something, I'm sure," he'd said as he led her out of the parlor and upstairs to a room she could use for the night.

Like the rest of the large house, the room was very tastefully furnished, and she'd politely remarked on that. "Very nice."

"You were expecting something tawdry?" He'd smiled when her look said as much. "I cater to the *ton*, dearie, and have found they are much more willing to part with their money if they feel at home while doing it." And then he'd laughed. "The lower classes can't afford my prices, don't even make it through the door."

"I see," she'd said, not that she did. Men would take their pleasures where they found them, and there were houses of ill repute all over London to prove that. This just happened to be one of the more expensive ones.

And before he left her, he'd stressed once more, "You *do* fully understand this arrangement you've agreed to and how it differs from a normal arrangement of this sort?"

"Yes."

"And that you will receive nothing for it yourself, other than what presents your gentleman decides to give you during your time with him?" She'd nodded, but he still wanted it perfectly clear, continuing, "A minimum figure will be set, the amount your uncle requires, and that will go to him. Whatever is paid beyond that I will have a share in, for arranging the sale. But no amount at all will go to you."

She did know that, and prayed a good deal more would be offered, at least enough to tide her family over until Elliott got a new job and stuck with it. Otherwise, she would have made this sacrifice for nothing more than a temporary postponement of disaster. But on their way to London, her uncle had sworn to her that he would get a job and keep it, no matter if it wasn't up to his standards, that he would never find himself in such a ruinous predicament again.

What worried her, however, considering just how much Elliott owed, and what she finally asked Lonny, was "Do you really think anyone *will* pay that much?"

"Oh, yes," he replied with complete confidence. "These rich nabobs have nothing else to spend their money on. Horses, women, and gambling are their major pursuits. I'm happy to supply two out of three, and any other vice they have a desire for, short of murder."

"Any vice?"

He'd chuckled. "Dearie, you would be surprised what some of these lords — and ladies — request. Why, I've got one countess who comes here at least twice a month and pays me to supply her with a different lord each time who will whip her — carefully, of course — and treat her like a lowly slave. She wears a mask, so no one will recognize her. In fact, the gentlemen I send to her merely assume she's just another one of my girls. Would be happy to supply the service myself, her being a looker like yourself, but that isn't what she wants. What titillates her the most is that she knows each of them personally, but they don't know it's her, and she sees them all at the *ton* gatherings, dancing with them, playing cards across the table from them, knowing their dirty little secrets."

Kelsey had gone red in the face, as well as being rendered speechless, after hearing that. That people actually did such things — and paid to do them and have them done. Never would she have conceived of such a thing!

Which was why Lonny said in disgust, "Gah, them blushes are well enough for now, but you better get used to such talk, girl. It's going to be your job henceforth to supply the man who buys you with sex, however he wants it, you understand? A man will do things with his mistress that he *won't* do with his wife. That's what a mistress is bloody well for. I'll be sending one of my girls by to explain that to you in more detail, since your uncle obviously didn't see fit to."

And he'd done just that, to Kelsey's further mortification. A pretty young woman named May had come by in the night, bringing the gaudy gown that Kelsey was now wearing, and had spent several hours discussing the facts of sexual life with her. May had covered everything from how to avoid unwanted pregnancies to every way imaginable to pleasure a man, ways to incite them to lust, and ways to get what *she* wanted out of them. The last had probably been something Lonny hadn't intended Kelsey to learn, but May had seemed to feel sorry for her, so had volunteered that information too.

It had certainly been nothing like the brief talk Kelsey had had with her mother more than a year before, when she'd turned seventeen, about love and marriage. Her mother had discussed lovemaking and babies in her forthright way, then went right on to an unrelated subject, as if they both weren't embarrassed to their toes by the previous one.

May had left her with the parting advice, "Just remember, it's likely a married man that will buy you, and the reason he wants a mistress in the first place is he gets no satisfaction from his wife. Hell, some of them ain't never seen their wives naked, believe it or not. Anyone will tell you — well, anyone of *my* acquaintance will tell you — that a man likes looking at a naked woman. Just give him what he don't get at home and he'll adore you."

And now it was time. Kelsey was nearly trembling with dread. Lonny had given her an approving look — a very approving look, actually — when he'd opened the door and seen her in the ruby-red gown with its deeply scooped neckline. That he felt she looked more appropriate for the occasion did nothing to bolster her courage.

Her future, for better or worse, was going to be decided that night by the man who would be willing to pay the most for her. He didn't have to be to her liking, she understood that. May had made it clear that she might even despise him right from the beginning, if he were old or cruel. She could only hope that that wouldn't be the case.

Lonny led her downstairs. He had to do a bit of tugging to get her to move when she heard just how crowded it was below simply from the level of noise, and worse, he didn't take her to the parlor, where she could have met the gentlemen and conversed with them.

Instead, he escorted her into the rather large gambling den, whispering when she halted completely, "Most of these gents aren't here to bid on you. They're here to gamble or for other pleasures. But I have found that the more present, the more active the bidding from those seriously interested. The others, well, it gives them a rousing good show, which is very good for business, don't you know."

And before she knew what he meant to do, he'd hefted her up onto one of the tables, and warned in a hiss, "Stay there, and do your part to look enticing."

Enticing, when she was paralyzed with fear and utter mortification? And because most of the men in the room weren't there to bid on her, as he'd said, and so had no idea why she was standing up on that table, Lonny made a little announcement to enlighten them.

"A moment of your time, gentlemen, for a very unusual auction."

The word *auction* had a way of gaining immediate attention, and this was no exception. Lonny had to wait only a few more seconds for the room to quiet down completely.

"For those of you pleased with your current ladyloves, please continue your gambling, this auction is not for you. But for those of you in the market for something new, I offer this vision of — blushing loveliness." There were a number of snickers because Kelsey's face had, in fact, turned nearly the color of her gown. "Not to sample, good sirs, but to call your own for however long you care to. And for such a privilege, bidding will begin at ten thousand pounds."

The amount, quite naturally, caused an immediate uproar, raising the volume in the room much higher than it had been before Lonny's startling announcement.

"Ain't no female worth that much, even m'wife," one man called out, generating laughter around him.

"Can you loan me ten thousand, Peters?"

"Made of gold, it is?" someone else sneered.

"Five hundred, and not a pound more" was called out in a drunken voice.

Those were just a few of the dozens of comments that Lonny wisely let run their course before he put an end to them by stressing again, "Because this little jewel will go to the highest bidder, the option will belong to her new protector of how long he

28

wishes to keep her. A month, a year, indefinitely . . . the choice will be his, not hers. This will be stipulated in the bill of sale. So come now, gentlemen, who will be the lucky one to be the first . . . *ever* . . . to sample this luscious young morsel?"

Kelsey was too shocked to hear much of what was said after that. She had been told she would be "presented" to the gentlemen, misleading her into believing that she would meet them and have a chance to speak with each of them, and that then they would quietly make their offers, if they intended to bid, to Lonny.

Never had she imagined that the whole thing would be done so publicly. Good God, if she had known she was going to be auctioned, *auctioned,* to a room full of men, half of them foxed, would she have still agreed to this?

A voice broke through her horrified thoughts.

"I'll meet the opening bid."

Kelsey's eyes moved to the sound of that tired voice to see an equally tired and ancient face. She had a feeling she was going to faint.

3

"Still don't know what we're doing here," Lord Percival Alden mumbled. "Angela's place is just as nice, was just as close from the White's dinner, and her girls are used to *normal* debauchery."

Derek Malory chuckled and winked at his cousin Jeremy as they followed their friend into the foyer. "Is there such a thing as normal debauchery? Sounds like a contradiction in terms there, don't it?"

Percy could say the most unusual things at times, but like Nicholas Eden, he'd been one of Derek's closer friends since their school days, and so he could be forgiven his occasional lapses into denseness. Nick, now, rarely chummed about with them anymore, and certainly not to places like this, not since he'd got himself leg-shackled to Derek's cousin Regina. Not that Derek wasn't delighted to have Nick in the family, as it were, but he was of the firm opinion that marriage could wait till after thirty, and that was still five long years away for him.

His two youngest uncles, Tony and James, were the perfect examples of the wiseness of that opinion. They'd been two of London's most notorious rakes in their day, had sowed their oats long and well, and hadn't settled down to raise families until their mid-thirties. Having Jeremy, James's illegitimate eighteen-year-old son, wasn't considered raising a family early, since he was conceived without the sanctity of marriage — just like Derek was. Besides, in Jeremy's case, Uncle James hadn't even known of his existence until a few years before.

"Oh, I don't know," Jeremy remarked on the subject in all seriousness. "I can debauch as well as anyone, and I do it normally."

"You know what I mean," Percy replied, gazing warily about the foyer and up the stairs, as if he expected the devil himself to appear. "Some mighty queer chaps known to frequent this establishment."

Derek raised a golden brow at that, scoffing, "I've been here a few times now, Percy, to gamble and to avail m'self of one of the rooms upstairs — and its occupant. Didn't notice anything out of the ordinary. And recognized most of the chaps here."

"Didn't say *everyone* who comes here is weird, old man. Gad, no. We're here, aren't we?"

Jeremy couldn't resist. "You mean we're not weird? Hells bells, I could've sworn —"

"Be quiet, scamp," Derek cut in, succeeding, just barely, to hold back his laughter.

"Our friend here appears to be quite serious."

Percy nodded emphatically. "Indeed I am. They say any fetish or fantasy can be found here, no matter how bizarre one's particular tastes run. And I believe it now, having seen Lord Ashford's driver outside. Would be afraid a girl here would hand me some chains the minute I walk in her room," and he shuddered.

The name Ashford brought an abrupt end to Derek's humor, as well as Jeremy's. They'd all three had a run-in with the fellow a few months before in one of the taverns down by the river, having been drawn by a woman's terrified screams to one of the upstairs bedrooms.

"Isn't that the fellow I beat senseless not so long ago?" Jeremy asked.

"Beg to differ, dear boy," Percy replied. "It was Derek here who beat the lout senseless. Didn't give either of us much of a chance at it, furious as he was. You did get a kick or two in after he was out for the count, though, as I recall. Come to think of it, so did I."

"Glad to hear it." Jeremy nodded. "Must have been foxed not to have remembered that."

"You were. We all were. And a good thing, too, or we might have killed the bloody sod."

"No more than he would have deserved," Derek mumbled. "The man's thoroughly demented. No other excuse for that kind of cruelty."

"Oh, I agree, indeed I do," Percy said, and then in a whisper, "I've even heard that without the blood, he can't — well, you know . . ."

Trust Percy to lighten the mood. Derek actually burst out laughing. "Good God, man, we're in the most notorious brothel in town. No need to quibble words here."

Percy actually blushed before he grumbled, "Well, I still want to know what *we're* doing here. The things they cater to in this house are simply not my cup of tea."

"Mine either," Derek agreed. "But as I said before, that isn't all that goes on here. They may cater to the depraved, but the girls here can still appreciate a nice, *normal* tumble when that's all that's required of them. Besides, we're here because Jeremy found out his little blonde Florence from Angela's establishment has moved here, and I promised him an hour or so with her before we show up at that ball we're due to make an appearance at later. Could have sworn I already mentioned that, Percy."

"Don't recall," Percy said. "Not to say you didn't, just don't recall."

But Jeremy was frowning now. "If this

place is as bad as you say, don't think I want my Florence working here."

"So cart her back to Angela's," Derek suggested reasonably. "The chit will likely thank you for it. Couldn't have known what she was getting into, even if she was promised more earnings here."

Percy nodded once in agreement. "And do be quick about it, dear boy. Can't say as I care to even play a few hands here while you find the gel. Not if Ashford is in the same bloody room." Yet he walked over to glance into the gambling den while he said it. Then with a bit of excitement, "Oh, I say, now there's a little bird I wouldn't mind spending an hour or so with, even here. But looks like she ain't available, more's the pity — or maybe she is. No, she ain't. Much too costly for my tastes."

"Percy, what *are* you going on about?"

Percy glanced over his shoulder to say, "An auction taking place, by the sound of it. Don't need no mistress at my age, when a few coins spread here and there does me just fine."

Derek sighed. They obviously weren't going to get an answer out of Percy that made any sense, but that was nothing new. Half the time Percy's remarks were a major mystery. But Derek didn't feel like trying to unravel them just now, when a few steps would let him see for himself what had set Percy off this time.

So he moved to stand beside his friend in the open doorway, as did Jeremy. And they both saw her right off, couldn't help but see her, standing up on that table like she was. A pretty young thing — at least, she appeared to be. Hard to tell, all splotchy with blushes as she presently was. Nice figure, though. Very nice.

And now Percy's remarks made sense. They heard the proprietor say, "Once again, gentlemen, this little jewel will make a splendid mistress. And so very easily trained to suit your own tastes, untouched as she is. Do I hear twenty-two thousand?"

Derek quietly snorted. Untouched? Coming from a place like this? Not bloody likely. But then, fools deep in their cups could be made to believe anything. The bidding, however, had obviously got out of hand, the current price absurd.

"Doesn't appear we'll find a friendly game of whist here, Percy, with that nonsense going on," Derek said. "Take a look, no one's paying any attention to the gambling."

"Don't blame 'em a'tall." Percy grinned. "Rather watch the gel m'self."

Derek sighed. "Jeremy, if you wouldn't mind hurrying up with your business here, I'd as soon get to that ball early after all. Fetch the chit and we'll drop her back at Angela's on our way."

"I want that one."

Since Jeremy still had his eyes on the girl up on the table, Derek didn't need to ask who. He said merely, "You can't afford that one."

"I could if you lent me the money."

Percy started chuckling at that. Derek wasn't a bit amused, was actually frowning. And his "No" was said in a tone that shouldn't have been brooked. But Jeremy, that scamp, wasn't easily daunted.

"Come on, Derek," he cajoled. "You can cover a loan that big easily. I've heard about the large settlement Uncle Jason gave you when you finished your schooling. It included several income-producing estates. And what with Uncle Edward investing the bulk of it for you, hell's bells, it's likely three times as much by now —"

"More like six times as much, but that doesn't mean I'm going to throw it away on lustful impulses, particularly when they aren't even *my* lustful impulses. I'm not about to lend you that much blunt. Besides, a woman like that, lovely as she is, would have to be kept in high style. You, cousin, can't afford that either."

Jeremy grinned, unabashed. "Ah, but I'd keep her *happy*."

"A mistress cares more about what's in your pockets than what's between them,"

Percy put in helpfully, then immediately blushed again for having said it.

"They ain't *that* mercenary," Jeremy protested.

"Beg to differ —"

"How would you know? You've never had one."

Derek rolled his eyes, cutting in, "There's no need to argue here. The answer is and is going to remain no, so give over, Jeremy. Your father would have my head if I put you that deep in debt."

"My father, better than yours, would understand."

Jeremy had a point there. To hear the stories, James Malory had done things just as outlandish in his youth, whereas Derek's father, being the Marquis of Haverston and the oldest of the four Malory brothers, had had to assume a responsible role at an early age. But that didn't mean the roof wouldn't still fall on their collective heads if Derek gave in to his cousin's request.

So he said, "Perhaps he'd understand, though you'll have to admit, Uncle James is much more conservative now that he's married. And besides, it's my father I'd be answering to. Furthermore, where the deuce would you keep a mistress, when you're still in school and still living with your father when you're home?"

Jeremy finally gave a look of disgust,

self-directed. "Damn me, didn't think of that."

"Besides, a mistress can bloody well be as demanding as a wife," Derek pointed out. "Tried one myself once, and didn't care for the arrangement a'tall. You want to be tied down like that at your age?"

Jeremy now looked appalled. "Hell no!"

"Then be glad I'm not going to let you waste *my* money on a silly whim."

"Oh, I am, indeed. Can't thank you enough, cousin. Can't imagine what I was thinking."

"Twenty-three thousand" was called out, drawing their attention back to the gaming hall.

"Now there's another reason to be glad you came to your senses, Jeremy," Percy said with a chuckle. "Sounds like the bidding ain't going to end."

Derek wasn't amused, had, in fact, stiffened upon hearing that bid, and not because the ridiculous price was still escalating. Bloody hell, he *really* wished he hadn't recognized the voice behind that last bid.

4

"Twenty-three thousand."

Never would Kelsey have believed the bid could have gone that high. But knowing she could fetch such a price did nothing for her vanity. In fact, she couldn't even be pleased that it would solve her aunt's and uncle's problems for a *very* long time. No, she was too horrified to be pleased.

He looked . . . cruel. That was the single word that kept coming to mind. She wasn't sure why. The slant of his thin lips perhaps? The narrowed, cold gleam in his light blue eyes as he watched her squirm beneath his gaze? The chill that had run down her spine when she first caught his eyes on her?

He was in his early thirties, she would guess, with coal-black hair and the patrician features common to many lords. He wasn't ugly. Far from it. But the cruelty in his looks detracted from the handsomeness that might have been found there. And Kelsey was hoping that the old man who had started the bidding, even with his disgusting leers, would continue to outbid that one.

And Heaven help her, it had come down to just the two of them. The few others who had offered a bid or two at the beginning had dropped out when they'd noticed the frigid looks coming their way from that other lord, looks ominous enough to chill the most hardy soul. The old man was still bidding because he simply hadn't noticed, possibly due to poor eyesight or because he was barely cognizant; he appeared foxed.

And then she heard a new voice upping the bid to twenty-five thousand, followed by a yelled-out question from another man nearby, "What do *you* need with a mistress, Malory? I hear you've got the ladies standing in a line waiting to get into your bed."

That remark produced a lot of laughter, and even more when the new bidder replied, "Ah, but those are *ladies,* m'lord. Perhaps I'm in the mood for something — different."

Which was an insult to Kelsey, but perhaps wasn't meant to be. He didn't know, after all, that she'd been every bit the lady until she walked into this house. In fact, there was nothing about her at the moment to indicate that she was other than what they all thought her to be, which was no lady at all.

She had been unable to see who the new bid had come from. The voice had sounded from the general direction of the doorway, but the exact position of the speaker was hard to distinguish with so much noise going on in the room. And there were more than a dozen men in that area, sitting as well as standing. It was impossible to tell. Yet the man she *didn't* want to buy her apparently knew who the new offer had come from, because he was now glaring in that general direction. But again, Kelsey couldn't tell exactly who had drawn his murderous look.

She held her breath, waiting to see what he would do. A glance at the old man showed that he likely wouldn't be bidding anymore. He'd actually nodded off, and no one seemed inclined to wake him. Well, he'd sounded pretty foxed when he had been bidding. Apparently the drink had done him in. But her savior, whoever he was, would he continue to bid against that other lord? Or would he be intimidated like those others?

"Do I hear twenty-five five?" Lonny called out.

Silence. And Kelsey suddenly realized that all of the other bids had jumped by five-hundred-pound increments — except the last one. The man called Malory was the first to raise the amount by two thousand. An indication that he was very serious? Or too rich to care? Or perhaps he was too deep in his cups to have been paying much attention.

"Do I hear twenty-five five?" Lonny repeated, a bit louder so as to reach the back of the room.

She kept her gaze on that blue-eyed lord, waiting, praying he'd sit down and bid no more. Veins were standing out on his neck, he was so furious. And then, amazingly, he stalked out of the room, knocking one empty chair over in the process, shoving men aside if they didn't step out of his way in time.

Kelsey looked to the owner of the house, to see his reaction, and Lonny's disappointment confirmed it. The departed lord was bidding no more.

"Twenty-five thousand then, going once . . ." There was only a brief pause before Lonny added, "Going twice . . ." Another pause, just a tad longer. "Very well, sold to Lord Malory. And if you will step into my office just down the hall, m'lord, we can conclude this business."

Again, Kelsey tried to see who Lonny was talking to. But he was lifting her down from the table, and short as she was at only five feet, three inches, she couldn't see beyond the men just in front of her.

She was thankful that the ordeal was finally over. But the relief she ought to be feeling wouldn't come, because she still didn't know who had bought her. And keeping her trepidation high was the thought that, good God, he *could* be just as ghastly as those other two. After all, the remark made to him, insinuating that women desired his company because they were lined up to get into his bed, could have been said in sarcasm, meaning just the opposite. Sarcasm of that sort would have drawn just as much laughter from this crowd.

"You did good, dearie," Lonny whispered to her as he escorted her out into the foyer. "Surprised me, it did, the price going that high." He chuckled then, more to himself. "But these nabobs, they can afford it. Now, run along and fetch your things, and don't dally. Come to my office, just over there" — he nodded to an open door at the end of the hall — "when you're ready." And he patted her backside to push her toward the stairs.

Dally? When her paramount concern was finding out who had bought her? She practically flew up the stairs. And she had nothing really to gather, not having unpacked much from her small valise the day before. So she was back downstairs in less than ten minutes, closer to five.

But one step from that open doorway she stopped short. Her desire to see who had paid such an exorbitant sum for her was abruptly superceded by her fear. It was a done deal. She had to honor it or deal with Lonny's subtle threat, which she didn't doubt for a minute had been life-threatening. But the unknown was paralyzing her. What if this man who had bought her wasn't even fit to be called decent but was a cruel, vicious man just like that other lord had seemed to be? Or what if he was a grotesquely ugly man who couldn't get women any other way than to purchase them like this?

What would she do? Horribly, there was nothing she *could* do. She'd either hate him or like him — or feel nothing at all. Actually, she hoped to feel nothing. She certainly didn't want to become attached to a man she could never marry, even if she was going to have to be intimate with him.

"I'm sure you will find you've made an excellent purchase, m'lord," Lonny was saying as he backed out the door of his office, then noticing Kelsey there, he pulled her into the room, adding, "Ah, and here she is now, so I'll bid you a good evening."

Kelsey almost closed her eyes, still not ready to face her future. But the contrary, brave side of her, small portion that it was, refused to put it off another second. She looked at the people in the room. And because of that, she got to experience her relief immediately. Immense relief. She still didn't know who had bought her, because there was not one man waiting in Lonny's office, but three. Yet of those three, one was handsome, one was very handsome, and one was incredibly handsome.

How could she have gotten this lucky? She couldn't credit it. Something must be wrong. Yet for the life of her, she couldn't tell what that might be. Even the least handsome of the three, who seemed to be the oldest, she felt she could deal well with. He was tall and lanky, with gentle brown eyes and an admiring smile. The word *harmless* came to mind when she gazed at him.

The tallest of the three also appeared to be the youngest, no more than Kelsey's age, though he had such broad shoulders and an expression that was clearly on the mature side, that he seemed much older. He was also too handsome by half, with raven-black hair and eyes the most beautiful shade of cobalt blue, just slightly tilted for an exotic slant. She had a feeling she could deal exceptionally well with him, and she was hoping, praying, that he was the one who'd bought her. Heavens, she could hardly take her eyes off him, he was so appealing to every one of her senses.

But she did force herself to look away to examine the third man standing in front of her. If she hadn't glanced at that blue-eyed young man first, she could have honestly said she'd never seen a man as handsome as this one. He had thick blond hair in an unruly, flyaway style. His eyes were hazel

— no, green, definitely green — and the look in them was a bit disturbing, though she couldn't say why exactly. He was shorter than the other two, though not by much, and certainly still taller than her by half a foot or more.

And then he smiled, and Kelsey's stomach fluttered — for the first time in her life. What a strange feeling. And the room had suddenly become too warm. She wished she had a fan, but she hadn't thought to pack one, hadn't thought to need one in the heart of winter.

"Might as well set that down . . . ?" he said to her, glancing at her valise. "And do hurry up, Jeremy, and do whatever fetching you intend to do."

"Gad, forgot all about the chit he came here for," the older of the three said. "Yes, do hurry it up, Malory. Interesting as this evening has been thus far, it still ain't over."

"Damn me, forgot about Flo m'self," Jeremy admitted with a sheepish grin. "Won't take me long to fetch her, though — if I can find her."

Kelsey watched the youngest of the threesome saunter out of the room. So she'd got her wish after all. He'd just been called Malory, and the man who'd paid such an exorbitant price for the privilege of having her for his mistress had been a Lord

Malory. So where was the relief she'd been positive she would feel?

"Kelsey Langton," she said, having finally realized, long after the fact, that the blond man had been asking her name when he'd suggested she set her valise down.

Now she blushed, however, to have blurted it out like that. And she still hadn't set down the valise, hadn't even realized she was still holding it, until that same blond man stepped forward and took it out of her hand.

"My name's Derek, and the pleasure is mine, Kelsey, you may be sure," he said to her. "But we'll have a bit of a wait while the youngun attends to the business that brought us here. So perhaps you'd like to sit down?" And he indicated one of the chairs next to Lonny's desk.

Not only handsome but kind. Imagine that. Yet still disturbing in some way. Her heart had fair tripped over when he'd come so close and his fingers had touched hers as he took the valise from her to set it aside. She had no idea what it was about him that was causing these strange reactions in her, but she was suddenly *very* glad he wasn't the one she'd be going home with.

She'd have enough to deal with just in becoming a mistress at the end of the day, the thought of which she had put in the far back of her mind or she never would have survived up to now. She didn't need any extra worries. And at least with young Jeremy, she imagined the worst problem she'd have would be to keep from staring at him like a ninny. But that, undoubtedly, was something that particular young man with his mesmerizing looks was very used to.

"Knew an earl over Kettering way by the name of Langton," the other man said suddenly. "Nice enough chap, though ended bad, I hear. 'Course, you wouldn't be any relation."

Thankfully, he hadn't put it as a question, had stated his own opinion, so she didn't have to lie. But that had been a horrible moment, when he'd mentioned her father. What could she have been thinking, to give her real name? Obviously, she hadn't been thinking, and it was too late now.

"Since she isn't any relation, Percy, why mention it?" Derek said a bit dryly.

Percy shrugged. "Was an interesting tale, is all, and her name reminded me of it. By the by, did you see the look on Ashford's face when he passed us?"

"Could hardly miss it, old boy."

"You don't think there'll be trouble from that quarter, d'you?"

"The man's a rotter and a coward. I *wish* he'd cause trouble, damn me if I don't. Give me a reason to wipe the floor with him again. But chaps like him only bedevil those who can't fight back."

Kelsey shivered at the anger she felt from the one called Derek. She wasn't sure, but she had a feeling they were speaking about the blue-eyed lord who had been bidding on her but had left in such a fury. And if that was so, then apparently these gentlemen had crossed paths with him before.

She wasn't going to ask, however. In fact, she moved over by the desk to sit down in the chair that had been offered, hoping to stay out of their notice. But that was a mistake, drawing both of their eyes back to her. She started to squirm, but was really sick and tired of the nervous, fearful state she'd been in all day.

A spark of anger formed, countering it, allowing her to say, "Don't mind me, gentlemen. Do go on with your conversation as it pleases you."

Percy blinked at her. Derek's eyes narrowed. And she realized immediately what she'd done wrong — again. She might not look like a lady in the garish red gown she was wearing, but she'd certainly just sounded like one. Yet this was something she couldn't help. Pretension was not her forte. Even if she'd tried to sound less cultured, and managed it for a time, she would have slipped at some point and then had even more explaining to do.

So she decided to brave through and lie. The truth, of course, was out of the question.

With an innocent look that she bestowed on both of them, she asked, "Did I say something untoward?"

"It's not what you said, m'dear, but how you said it," Derek replied.

"How I said it? Oh, you refer to my speech? Yes, it does surprise people occasionally. But you see, my mother was a governess, and I was able to benefit from the same tutors assigned to her charges. A very uplifting experience, if I do say so myself."

She had to smile at the pun, whether they caught it or not. Percy relaxed, taking her word for it. Derek was still frowning, however.

And he didn't take long to say why. "I find it hard to imagine that being allowed, when most lords are from the old school and believe the lower classes should be kept the lower classes, as to say, ignorant of higher learning."

"Ah, but there was no lord to say yea or nay, just a lord's widow my mum worked for who really couldn't have cared less what the children of her live-in servants were up to. She did, in fact, give her permission. My mum wasn't one to take such liberties on her own, after all. And I will be forever grateful to the lady — for not caring one way or another."

Percy coughed at that point, followed by a snicker. "Give it a rest, old man. What you were thinking ain't possible and you know it."

Derek snorted at his friend. "As if you didn't think the same thing."

"Only for the briefest second."

"And what, may I ask, are you both referring to?" Kelsey asked, keeping up her pretense at innocence.

"Nothing that matters," Derek replied in a low grumble, and stuffing his hands in his pockets, he moved to stand in the open doorway, leaning against the frame there, giving his back to the room.

Kelsey looked to Percy for a clearer answer, but he just smiled sheepishly, shrugged, and stuffed his hands in his pockets as well, rocking back on his heels. She almost laughed. Of course they wouldn't admit they had, however briefly, thought she might be a lady. The very thought of it wasn't to be borne by men of their class. And that really was her protection. Her family had endured one scandal. She wasn't going to be the cause of another if she could help it.

5

"You sure you don't want me to be in your debt for life, Derek?"

"Getting greedy now, are we? I could've sworn we'd finished that subject."

"Well, that was before you ended up with the prize," Jeremy said with an engaging grin.

Kelsey had no idea what they were talking about and didn't care. She was getting nervous again now that they were on their way to, she assumed, her new home. Too soon she would have to begin her mistressing and . . . She shuddered, unable to finish the thought.

They were in a well-appointed, plush carriage that apparently belonged to Derek, and it was moving along at a brisk pace. And there were five of them now. Jeremy had returned to Lonny's office with his arm around a young blonde girl dressed as gaudily as Kelsey was. She'd been introduced as Florence, and it became apparent within seconds that she fair worshiped Jeremy Malory. She couldn't keep her hands off him, or her eyes, and even now, in the carriage, she was practically sitting in his lap.

Kelsey felt complete indifference. It wasn't

as if she and Jeremy had started their relationship yet, but even if they had, she knew she had no right to demand fidelity from him. He would be paying her support. Even if their situation wasn't highly unusual, in that he'd bought her outright, for the support alone he would expect complete faithfulness from her. But in such arrangements, the gentleman wasn't constrained to behave likewise. Far from it. Most of them had wives, after all.

As the men continued to banter with each other about prices and lifelong debts, Kelsey continued to do her best to ignore them. But it did occur to her to wonder, after Jeremy had spoken of debts, how a young man his age could possibly have afforded the outrageous price he'd paid for her, when most young people had to make do with quarterly allowances from their parents or from estates they were due to inherit.

He must be independently wealthy, which she could only be grateful for. If that weren't the case she'd be with that other lord right now, rather than with these gentlemen, going . . . she had no idea where.

When the carriage did stop shortly thereafter, only Jeremy and Florence alighted from it. No explanation was given, and there was no request for Kelsey to follow along. But Jeremy was back in a few minutes, without the clinging Florence, and since neither of the other two men asked him what he'd done with the girl, Kelsey had to assume they already knew.

The carriage moved along again, and it was a good fifteen minutes before it stopped once more. Kelsey didn't know London at all, had never been there before Elliott had brought her the day before, but a glance out the window showed a very fine looking neighborhood with stately mansions and carriage houses, the town houses of the upper crust.

She shouldn't have been surprised, not with the amount of money that had exchanged hands that night. But she was mistaken in thinking that this was where she was being taken, since it was Derek who left the carriage, not Jeremy. So it was Derek who lived there, and she could only surmise that both Derek and Percy were being let off at their respective homes first, before she and Jeremy reached their final destination.

But she was wrong again, because Derek turned back to the carriage and reached his hand inside to help her out. And Kelsey was surprised enough to take his hand without thinking about it, and was led halfway to a pair of imposing double doors before she even thought to ask, "Why are you escorting me rather than Jeremy?"

He looked down at her, clearly puzzled by her question. "You won't be staying here long. Just the night. Other arrangements will be made tomorrow."

She nodded and flushed with color, afraid she understood now. Jeremy, as young as he was, might well still live with his parents, so of course, he couldn't take her home with him. Derek must have offered to put her up for the night, which was kind of him. Hopefully, he wouldn't have someone here that he would need to explain that to.

"You live here, then?"

"When in London, yes," he replied. "It's m'father's town house, though he's rarely in residence. Prefers the country and Haverston."

The door had opened before he finished, and a portly butler was giving a slight bow and a "Welcome home, m'lord," and was carefully keeping his eyes averted from Kelsey.

"Won't be staying, Hanly," Derek informed the servant. "Just dropping off a guest who needs putting up for the night. So if you'll fetch Mrs. Hershal to take care of the girl, I'd appreciate it."

"A guest for above stairs — or below?"

Kelsey was amazed to watch Derek blush at that impertinent, though necessary, question. She might have donned her spencer to cover a good portion of the god-awful gown she was wearing, but enough of it was still showing to proclaim what profession she had embraced.

"Below stairs will do," Derek answered curtly. "I did say I'm *not* staying."

And now Kelsey was blushing again at what that insinuated. The butler, however, merely nodded and walked off to fetch the housekeeper.

Derek mumbled at his back, "Comes from keeping servants around so long they knew you when you was in knickers. Gives 'em airs, by God."

Kelsey might have laughed if she wasn't so embarrassed. Handsome as he was, Derek looked very funny disgruntled as he was just now. He wouldn't have appreciated her humor, however, even if she'd managed to find it. So she just stared at the floor and waited for him to depart.

And ready to do just that, he said, "Well, then, get a good night's sleep. You will be traveling most of the day tomorrow. Can wear a body out if they aren't rested."

And before she could ask where she would be traveling to, he'd closed the door behind him and was gone.

Kelsey sighed. And then a new dose of relief set in. She was actually going to be spending the night alone; what she had been avoiding thinking about was to be delayed — for another day at least. Perversely, now that it was put off, she couldn't get it to retreat back into the recesses of her mind.

For her, starting her mistressing was going to be like a wedding night, though lacking a certificate of marriage and lacking any tender regard between the two participants. She knew that, historically, marriage between strangers was a frequent occurrence. The pairings were arranged by parents or by kingdoms, with mere days for couples to become acquainted — or even less time, depending on circumstances. But such marriages were very, very rare in this modern age. Today, if the partners didn't do the choosing themselves, they were at least given an abundance of time before the nuptials.

How much time would Kelsey have? This reprieve had been unexpected. She had assumed she would *not* be spending the night alone. And tomorrow there would be traveling. Might that constitute another delay?

She could hope. But delays weren't going to do her much good if they didn't give her an opportunity to get to know Jeremy somewhat better. And so far, come to think of it, she hadn't said one word to that young man, nor he to her. How the deuce was she supposed to develop a relationship with him if they had no conversations?

She supposed she would find out tomorrow. Right now, she should be setting her mind to deciding how to deal with the housekeeper here. In her usual manner? Or in a manner more suited to her new status?

As it happened, the decision wasn't hers to make. Mrs. Hershal showed up just then and, taking one long look at Kelsey, humphed and headed back into the recesses of the house, leaving Kelsey to meekly follow or not. So be it. She would have to get used to such treatment henceforth. She just hoped the scalding embarrassment that went hand in hand with it would get easier to bear.

6

Derek should have known his bosom companions wouldn't leave it alone. He'd no sooner stepped back into his carriage than Jeremy said, "I bloody well don't believe it. You're still going to that ball? Damn me if I would."

"And why wouldn't I?" Derek asked, raising a golden brow. "The chit isn't going anywhere, and our cousin Diana personally requested our appearance tonight at her friend's coming out. Seeing as how we both agreed to attend, Jeremy, what would you say is more important?"

"Exactly my point," Jeremy all but snorted. "Least *I* know what's more important, and it ain't adding to the numbers of what is rumored to be *the* ball of the season. Diana prob'ly won't even notice us there in the crush."

"Whether she does or not, having agreed to attend, we are obligated to do so. Percy, will you endeavor to explain obligations to this irresponsible youngun?"

"Me?" Percy chuckled. " 'Fraid I'm seeing things from his perspective, old man. Can't say as I'd have the fortitude to leave a brand-spanking-new mistress to hie off to a *ton* gathering that doesn't promise to be any different from any other gathering that we've attended. Now, if one of your uncles was going to be present, or your lovely cousin Amy, that'd be different. Your uncles know how to put a little spark into the dreary, and Amy ain't wed to that Yank of hers yet, so in my book she's still available."

After that long-winded account from their friend of few words, Derek and Jeremy both were left a bit speechless. Derek recovered first to say, "Amy might not be married yet, but the wedding is scheduled for next week, so *do* cross her out of your book, Percy."

And then Jeremy added, "And you can't be naming m'father as entertainment anymore. He's too thoroughly domesticated now to be starting the gossip mills churning. So's Uncle Tony, for that matter."

"Beg to differ, dear boy. Those two particular Malorys will never be so domesticated that they won't raise a brow or two. Gad, witnessed it m'self not long after your sister Jack was born, your father and uncle dragging the American into a billiards room, and the Yank barely limped out."

"That was when they had just found out about, and objected to, Anderson's interest in Amy. And it was to be expected that they'd react like that. But, then, we've already explained that to you, Percy, when you were thinking of courting her yourself.

Comes from their each having a hand in raising our cousin Regan after their sister died, and the fact that Amy looks so much like Regan —"

"Reggie," Derek interrupted, just like his father would have were he there, though with much less heat. "I understand why your father persists in calling her by a different name, just to irritate his brothers, but you don't have to take the leaf from his book."

"Ah, but I like his leafs." Jeremy grinned unrepentantly. "And he don't do it to irritate them — well, maybe just a tad, but that ain't why he started calling her Regan. The reason started way back, 'fore I was even born. With three brothers, two of them older than him, he just felt the need to be different in all things."

"Well, he certainly succeeded there," Derek said with a knowing wink.

"Didn't he though."

The cousins were referring to James Malory's pirating days, when he'd been known as the Hawk and the family had disowned him. It was during his infamous career as the Hawk that James had discovered he had a nearly full-grown son, and he'd not only acknowledged Jeremy but took him along, which was why the lad had such an unorthodox education, having learned too much about women, fighting, and drinking from James's motley crew of pirates.

But Percy didn't know that and never would. Percy might be a dear friend, but he was a dear friend who simply couldn't keep a secret to save his soul, and James Malory's past nefarious exploits were a well-kept secret that only the family would ever know of.

"Besides, Percy," Jeremy said, getting back on the subject, "m'father hates balls, positively, and only gets dragged to 'em these days at his wife's insistence. Same with Uncle Tony. Definitely know how they feel. Feels like I'm being dragged to this one, damn me if it don't."

Derek frowned. "I'm not dragging you, dear boy, only pointing out your obligations. You didn't have to agree to Diana's request."

"I didn't?" Jeremy replied. "When I have the worst bloody time telling a female no? Any female, for that matter. Just can't stand to disappoint 'em. And I certainly wouldn't have disappointed the one you just left behind."

"If all she wanted was to be left alone, Jeremy, then I'd hardly say I disappointed her."

"Left alone?"

"You find that hard to believe?"

"Women scheme and fight to get into your

bed, cousin, not to leave it. I've seen it firsthand —"

Derek cut in. "And sometimes women just don't want to be bothered, for one reason or another, and that is the distinct impression I got from this girl. She looked exhausted. Could have been no more'n that, but as I already had other plans anyway . . . Besides, Jeremy, I didn't fork up all that blunt just to bed the girl, so I am hardly impatient to do so. Didn't *want* a mistress in the first place, but now I've got one, I'll bloody well see to her in my own good time, if it's all the same to you."

"Indecent amount for something you *didn't* want," Percy remarked.

Jeremy chuckled. "Wasn't it though."

Derek slouched down in his seat, grumbling, "You know why I did it."

" 'Course we do, old boy," Percy replied. "And commend you for it, 'deed we do. Don't have the blunt to be so noble m'self, but at least one of us did."

"Aye," Jeremy agreed. "Thwarted Ashford and got a splendid bonus for doing so. A fine night's work, if I do say so m'self."

All but blushing at the unexpected praise, Derek said, "Then perhaps you will both cease the ribbing about leaving the girl behind?"

Jeremy grinned. "Must we?"

A scowl from Derek had Jeremy glancing

out the window beside him and whistling a merry ditty. Incorrigible scamp. Uncle James really was going to have his hands full trying to reign this young pup in to responsibilities when the time came. 'Course, Derek's father had been lamenting about the same thing where he was concerned. But then, of the four Malory brothers, Derek had to be stuck with the head of the family, and being so, Jason Malory, Marquis of Haverston, was the most stern out of the lot of them, and the hardest to please.

7

Derek usually enjoyed balls, though not ones with over three hundred people in attendance, as that night's turned out to be. But he liked to dance, could usually find a friendly game of whist or billiards, and invariably there would be a fresh new face or two there to intrigue him.

The intrigued part never lasted long, however, since most young ladies who decked themselves out so splendidly for these occasions, and flirted so coyly, were after only one thing: marriage. And the very minute their motive was established, Derek would bid them adieu, because marriage was the very last thing he was interested in.

There were a few exceptions to that rule, but those didn't come along very often. Even if a girl didn't want to get married right away, she'd be dealing with pressure from her relatives to get the matter seen to. It was the rare young lady who could withstand that pressure and devote some time to just enjoying herself.

Derek actually liked those independent-minded young ladies the most, and had gotten to know several fairly well. These were innocents still, so the relationships involved were not of a sexual nature. Far from it. Derek respected the rules of society and found it quite refreshing to associate with them on other terms, good conversation, shared interests, and to simply be able to relax his guard with them.

Which wasn't to say he wasn't constantly on the lookout for his next bed partners. He just didn't pick them from the crop of new innocents who descended on London each season. No, his sexual pursuits were culled generally from young wives and widows, the former unhappy with their marriages, the latter free to do as they chose — with discretion, of course. And he rarely left one of these large London affairs without a tryst arranged for later in the week, or even that night.

At this ball, however, nothing seemed to interest him. He did his requisite dancing to keep the hostess happy, and had to take pains not to yawn before he relinquished each partner to the next gentleman on her dance card. He tried a few hands of whist, but again, he couldn't manage to concentrate on the game, even when the stakes rose perilously high.

Two of his former lovers had tried to interest him in another rendezvous, but where he would usually put them off with promises of another time, he had simply told them he was otherwise involved at the moment. Yet he wasn't. The girl he had dropped off at his home couldn't be considered an involvement — yet. Besides, a mistress was never considered an involvement, not a true involvement. A mistress was simply a very nice — and expensive — convenience.

And he still couldn't believe he had one now. The one and only other time he had agreed to pay the support of a woman in return for her favors had been an utter disaster.

Marjorie Eddings had been her name. She was a young widow of good breeding who couldn't quite make ends meet to continue living in the style she had been born to. He had paid her debts — actually, most of them had been her departed husband's debts — refurbished the house she had inherited, gave in to her desire for costly little trinkets.

He'd even agreed to be her escort to the many gatherings she was still invited to, when he'd had no desire to fill that role. All aboveboard, naturally, and highly respectable, even to dropping her off at her residence, as was proper, and having to wait hours before it was safe to sneak in for the favors he was due — which, half the time, she claimed she was too tired to supply. And during the entire six months of their relationship, knowing full well that he had no interest in marriage, she had plotted to get him to the altar.

Even if he had liked her well enough to make their relationship permanent, which he hadn't, he didn't like being tricked and lied to, which she had done. She claimed she was with child when she wasn't. Then she had let their real association leak through to the gossip mills, while claiming that he'd promised to marry her. That had been the last straw. And she'd made *that* claim directly to his father.

Of course, Marjorie had underestimated the Malory family. It was impossible to insinuate herself into their ranks with lies. Derek's father knew him well enough to know he'd never make such a promise. As it happened, Jason Malory would have been delighted if it were otherwise.

But Jason knew his only son wasn't ready to settle down any time soon, and thankfully, he'd never tried to force Derek to change his mind. Derek knew the day would come when the pressure would be turned on. Responsibility and all that, carrying on the line, and in Derek's case, the title he would eventually inherit, were large considerations.

As for Marjorie, well, Jason didn't like liars either. He was a man of rigid principles. And having been head of his family for so long — since he was sixteen, actually — and having had to call his younger brothers on the carpet so often for their misdeeds through the years, as well as Derek and Reggie, whom he'd had the raising of, he had that sort of thing down to an art.

A hot temper should also be mentioned. It was only the most innocent who could stand up to one of Jason's furious sermons. The guilty would quickly crumble in shame, and in the case of women, tears, since it was very unpleasant getting the roof dropped on your head, as Uncle Tony was fond of putting it.

Marjorie had left in tears and disgrace and had troubled Derek no more. She'd gulled a great deal of money out of him during their short relationship, so he was feeling no guilt himself that it had ended so badly. And he'd learned his lesson — at least he'd thought he had.

To be fair, though, the woman he had acquired earlier that night wouldn't — at least shouldn't — be anything like Marjorie. Kelsey Langton wasn't gentry, even though she might *sound* like it, wasn't raised to privilege, so she would be genuinely grateful for anything he might do for her, whereas Marjorie had expected it as her due.

Furthermore, he'd actually bought her. He had the bill of sale in his pocket to prove it. And he still didn't quite know what he thought of that. But she'd put herself up for sale. It wasn't as if she'd been sold without her permission and . . . better not to even think about the bought-and-sold part of it. He'd acquired a mistress, and he hadn't even done it to acquire one but to keep that blackguard Ashford from brutalizing still another woman, and this one without an avenue of escaping his cruelties.

Beating Ashford senseless obviously hadn't put an end to his perverted ways, as Derek had hoped. He was just going about it more legally now, as in that absurd auction and in making use of houses like Lonny's that supplied women for such purposes.

Previously, David Ashford had bought cheap whores for a night. Such women had no recourse against lords of Ashford's ilk, and worse, probably felt the few pounds he tossed them was ample compensation for whatever scars he left. Pathetic, but true. And even if Derek brought charges against Ashford, having witnessed firsthand the man's sick excuse for pleasure, he knew no victims would be found to bear witness against the man. They'd be bought off, or disposed of, before it ever came to trial.

But Derek felt so strongly about this that he was going to have to do something further now that he knew for a fact that Ashford was still at it. And he couldn't go around buying up every female Ashford tried to purchase outright, even if he caught wind of every auction of that sort. He didn't have an endless supply of money. Tonight he'd acted on impulse.

Perhaps he ought to talk to his Uncle James about what to do. James had dealt a great deal with the unsavory side of life during his pirating days. If anyone would know how to deal with scum like Ashford, he would.

But that was for tomorrow. Tonight, he was having a devilishly hard time enjoying himself. And he finally began to wonder, when he kept seeing a pair of soft gray eyes in front of him instead of the blue ones belonging to his present partner, if Jeremy and Percy hadn't been right. What the bloody hell *was* he still doing at the ball when there was a lovely young woman — under his own roof, for that matter — who'd probably gone to bed tonight wondering why he wasn't with her?

Of course, "under his own roof" put a damper on matters. One reason he got along with his father so well, and was rarely taken to task for anything, was because he understood that his father wasn't going to try to curtail his pleasures as long as he practiced them with complete discretion. And Derek had always done so.

Which meant he'd never dallied with a

wench in the London town house, not even at the two estates that had been turned over to him. Servants' gossip could be the worst gossip there was, there being no faster grapevine than the one that connected each house down a street and beyond through their butlers, their drivers, their maids, their footmen, and so forth. And that meant he wouldn't be getting to know his new mistress any better tonight.

Finally he gave up the pretense of enjoying himself and found Jeremy and Percy to let them know he was leaving and would send the carriage back for them later. They, of course, gave him knowing winks and smirks, thinking he was heading home to enjoy himself. But, then, they didn't have fathers like Jason Malory.

Which wasn't to say he didn't give going to her a lot of thought on that ride home. Kelsey Langton wasn't one of the servants, after all. And she wouldn't be in the house long enough to gossip with any of the regular servants. He could, in fact, visit her with none the wiser and be tucked into his own bed by morning. His valet wouldn't be up to know the difference, since he never kept the man waiting up for him.

Actually, it didn't take much to talk himself into paying Kelsey a short visit. So it was rather disappointing to be met at the door by Hanly again, even at that bloody late hour, and having that put an end to those plans.

Nosy old coot. If Hanly hadn't stood there in the foyer and watched him ascend the stairs, every single step of them, Derek might still have gone down to the servants' quarters to search out the girl. But he didn't doubt for a moment that Hanly would be lurking about down there, watching for him.

And then Derek's father would hear about it within the week, and he'd end up called to task about propriety, discretion, and ensuring the servants' gossip had to do with other people's households, not one's own. All for one little tryst with a chit he could have access to at any time — after tonight? Not bloody likely.

But it was deuced hard getting to sleep that night.

8

"It's my own fault," Mrs. Hershal mumbled. "Should've seen it right off, but I'll admit my eyesight ain't what it used to be, 'specially at night."

Kelsey rubbed the sleep from her own eyes as she listened with half an ear to the housekeeper. She didn't comment, since she didn't know what the woman was talking about. Obviously, she must have missed that part, having awakened to find Mrs. Hershal taking one of her dresses out of her valise to smooth out the wrinkles.

The room had already been tidied up, not that she had been awake long enough last night to make much mess. And there was fresh water awaiting her, fluffy towels, and what looked like a pot of tea.

She yawned, thankful that she hadn't awakened disoriented and wondering where she was and who the devil this woman was who was rummaging about in her room. Brown hair twisted into a severe bun, broad shoulders and an overly large bosom making her a bit top-heavy, and thick brows that seemed slanted into a perpetual frown.

Oh, yes, she remembered the housekeeper all right — too clearly, in fact, the woman's contemptuous tsking and disparaging looks that had made Kelsey feel like the lowliest gutter rat. And her parting remark the night before that Kelsey would never forget.

"And don't be wandering about and stealing anything, 'cause we'll know who done it, we will."

It was extremely hard to stomach such disdain when she had never experienced anything approaching scorn in her life, but she'd already figured that she would have to get used to such attitudes. She'd just have to put a shell around her feelings so eventually it wouldn't hurt or embarrass her as it did now.

Kelsey wished the housekeeper would hurry up and leave. But she was still mumbling to herself, apparently not aware yet that Kelsey was even awake. And then Kelsey changed that opinion when she started listening more intently to what the woman was saying.

"Comes from trusting Hanly's opinion. But what does he know, I ask you? Tells me you're a tart His Lordship's brought home and I go and believe him. My own fault, though. I know it. I admit it. I should've had a closer look-see. It's in the bones, you know. The bones won't deceive you, and you've got 'em."

"I beg your pardon."

"See? What did I tell you? You should've begged my pardon last night, m'lady, and I'd have known right off that you didn't belong down here. It was that dress, you see. And my eyesight ain't so good, like I said."

Kelsey stiffened, sitting up in the lumpy bed. Last night she hadn't even noticed it was so uncomfortable. Good God, the woman was *apologizing*. That's what all her mumbling was about. For some unknown reason she'd decided that she'd made a mistake in classing Kelsey with gutter rats. And how was Kelsey supposed to deal with that? She didn't *want* anyone thinking she was a lady.

She could just say nothing. Let the woman think whatever she liked. It wasn't as if she would be staying in this house, where she'd have to deal with her on a daily basis. But there was a chance that Mrs. Hershal might take her guilt straight to Lord Derek to continue her apologizing to him, and that wouldn't do at all.

So she gave the woman a somewhat weak smile and said, "It's not what you're thinking, Mrs. Hershal. It's true that gaudy dress wasn't mine, and if I never see it again, I couldn't be happier. But I'm not gentry, really I'm not."

"Then how do you explain —"

Kelsey quickly interrupted. "My mum was

a governess, you see, and we didn't have it so bad. She was employed by the same family for most of my life, and we got to live in a nice house like this. I was even privileged enough to get to share the same tutors with the young ladies my mum had charge of — which is probably why you're thinking I'm other than what I am. Believe me, you're not the only one to have made that mistake because of the way I talk."

That lie was getting easier with repetition, but Mrs. Hershal was frowning doubtfully and studying Kelsey's face as if the truth were written there for any discerning eye to note. In fact, that was exactly what she was still thinking. "That don't explain the bones, m'lady. You've got the fine bones of the upper crust, you do."

Kelsey thought frantically for a moment, then said the only thing that came to mind. "Well — I've never met my father, actually." And there was no need to try to simulate the blush that came with that lie.

"A by-blow then?" Mrs. Hershal replied thoughtfully, then nodded to herself, seeming well pleased with such a logical, obvious answer. Then sympathetically, "Ah, well, there's enough of that goes around, ain't there now. Even Lord Derek, bless him, came out on the wrong side o' the blanket. 'Course his papa, the marquis, acknowledged him and made him his heir, so he's accepted well enough by the *ton*, though it weren't always so. Had many a fight, he did, younguns being as cruel as they are, up until Viscount Eden befriended him in their college days."

Kelsey certainly hadn't expected a history of Jeremy's friend Derek, and didn't know quite what to say. His illegitimacy was none of her business, certainly, but since she had just, sort of, claimed to be the same thing, she supposed she should pretend some understanding.

"Yes, I know how that is."

"I'm sure you do, miss, I'm sure you do."

Kelsey relaxed then, hearing Mrs. Hershal using "miss" instead of "m'lady." Mrs. Hershal didn't look so fretful either, apparently having been satisfied that her mistake wasn't *too* far off the mark, so she wouldn't be getting into trouble for it.

And the housekeeper was quick to conclude on her own, "Having a bit of trouble then, are you, for Lord Derek to be helping you out?"

It was easiest to just say "Yes" and let it go at that, but wouldn't you know, the housekeeper was too nosy to take the hint.

"You've known His Lordship long, then?"

"No, not a'tall. I was — stranded. I don't know this city, you see, only just arrived and had been lucky enough to find lodging right away, but unlucky enough to have the building catch fire last night. That's why I was wearing that horrid dress. Someone had lent it to me before my valise was recovered, and — and Lord Derek had been driving by, saw the smoke, and stopped to help."

Having improvised as she went along, Kelsey was feeling rather proud of creating a fire to explain the dress as well as her presence here. The housekeeper nodded with approval.

"Yes, our Lord Derek is kindhearted, he is. I remember once —"

A knock at the door interrupted her reminiscing. A young maid opened it and poked her head in to say, "The carriage has arrived and His Lordship's awaiting."

"Goodness, this early?" Mrs. Hershal said as she waved a hand to dismiss the maid, then with a glance to Kelsey, "Well, then, no time to press this, is there? But I think I've worked out enough of the wrinkles for it to do, and I'll leave you to ready yourself. No time for breakfast either, so I'll have Cook do you up a basket to take with you."

"That isn't necessa—" Kelsey quickly began, but the woman was already out the door.

Kelsey sighed, hoping the whopping lie she'd just told wouldn't go any further. Not that it mattered, since she wasn't staying there.

But this lying business didn't sit well with her. And she certainly wasn't very good at it, never having had the practice. She and Jean had both been raised to be scrupulously honest, and neither of them had ever had cause to deviate from that — at least Kelsey hadn't — until now.

The tea wasn't quite hot any longer, but she gulped down a quick cup as she hurriedly washed and dressed. She thought about leaving that red dress behind, she really did, but she recalled some of the advice that May had imparted to her at Lonny's about always looking her best and enticing for her lover, and she had nothing else that fell into the category of enticing. *She* might think the dress was in appalling bad taste, but apparently men didn't, or the bidding would never have gone quite so high.

But if she ever did wear it again, it would only be late of an evening, and only behind closed doors. For now, she dressed in the gown Mrs. Hershal had brought out, the winter-thick woolen beige that matched her spencer jacket. And goodness, it felt good to dress decently again, even if "decent" wasn't going to be part of her future.

When she went downstairs, she found Lord Derek waiting in the foyer, rather than Jeremy, and he was slapping a pair of gloves against his thighs in an impatient manner. He looked different in the lighter colors of day wear, though no less handsome.

Actually, the strong light in the foyer pointed out just how handsome he was in every way, from his tall, lean physique to his finely chiseled face and . . . his eyes really were hazel. It must have been a trick of the light last night that had made them appear green.

And they were certainly going over her in a critical manner this morning, giving her the impression that he didn't care for her demure dress. Which was quite likely. After all, now she looked like a lady, and he wouldn't have expected that. But he wasn't the one she needed to impress or entice, so she wasn't going to worry about it.

She had assumed "His Lordship's awaiting" had meant that Jeremy had come to fetch her, but the younger lord was nowhere about. Of course, he could be waiting in the carriage.

"You slept well, I trust?" Derek asked her when she reached him, his tone somewhat challenging, as if he didn't think that was possible.

"Yes, very."

She was amazed that that was true, but now she thought of it, she must have fallen asleep the moment her head touched the pillow. But, then, the fear and anxiety she had undergone the day before had seriously worn her out.

"This is for you, I believe."

She hadn't noticed the basket he'd been holding partially behind him. She nodded, hoping Mrs. Hershal hadn't handed it over herself, or if she had, that she'd done so without comment. But no such luck . . .

"So I'm credited with doing a good deed I don't quite remember doing?"

Kelsey blushed furiously to have been caught in the lie. "I'm sorry, but your housekeeper was badgering me with questions this morning, and I didn't think you'd want the truth known to her."

"Quite right, and none of her business in any case. You really slept well?"

She was surprised that he'd ask that again, and again in a tone that implied he found it impossible to believe that she could have.

"Yes. I was apparently exhausted. It was a . . . trying day."

"Was it?" More doubt that was impossible to mistake, but then he smiled. "Well, hopefully today will be better. Shall we?" He indicated the door.

She sighed and nodded. The man was behaving exceedingly strangely, but it was nothing to her. Perhaps it wasn't strange at all and he was naturally skeptical about every little thing. Not that it mattered, when she doubted she'd be seeing him again after today.

He assisted her into the waiting carriage, and the moment his hand touched hers, she felt one of those disturbing reactions again. But that wasn't why she frowned as he settled into the seat across from her. It was because the carriage was empty.

She didn't put off asking, "Will we be picking up your friend Jeremy?"

"Jeremy?"

His momentary confusion annoyed her, coming on top of her own confusion, but she repeated calmly, "Yes, Jeremy. Will we be picking him up this morning?"

"Whatever for?" he countered. "We hardly need his company on the way to Bridgewater." And then he smiled, and she could have sworn his eyes were green again. "Besides, this is a perfect opportunity for us to become better acquainted, and I find I can't resist another moment finding out what you taste like."

Before she realized what he was going to do, he was pulling her onto his lap. But she wasn't the least bit slow in reacting. Before he'd barely got his lips close to hers, she slapped him. He looked at her then as if she had gone crazy. She looked at him in a like manner.

And then he was dumping her back on the seat across from him and saying, albeit quite stiffly, "I don't know if I'll be begging your pardon or not, Miss Langton. Considering the hole you put in my pocket yesterday for the exclusive use of your sweet self, I believe an explanation is in order. Or are you under the mistaken impression that I'm like those select few who frequent Lonny's place because they like their sex a little rough? I can assure you that isn't the case."

Her mouth had dropped open at the same time her cheeks had flamed with color. *He* had bought her. Not Jeremy. And she'd just begun their relationship by slapping him.

"I — I can explain," she said, feeling a bit sick to her stomach.

"I do hope so, m'dear, because at the moment I'm about to demand my money back."

9

Kelsey was feeling rather sick. She didn't know how to explain what she'd just done. And she didn't know how to explain it because she couldn't think clearly with Derek scowling at her. The only thing that *was* clear in her mind just then was that he'd bought her. Him. The one who disturbed her. The one out of the three she had hoped wouldn't be the one.

And goodness, now she knew why she had hoped it wouldn't be him. He flustered her so much, she couldn't think.

"I'm waiting, Miss Langton."

For what? For what? Oh, yes, for why she'd slapped him. *Think*, you ninny!

"You startled me," she said.

"Startled?"

"Yes, startled. I wasn't expecting you to attack me like that."

"*Attack* you?"

She cringed at the volume he was fast reaching. She was making a muck of explaining. How to make him understand without admitting what an idiot she was. Why hadn't she asked immediately which one of them had bought her? She *should* have asked. Actually, she should have been told. But she never should have assumed.

"A bad choice of words," she allowed. "But I'm not used to being yanked onto men's laps and — well, as I said, it startled me and — and I reacted before I thought . . ."

She didn't finish. He was still scowling, and she'd run out of excuses. There was nothing for it but to own up to the truth of the matter.

"Very well, if you must know, I didn't see which of you had bid on me. I only heard Lord Malory mentioned, and when Jeremy was called Lord Malory —"

"Good God!" he exclaimed. "You thought my cousin Jeremy bought you?"

His amazement showed. She was blushing as she nodded.

"Even after you were brought to *my* home?" he wanted clarified.

She nodded again, but added, "You said that was only temporary. I guessed that as young as Jeremy is, he might still be living with his parents, and so he must have asked you to see me settled for the night. Why else do you think I asked if we would be picking him up this morning?"

At that point he confounded her by smiling. "Actually, dear girl, I was worried that you might have become smitten with the scamp. It wouldn't be the first time. He has that effect on the fairer sex despite his tender years."

"Yes, he is unusually handsome," she

agreed, then wished she hadn't commented at all. He stopped smiling.

"I suppose you are disappointed now, to be stuck with me instead?"

It was really unfortunate that he asked that question. The truth was written on her face before she took the lie in hand to try to assure him. "No, of course not."

It was immediately apparent by his skeptical expression that he didn't believe her, but she wasn't going to make matters worse by trying to explain. Jeremy had simply boggled her with his good looks, but this Malory stirred things up in her that she didn't understand. With Jeremy, she had suspected things would be quite simple. With this man, she didn't think anything would be simple. So certainly she would have preferred Jeremy, for the relationship she entered with him wouldn't have been all that complicated.

When he said nothing, just continued to look doubtful, despite knowing she shouldn't, she got defensive and said stiffly, "I can assure you, Lord Malory, that I find you infinitely preferable to those other two gentlemen you outbid. However, I didn't realize that my preferences mattered in the least in your transaction. I wasn't asked if you will do. That option wasn't included in the bargain I made. Or did you want it to be?"

Turning the tables on him made him smile, though the expression didn't quite reach his eyes. And his tone was on the dry side as he said, "Excellent point, m'dear. Perhaps we should start again. Come here, and I will endeavor to make you forget it isn't Jeremy sitting here. And you can endeavor to make me believe that you have forgotten."

She stared at the hand he held out to her. She couldn't very well refuse it. But already her belly was starting to churn with those strange feelings, and when she actually put her hand in his, she almost gasped, the feeling leapt with such strong currents.

"Much better," Derek said as he settled her back on his lap.

Kelsey was positive her cheeks were burning in expectation of his kiss. But he didn't kiss her. He moved her a tad this way, and a little that way, then his arms settled around her and she heard him sigh.

"You can relax, m'dear," he told her in a somewhat amused tone. "Rest your head wherever you like. I believe I'm just going to get used to holding you for a while."

She hadn't expected that, but some of the stiffness went out of her upon hearing it. "I'm not too heavy?"

He chuckled. "Not a'tall."

The carriage continued to rattle along the city streets, which were heavily congested at that time of the morning with delivery carts and wagons and so many people on their way to work. By the time they reached the outskirts of the city, Kelsey was feeling relaxed enough to finally rest her head against his chest. One of his hands came up to her head when she did, a thumb smoothing against her cheek, which she didn't mind in the least. The scent of him was so pleasant, clean and spicy, and she liked that too.

"How far is it to Bridgewater?" she thought to ask after a while.

"Since we will be stopping for lunch along the way, most likely it will take all day."

"And what's in Bridgewater?"

"I have a house in the country near there. Was due for a visit anyway, and there is a cottage nearby that I believe is empty, which you should be quite comfortable in for a week or two, until I can make arrangements for something for you in London."

"I'm sure it will do nicely."

They fell silent for the next hour. Kelsey was warm, and comfortable, and nearly falling asleep when she heard . . .

"Kelsey?"

"Hmmm?"

"Why did you put yourself up for sale like that?"

"It was the only —" she started, but stopped abruptly, realizing that she'd been so relaxed and off guard that she'd nearly blurted out the truth. She quickly corrected that blunder with, "That is to say, I'd rather not talk about it, if it's all the same to you."

He tilted her chin up until her eyes met his looking down at her. They were most definitely green, and curious, and something else was there that she couldn't define.

"I'll accept that answer for now, love, but I can't say that I will next time I ask," he said gently.

And then his head bent, and she felt the soft caress of his lips on hers, nothing threatening, nothing alarming, just the barest touch. She sighed in relief. This wasn't so bad, was certainly nothing to be frightened of.

She'd had several young men courting her in Kettering, but none had ever dared to kiss her. Her mother's eagle eye was always upon them, as was proper. And for a first kiss, this was very nice indeed. She certainly couldn't see the harm in it, or why parents frowned on their daughters' participating in such sport.

His thumb was still rubbing soothingly against her cheek. After a while, though, it moved to the corner of her mouth and tugged very slightly until her lips parted. Then she felt his tongue tracing a path over her lips first, widening them still more, then over her teeth, then beyond.

This wasn't the least bit relaxing. In fact, her insides were suddenly rioting with sensations, but as it continued, she realized that they weren't unpleasant sensations, far from it, just like nothing she'd ever experienced before.

She tried frantically to recall some of May's advice. *Never lay there like a wet blanket. Caress him at every opportunity when you are alone. Make him think you want him constantly, whether you do or don't.*

Kelsey had no idea how to make Derek think she wanted him. But caressing him was a simple enough matter — if she could get her mind off what she was experiencing and onto what she ought to be doing. She brought her hand up to his own cheek, spread her fingers up into his hair. Soft and cool it was compared with the heat from his mouth . . .

His mouth. It was working magic on hers, keeping her from concentrating on what she was doing. She was gripping his hair without realizing it. Her other hand was digging into his back, pulling at him, as if she could get him any closer to her, as close as he already was. And it was getting so hot she was feeling faint.

And then his mouth left hers abruptly. Kelsey thought she heard a groan, but whether from her or him she wasn't the least bit sure.

But before she could come out of her daze and get her eyes open, she heard him say in a strained tone, "Very well, I can see this wasn't such a good idea after all."

She hadn't quite grasped his meaning. He was setting her back on the seat across from him, his hands leaving her rather quickly, so she assumed her sitting on him had something to do with it. She couldn't bring herself to look at him as she struggled to regain her composure and combat the blush that she just knew was staining her cheeks.

When she did finally glance up, he didn't look too composed himself. He was loosening his cravat and fidgeting on his seat as if nails had suddenly poked through the velvet upholstery under him.

And then he met her gray eyes and must have detected her confusion. He made an effort to explain, "When I make love to you, Kelsey, it will be in a decent bed, not bouncing around in discomfort in a carriage."

"Were we about to make love?"

"Yes, we most definitely were."

"I see."

But she didn't see at all. They were still fully clothed. May had been rather derisive when she had explained that some men still made love to their wives in the dark and without removing any of their nightclothes, but with a mistress, they would most definitely get naked.

Kelsey supposed that she would just have to take Derek's word for it that, in their case, they had been about to make love. But she hoped all the advice and warnings she had received would make sense to her once she *did* make love. Right then it was all just very confusing.

10

They stopped at a rustic inn in Newbury for lunch. Derek had frequented the establishment many times since the property in Bridgewater had been turned over to him, enough to know the place was cleaner than most and the food excellent. More important, it offered a private dining room for those who didn't want to rub elbows with the locals; the room was expensive enough that only the gentry could afford its use. And not knowing Kelsey's habits yet, he preferred not to find out that she ate like a pig with the entire establishment watching.

Her table manners proved impeccable, however. He'd never have to worry about being embarrassed on that count, if and when they dined with others of his acquaintance. And he saw no reason to keep her exclusively hidden once he moved her to London. There were, after all, many places one could take one's mistress without worry of running into gently reared females who would be affronted by the presence of someone of Kelsey's class and profession.

He had studied her for quite a while in the carriage while she pretended not to notice. She could have been a duke's daughter, sitting there so rigidly proper, with such decorum, her clothes not the most expensive, yet still fit for any lady to travel in.

Those clothes had surprised him when she'd come downstairs. He hadn't expected her to look so *un*like a mistress, even if it was early in the morning. He was going to have to buy her some that were more appropriate, if that was the best she could come up with from that valise of hers.

It was bloody well disconcerting, listening to her fine speech, too. Her diction was better than that of half the *ton,* who, like himself, tended to butcher a sentence down to the briefest thought.

But Kelsey by daylight was a revelation, much prettier than the night before, when she had been so stiff and wide-eyed in her nervousness. Her complexion was flawless cream, making her blushes all the more telling. Her brows were thin and arched just enough to highlight her oval-shaped eyes, which were made even more prominent by some very thick black lashes outlining them. High cheekbones complimented a slim nose and delicate chin.

Her black hair held a natural curl, so there was very little that needed to be done to it to make it quite stylish. She wore it now in a braid that wrapped about her head, the flyaway bangs and soft curls at her ears very becoming. And those eyes, softest gray they were, and so telling when they filled with innocence, or rancor, or simple confusion. He had to wonder how much of what he saw in them was actually true and how much was artful contrivance.

He was finding her fascinating, no doubt about that. He had had the devil's own time falling asleep the night before because of her, for thinking about her being under the same roof, while she had slept like a baby. And that had annoyed him too. She hadn't laid awake, expecting a visit from him, because she hadn't realized she was in the house of the man who'd bought her. She'd thought that man was Jeremy.

Derek still didn't know what to make of his reaction to that. He barely knew the girl. Just because he owned her was no reason to be experiencing jealousy of any sort — at least not this soon. And over Jeremy?

Granted, his scamp of a cousin had made no bones about wanting her for himself. And she had owned up to how handsome she'd found him. Of course, had she said otherwise, he would have known she was lying. *All* women found Jeremy exceptionally handsome. And it had rankled, indeed, when she'd tried to convince him that she preferred him. He *knew* she was lying through her teeth.

But he would come to grips with that. After all, he had no desire for her to fall in love with him and start thinking about babies and homemaking. That was hardly what a man wanted from his mistress. And he couldn't deny now that he did indeed want her, after what had happened earlier.

Her lack of finesse combined with her passion was a strange mixture that had sent his own desire soaring nearly out of control. He still found it hard to believe how much he'd wanted her right there in the carriage, and how long it had taken to get the urge to ravish her under control.

Lust. A right and proper feeling to have for one's mistress, he had to allow, so he wasn't displeased. She might prefer Jeremy and wish that she'd ended up with him instead, but where Derek was concerned, her response had been more than satisfying.

Still thinking about it as they finished their meal, Derek remarked, although more to himself, "I'm tempted to rent a room here, damn me if I'm not. But I have a feeling it will take several hours to make love to you the first time, and that would have us arriving too late in Bridgewater to get you settled . . . Why do you blush?"

"I'm not used to such talk."

He chuckled, finding her continued pretense of innocence rather amusing. He was curious to know how she hoped to carry the pretense beyond the first time they came together. But he'd find that out to-night, wouldn't he? And that was a very pleasant thought.

"Don't worry about it, m'dear. You'll get used to it soon enough."

"I hope so," she replied. "Or I am sure to need cooler clothing — that is to say, this constant blushing keeps me rather warm."

He burst out laughing. "And here I'd hoped I would be doing that."

"There, you see?" she said with yet another blush, and brought her hand up to fan against her cheeks. "It might as well be summer, with as warm as I'm keeping."

"I expect by summer we'll be hard-pressed to get a blush out of you," he replied somewhat dryly, though he knew it made no difference, if she could blush on command as she was doing now. But he had no desire to end her pretense, amusing as it was. "Shall we be off then, before I change my mind about letting a room?"

To give her credit, she didn't shoot out of her chair and run for the door, but it was close, and very apparent that it *was* close, that she was fighting the urge to do just that. Derek shook his head as he followed her out. Strange girl. If she were to be taken at face value, he would be truly confounded. But he'd been with enough sophisticated women to know that it was all part of the game, these little contrivances, done to amuse their gentlemen, not to deceive or give false impressions.

There was perhaps an hour left of daylight when they finally reached the little tenants' cottage on Derek's property. It had one room combining a kitchen area on one wall, with a dining table in the middle, and on the other side of the room, a small area that could be construed as the parlor only because it contained a large stuffed chair. There was a single bedroom off the back with a tiny water closet, replete with a round barrel bath rather than a tub. No modernizations here.

The cottage was sparsely furnished and quite dirty at the moment, attesting to a long vacancy. There were a few rusted cooking pots hanging on the wall by the sink, a small table with two chairs for eating, the one large stuffed chair with a dust blanket covering it, and the bedroom containing only a bed, no wardrobe, no bedding. But the cottage was sturdily made, no drafts sneaking in through cracked or rotting boards. All it really needed was a good cleaning and a few necessities to make it quite cozy.

After a sigh over the condition of the place, Derek fetched an armload of firewood from a shed that was out back and got a fire going. Dusting his hands off after he'd finished, he turned to Kelsey expectantly.

"I need to check in at the house," he told her, "to let them know I've arrived. I'd as soon it not become common knowledge who you are and why you're here, so the less people who see you, the better. I've never kept a woman here before, you understand, and having it known will raise brows among my staff and get back to m'father, which I'd rather not happen. But I'll have bedding and other essentials sent down to you, and return shortly m'self. You'll be all right here alone for a little while?"

"Certainly," Kelsey replied.

He gave her a bright smile, apparently pleased that she wasn't going to complain about the accommodations. "Splendid. And perhaps dinner in town when I return? They have several excellent eating establishments as I recall, and it's only about a mile from here." He said that as he approached her, where she was sitting at the table, and he bent to give her a brief kiss. "I'm looking forward to tonight, m'dear. I hope you are as well."

The blush was quick to come, but he didn't stay to notice. Kelsey sighed as the door closed behind him. Tonight? No, she wasn't looking forward to it in the least. And to keep her mind from dwelling on it, she set about doing what she could in the way of cleaning after a bit of exploring turned up two crates in the shed out back, one filled with broken dishes, the other with a bucket and rags.

She made use of the rags, dusting the few pieces of furniture and wiping down the windows and the few empty kitchen cupboards. But there wasn't much else she could do without some strong soap and a broom. So she was soon back to waiting for Derek's return and the arrival of the things she needed to make the cottage habitable.

It was soon dark, however, and the strain of the day was fast catching up to her. Kelsey had been much more comfortable sitting on his lap for that short while in the carriage than sitting across from him the rest of the day, knowing he was watching her, wondering what he was thinking. That had been quite tiring indeed. So she was asleep in the stuffed chair with only a single blanket and the fire for warmth before anyone came by.

11

Kelsey had no idea what to think when she awoke the next morning to find the cottage just as it had been the previous night. Apparently Derek hadn't returned, or if he had, he hadn't bothered to wake her. Obviously he hadn't stayed, because he wasn't there now. Neither were the essentials he'd promised would be delivered.

She fretted about it for several hours, wondering what could have happened to change his plans. Nothing occurred to her. And all she could do was wait. He'd made it clear, before he left her the night before, that he didn't want her appearing on his doorstep, so she couldn't even go looking for him to find out what had happened.

At least the basket that Mrs. Hershal had had prepared for her, and that she'd never gotten around to opening yesterday, had been brought into the cottage. She was ravenous. Upon examining the basket, she found a plate of assorted pastries wrapped in a towel and a jar of jam with a knife for spreading it.

The four pastries, stale now, would have served her well enough for her missed breakfast yesterday. Today, however, having missed her dinner last night as well, they didn't keep her belly quiet for more than a few hours, making her wish that she'd slept longer, rather than waking with the first daylight that slipped through the curtainless windows.

Toward noon, she was too worried to heed Derek's warning about not raising eyebrows with her presence. Whatever he'd meant to send to her no longer mattered; it was food that concerned her the most now, and her lack of means for obtaining any. He'd left her no money and no transportation. If he didn't show up soon, she was going to be in serious trouble, the very kind she'd sold herself to avoid.

But, of course, he would show up. She had no doubt of that. It was just a matter of when. But he'd undoubtedly forgotten that there was no food in the cottage, and when he still hadn't made an appearance by that afternoon, her hunger prompted her to ignore his warning about showing up on his doorstep. There was no help for it. She had to make an effort to find him.

The moment she opened the front door she found his letter instead. It had been tucked into the edge of the door and fluttered to the ground when she opened it. Of course, she didn't know it was from him until she broke the seal and read it.

Dear Kelsey,

My father's messenger pounced on me as soon as I walked in my house. I've been summoned to Haverston with all due haste, which means I should have been there yesterday. I don't dare waste another moment, which is why I'm sending this note rather than myself.

Don't know what this is about, but I should return within a day or so. If not, I will send word. But you should be fine until we meet again. Until then . . .

Yours Respectfully,
Derek

She should be fine for a day or two? When he'd obviously left so quickly that he forgot to arrange for the things she needed to make the cottage livable? And how soon would it be before he realized he hadn't made proper arrangements for her and rectified that? When he was worried about why his father had summoned him and so would be thinking about that rather than about her? It could be several days . . .

This was so inconsiderate! So thoughtless! And because she was already so hungry, Kelsey lost her temper completely and tossed his letter into the fireplace, where she would have liked to toss Derek Malory instead.

It took her about thirty minutes to track down his house, which was the largest in the area, very large indeed. It wasn't just a country house, as she'd been thinking; it was a full-blown estate, with stables and working farms, and an abundance of tenants.

She asked to speak to the housekeeper and explained to the woman that Lord Malory had rented her the cottage for a short time while she was vacationing and had promised it would be properly furnished and stocked with provender, which it wasn't. A simple matter to be rectified, or so she had hoped. The housekeeper didn't make it so simple.

"I don't have anything to do with the tenants on Lord Jason — er, Lord Derek's land, m'lady. I've got enough to do seeing to this big old manor and the lazy help I've got to work with. Lord Derek's factor sees to the tenants and keeps 'em happy, he does, and I'll send him 'round to you just as soon as he returns at the end of the week. He'll take care 'o your complaints right quick I'm sure."

"You don't understand," Kelsey tried to explain. "I've already paid for the use of the cottage and didn't bring any money with me, only the few clothes I would need, because I was assured that food and bedding and everything necessary would be provided."

By then the housekeeper was frowning. "Let me see your lease, then. I have to account for everything in this house, including the food. I can't be handing it out to His Lordship's tenants without his say-so, and he didn't say so to me when he was here last night."

There was no lease, of course. And the only proof Kelsey had that she even knew Derek was the letter she'd tossed into the fire.

Because of that, she was forced to say, "Never mind. I'll make arrangements for credit in Bridgewater if you'll just direct me to it."

"Certainly, m'lady," the housekeeper said, agreeable again now that she didn't have to dole out anything from her larder. "It's just down the east road a'ways." And she pointed in that direction.

Kelsey left the manor in a quandary. If she hadn't lied in saying she'd rented the cottage, she might have gotten the help she needed. But she'd tried to keep her relationship with Derek quiet, as he'd wanted, and look what that got her. A persnickety housekeeper who hadn't even offered her tea and cakes.

She returned to the cottage even more

downhearted and much more hungry. She had no way to obtain credit, of course. She could just see herself asking for a loan on the basis of being Derek Malory's mistress. A banker would laugh her right out of his office.

But she did have a few things she could sell in town to at least buy some food for the moment. She had a pocket watch, which was a fine piece with two inset diamonds, a gift from her parents on her fourteenth birthday. She also had that horrid red dress. She was going to hate giving up the watch, but she really had no choice.

She stuffed the dress into Mrs. Hershal's basket, which she would need to carry back the food she was going to buy, and set out on the long walk to town. The cottage might not have any of the proper necessities, but there was plenty of fresh water from the pump in the kitchen and plenty of firewood in the shed out back to at least keep her warm. And she even had one plate to eat on, and a jar of jam.

Kelsey was almost feeling a little better as she walked to Bridgewater late that afternoon. Almost. But the small bit of optimism she was clinging to didn't last long, not when each jeweler she found and talked to had no interest in buying the watch from her.

It was almost dark when she gave up on

the watch and tried to sell the red dress.

The seamstress, a Mrs. Lafleur, had been about to close her shop for the day when Kelsey arrived and pulled the red dress out of the basket for her to examine. But after she explained that she would like to sell it, you'd have thought she'd insulted the woman.

"In *my* shop?" the woman exclaimed, eyeing the dress as if Kelsey had let a snake loose on her counter. "I don't cater to that sort of clientele, miss, nor will I ever."

"I'm sorry," Kelsey was forced to say. "Perhaps you know someone who does?"

"Not likely," Mrs. Lafleur huffed. "I might give you a few coppers for the lace — if you can remove it without damaging it. Don't have time to do it myself. Lost the girl was helping me, and Lady Ellen has ordered a new wardrobe for her daughter, to be delivered next week. She's my best customer, and I'm going to lose her if I don't get it finished on time."

Kelsey hadn't asked to hear the woman's troubles, when she had so many of her own. But at least they did give her an idea.

She suggested, "Buy the dress from me for five pounds and I'll help you with Lady Ellen's order — for further compensation, of course."

"*Five pounds!* When all I can use is the lace? One pound for the lace, and you finish three dresses that need completing — without further compensation."

"One pound for the lace, and another ten pounds to finish two dresses," Kelsey countered.

"Ten pounds for two dresses?" the woman sputtered, her already ruddy face getting even redder. "I don't even pay that much for a month's work!"

Kelsey rubbed the sleeve of her spencer. "I happen to know what clothing of good quality costs, Mrs. Lafleur. If you weren't paying your helper that much per month, then you were robbing her."

Unfortunately, Kelsey's stomach growled very loudly at that moment. By the look that entered Mrs. Lafleur's eyes upon hearing it, Kelsey knew right then that the woman had the upper hand.

Kelsey was once again forced to change her tune, saying, "Very well, ten pounds for the completion of three of the dresses — and my stitching is excellent, by the way."

By the time Kelsey finished haggling with the woman, it was full dark. But she had a one-pound note in hand, with the promise of another four when she completed the *five* dresses that were now stuffed into her basket along with needles and thread and scissors. At least Lady Ellen's daughter was under ten years of age, so there wasn't that much yardage involved in the sewing.

Unfortunately, she couldn't find a single food vendor or shop still open at that hour, so she was forced to eat at an inn instead, which cost her three times what she had hoped to spend for the same amount of food. But she had a few coins left to buy a bit more food the next day at normal prices. However, she'd need to buy a candle too, so she could work on the dresses at night. And at least one decent cooking pot, and some soap, and . . .

It had not been a pleasant day by any means. Ironically, she'd found herself in the exact situation that she'd sold herself to avoid, her only boon being that her family had been saved from facing the same.

She had the sniffles by the time she got back to the cottage, which was now as cold inside as it was outside. But her belly was full for the time being. And she had hope of more moneys being available once she finished the work she'd contracted for.

She was going to survive — at least long enough to murder Derek Malory when he returned.

12

Derek hadn't been home to Haverston in several months. Like most young men his age, he preferred the excitement, the sophistication, and the variety of entertainments to be had in London, rather than the country life. But he loved Haverston. The two estates he'd been given to cut his teeth on, as it were, weren't home to him yet, not like Haverston was.

He imagined his uncles — Edward, James, and Anthony — felt the same way, having each been raised at Haverston. His cousin Regina had also been raised there, having come to live at Haverston after her parents died. In fact, Reggie, only four years younger, was more like Derek's sister, the two of them having grown up at Haverston together.

Derek had arrived in the middle of the night. He'd taken one of the horses from his stable, rather than the carriage, to expedite the trip. And he'd been damn tempted to wake his father to find out what he'd been summoned for. But the appalled look on the face of the footman who'd let him in, when he'd asked "I don't suppose you'd care to go wake m'father?" had sent him off to his old room instead to await the morning.

And calmer reasoning surmised that that had been the proper thing to do. After all, if he'd been called home to get the roof dropped on his head, annoying his father even more by waking him would just make that roof a bit heavier. Not that he could think of anything he'd done recently that would have Jason up in arms. In fact, he couldn't come up with a single thing to account for this summons.

Of course, Jason Malory didn't need a specific reason to summon a member of his family to him. He was the oldest living Malory, which made him head of the family, and it was his habit to bring the family to him, rather than vice versa, whether he just wished to chat or impart some information — or drop the roof. That Derek had other things on his agenda, in particular, a fascinating woman who was just waiting for him to bed her, wasn't the least bit pertinent. When Jason demanded your presence, you went. It was that simple.

So Derek waited until morning. But he was downstairs and looking for his father not an hour after dawn. He ran into Molly first, which wasn't surprising. Molly always seemed to know when he was visiting, and always made a point of seeking him out to welcome him home. It had become such a habit that if he didn't see her on one of his visits he'd think something was wrong.

Molly Fletcher was an exceptionally pretty woman of middle years, with ashen blond hair and large brown eyes, who'd worked her way up from being a downstairs maid to the top honor in the servants' hierarchy, being Haverston's housekeeper for the last twenty years. She'd worked hard to better herself over the years, too, getting rid of the cockney accent that Derek could remember her having when he'd been a child, and developing a calm composure that would do credit to a saint.

And like every other female in the house, from the cook right down to the laundress, Molly had always treated both Derek and Reggie in a motherly fashion, imparting advice, caution, scoldings, and concern as she saw fit.

That, of course, was a natural result of there not being a true mother figure present when the two children had needed one. Jason had done his duty and married his wife, Frances, for just that reason, to give the two tykes a mother.

Unfortunately, he hadn't got what he'd bargained for. Lady Frances turned out to be a sickly woman who insisted on taking the water cures at Bath so frequently that she was away to Bath much more often than she was ever at home. She was a nice enough woman, Derek supposed, if a bit on the nervous side, but no one in the family had ever gotten to know her very well.

He'd often wondered if even Jason knew her well, or if he cared to. They were such a mismatched pair, Frances so thin and pale and jittery, Jason so big, robust, and blustery. And Derek couldn't ever recall hearing a tender word pass between them when they were together. Not that it was any of his business. He'd just always felt a little sorry for his father, for the bargain he'd made in Frances.

Molly had come up quietly behind Derek while he was peering into his father's empty study. Her "Welcome home, Derek" had given him a start, but he turned to bestow a fond smile on her.

"G'morning, Molly, luv. I don't suppose you'd know where m'father is this bright and early?"

"Certainly," she said.

And come to think of it, she always knew where anyone was in the house at any given time. Derek couldn't imagine how she managed that, as big as the house was and with as many servants as it had, but she did somehow. Perhaps it was just that she knew where everyone was *supposed* to be, and with her calm but firm control of the entire household, no one dared be somewhere else without letting her know.

"He's in the conservatory this morning,"

she continued. "Puttering with his winter roses and having fits because they aren't blooming on *his* time schedule — or so the gardener tells me," she added with a smile.

Derek chuckled. Horticulture was one of his father's hobbies, and he took it very seriously. He'd travel clear to Italy if he happened to hear of a new specimen he might be able to obtain for his garden.

"Would you also happen to know what I've been summoned home for?"

Molly shook her head. "Come now, why would I be privy to his personal business?" she gently chided. Then she winked and whispered in an aside, "But I can say that he hasn't been ranting and raving this week over anything in particular that I've heard about — aside from the roses."

Derek grinned in relief and resisted the urge to hug her — for all of five seconds. She oofed at his squeeze and said, "Here, now, none of that. Can't be giving the servants the wrong idea."

He laughed and swatted her on her backside before sauntering down the hall, shouting over his shoulder so every servant within a five-room radius was bound to hear him, "And here I thought it was already a well-known fact that I love you to distraction, Molly! But if not, I'll keep it a secret if you insist!"

And that had her blushing furiously even

as she smiled after him, more love in her brown eyes for the charming rascal than should have been there, though she quickly got those motherly feelings under control and went about her morning business.

The conservatory, constantly filled beyond its capacity over the years, had finally been moved away from the house several years before. Behind the stables now, it was a huge glass-roofed building, nearly the length again of the main house and rectangular in shape. Its two longest walls were also mostly glass, and in the winter especially, they were usually clouded with moisture from the humidity within, caused by dozens of braziers scattered about and kept burning day and night.

Derek was slinging off his jacket as soon as he stepped inside, the heavy scent of flowers, earth, and fertilizer overpowering. And it was a chore finding his father in such a mammoth place, when there were usually a half dozen gardeners also present.

But he did finally locate the rose beds — and Jason Malory, bent over some exquisite white blooms that he'd been transplanting. A stranger would be hard-pressed to deduce that this was the Marquis of Haverston, with his shirtsleeves rolled up, a fine coating of dirt up to his elbows, splotches of it on his shirt — another white lawn shirt ruined beyond redemption — and a streak across his damp forehead from when he'd absentmindedly wiped the sweat from his brow with the back of his hand.

He was big, blond, and green-eyed, as were most of the Malorys. Only a select few had the black hair and cobalt-blue eyes of Derek's great-grandmother. She was reputed to have Gypsy blood, though neither Jason, nor any of his brothers, had ever confirmed this.

Derek had to clear his throat a couple of times to announce his presence, Jason was so consumed with his task. But when the big man finally turned to him, his handsome face lit up in a smile, and he gave every indication that he was about to hug his son in greeting.

Derek jumped back, put up a hand with an appalled expression. "If you don't mind, I've already had my bath for the day."

Jason glanced down at himself and chuckled. "Point taken. But it's good to see you, lad. You don't visit often enough these days."

"And you don't come to London often enough," Derek countered.

"True."

Jason shrugged and headed for a nearby water pump to thrust his arms into the filled tub beneath it, dozens of watering cans stacked all around it. The closest flowers got an extra spray as he shook the water off in their direction.

"Business — and weddings — are about all that can drag me to that congested city," Jason added.

"I rather like the congestion m'self."

Jason snorted. "Spoken like any young pup, with the amusements that can be found there. You're taking after my brothers James and Tony in that respect."

There was censure in that remark, however lightly phrased, but not enough to cause Derek alarm. "But they're *married*," he replied with feigned horror. "Egad, I certainly hope I haven't fallen into *that* trap without noticing."

"You *know* what I meant," Jason grumbled, his expression going stern.

The nice thing about being the son of the austere, serious-minded head of the family was not having to curb the urge to tease or banter with him, as other members of the family might do. Derek had learned at an early age that his father might always give the appearance of being stern, but his bark was most times much worse than his bite, at least where Derek was concerned.

Derek grinned unabashedly. After all, who didn't know that James and Anthony Malory had been two of London's most notorious rakes, and neither of them had settled down until they were in their mid-thirties.

" 'Course I do," Derek said, still grinning. "And when I'm their age, I'll likely have made you a grandfather twice over. But that's a ways off, and until then, I rather like following in their footsteps — without the scandals they were known to create, of course."

Jason sighed. He'd raised the subject, and as usual, Derek had lightly sidestepped it. So he got on to the matter at hand.

"I expected you yesterday."

"I was on the way to Bridgewater yesterday. Your messenger had to track me down there, and as it happens, he arrived just as I did, not giving me time to even grab a bite to eat before I had to leave again to get here."

"Bridgewater, eh? So you *are* keeping abreast of your properties. Couldn't tell it, according to Bainsworth. Had a missive from him that he's been trying to reach you for a week with no luck. Claims the matter is urgent. That's why I sent for you."

Derek frowned. It was true he hadn't gone through his mail recently, but with the season being in full bloom and with so many invitations coming in, the huge pile had proven too daunting. However, he didn't like the idea that Bainsworth was still running to Jason with any problems that arose. The properties in the north that Bainsworth managed had been signed over to Derek. His father no longer had any dealings with them.

"Perhaps it's time I hired my own secretary. But Bainsworth, as I'm sure you remember from your own experience, can get excited over the smallest mishap. Did he happen to mention what he considered urgent?"

"Something about an offer that was submitted to buy the mill, with a time limit on it, which was why he was desperate to locate you."

Derek swore under his breath. "Perhaps it's time I found a new manager as well. The mill isn't for sale. Bainsworth *knows* that."

"Not even for a *very* lucrative offer?"

"Not for twice what it's worth. Not for any reason," Derek said emphatically. "I didn't accept the properties to turn around and sell them off."

Jason smiled and clapped him on the back. "Glad to hear it, lad. Truth to tell, with the man coming to me, I thought it might be an offering you were aware of, so I didn't think it could wait until I saw you later in the week at the wedding. But now we've had this little chat, I'll know better next time — if there is a next time."

"There won't be," Derek assured him as

they headed toward the exit together.

"Speaking of weddings —"

Derek chuckled. "We were speaking of weddings?"

"Well, if we weren't," Jason grumbled, "we ought to be, with Amy's wedding only four days away."

"Will Frances show up, d'you think?"

That Derek referred to his stepmother by her given name wasn't a matter of disrespect. It was merely that it had always felt bloody awkward calling her "Mother," when he barely knew her.

Jason shrugged. "Who knows what my wife will do. God knows I don't," he said with marked indifference. "But you know, son, it occurred to me the other day that my brother Edward, younger than me, is seeing his third child married this week, while I —"

"He's marrying off his third *girl*," Derek was quick to cut in, knowing full well where his father would like to lead this discussion. "His boys ain't getting leg-shackled yet. And that's quite a difference there, when girls do get married right out of the schoolroom, but boys bloody well don't."

Jason sighed again, having that line of reasoning thwarted. "Just seemed . . . unbalanced there."

"Father, you have only one son. If you'd had more, or some daughters, I'm sure you'd have most of them married off by now too. But don't compare one child to Uncle Edward's brood of five."

"I know I shouldn't."

They fell silent on the walk back to the house. And it wasn't until they'd reached the breakfast room, where an assortment of dishes was being kept warm on the sideboard awaiting their arrival, that Derek's curiosity got the better of him.

"Do you *really* want to be a grandfather already?"

Jason was startled by the question, but after giving it a moment's thought, he said, "Yes, actually, I do."

Derek grinned. "Very well, I'll keep that in mind."

"Excellent, but — ah, don't be following in James's footsteps in that regard too. The bloody wedding is supposed to come first, the babies after."

Derek laughed, not because James Malory's daughter had been born less than nine months after his wedding but because it was a rare occurrence indeed to see his father blushing, and he knew why he was in this case. Having made that statement, Jason had realized immediately his faux pas. Derek was a bastard, after all, and there wasn't anyone who knew the Malorys who wasn't aware of that fact.

Jason was scowling now at Derek's humor, and as was frequently his way, he turned the tables around with the remark "By the by, who's the chit you brought home the other night to the London house?"

Derek rolled his eyes. He always found it amazing, the things his father knew about that he shouldn't know about, and how quickly he knew about them.

"Just someone who needed a little help."

Jason snorted. "I had conflicting reports, Hanly calling her a tart, Hershal calling her a lady. Which was it?"

"Neither, actually. She's had a superior education, prob'ly better than most ladies, but she's not gentry."

"Merely caught your interest?"

There was no merely about it, but Derek would prefer his father didn't know that, so he said with an expression of indifference, "Yes, something like that."

"You *will* refrain from bringing her home again?"

"Certainly. That wasn't very wise of me, I admit. But really, Father, she's nothing to concern yourself over. You won't be hearing about her again."

"It's the servants that I don't want hearing about her, neither those in London nor here. This family has supplied more than enough gossip for the mills, enough for several lifetimes. We don't need to be contributing anymore."

Derek nodded, in perfect agreement. After all, other than the fact of his birth, he'd always managed to keep his affairs discreet enough that no scandal had ever been attached to him. He prided himself on that fact. And intended to keep it that way.

13

Derek never did get back to Bridgewater. He had stayed the rest of the day at Haverston to visit with his father, and had left the next morning to return to London to go through his mail and get a long letter off to Bainsworth. And as long as he was there, he started checking on a house to rent for Kelsey.

It would have been much easier if he could have gone to his Uncle Edward. Edward owned property all over London that he rented, and more than likely had available just what Derek was looking for. But Edward would ask what he required it for, and that wasn't something he wanted to divulge to the uncle who was closest to his father. With his other two uncles, there would have been no problem. They would have understood perfectly, having each kept countless mistresses themselves — at least previous to their marriages. But Edward was a family man, had always been a family man.

Unfortunately, his uncles Tony and James didn't own rentals in the city, or if they did, they left them to Edward to manage, as he did all of the family's investments. So Derek was forced to go through a normal search, and that had him running about the city, looking at town houses that were either too large, too expensive, or in need of too much repair. By the time he found just what he was looking for, it was the day before his cousin Amy's wedding. So there was no point in hieing off to Bridgewater then, just to turn right around and return to the city.

On the other hand, there was no point in keeping Kelsey in the country any longer either, when he had a signed six-month lease on a town house for her that came fully furnished and was ready for immediate occupancy. The only thing still needed for it was a small staff of servants, which she should be involved in the hiring of anyway. So he sent off a missive to his driver to fetch her back to the city.

Actually, he was too eager to see her again to wait until after Amy's wedding, when he would be free to fetch her himself. This way, she would be ensconced in the London flat by the next night, and they could get around to starting their relationship on a more intimate level a day sooner.

It wasn't often that the entire Malory family gathered under one roof at the same time. Even the two newest members of the family, James and Georgina's daughter Jacqueline, and Anthony and Roslynn's daughter Judith, were tucked away upstairs so their mothers wouldn't have to return home to feed them. Reggie's son was up there too, though he was old enough to feed himself now.

Reggie looked around the room at her expanding family. The other newest member of the family was, of course, the bridegroom, Warren Anderson, well and truly leg-shackled now, after that beautiful wedding ceremony they'd all just come from. Reggie smiled fondly at the newlyweds across the room. They made such a lovely pair, Warren taller than any of the Malorys at six feet four, with his golden brown hair and light lime-green eyes, and Amy, a stunning bride all in white, with her black hair and cobalt-blue eyes.

Reggie had that same coloring, as did Anthony and Jeremy, and Reggie's mother, Melissa, who'd died when Reggie was only two. The five of them were the only ones in the family who had taken after Reggie's great-grandmother. Everyone else was on the fair side, mostly all blond and green-eyed, with only Marshall and Travis taking after their mother, Charlotte, with brown hair and eyes.

The reception was in Uncle Edward's mansion on Grosvenor Square. Large, jovial, always good-humored, unlike the rest of her uncles, Edward was beaming proudly even as he patted the hand of his wife, Charlotte, who was quietly sniffling beside him. In fact, Aunt Charlotte had cried all through the ceremony. But, then, Amy was her youngest child — although, come to think of it, Aunt Charlotte cried at *all* weddings.

All of Reggie's other cousins were scattered about the room. Edward's brood included Diana and Clare, with their husbands, and Amy's brothers, Marshall and Travis. Reggie's cousin Derek, Uncle Jason's only child, was talking with her husband, Nicholas, and her uncles Tony and James. Derek and Nicholas had been best of friends ever since their school days, long before Reggie had ever met Nicholas and fallen hopelessly in love with him. But she had to worry anytime her two youngest uncles were around her husband.

Reggie sighed, wondering if they would *ever* get along. Not likely. In Uncle Tony's case, he hadn't thought Nick was good enough for her, Nicholas having been a rake. In Uncle James's case, well, feelings ran a little deeper, since Nick had unfortunately had a run-in with James on the high seas during James's pirating days. James had lost that battle, and his son Jeremy had been injured in it, though not seriously. But that had been the start of many confrontations between those two, the last serious one ending with Nicholas so soundly beaten he'd nearly missed their wedding; James had ended up in jail and nearly hung for piracy.

Of course, now that Nicholas was a member of the family, and had been for several years, they no longer tried to kill each other at each meeting. It was quite possible they even liked each other now, though neither one of them would ever admit it, and listening to them, you'd certainly never guess it. Mortal enemies is more what they sounded like when they were together. And Reggie didn't doubt for a minute that they both enjoyed baiting each other. But that did run in the family, leastwise with the men in the family.

It was a known fact that the four Malory brothers were happiest when they were arguing among themselves, though they would stand united against any other opposition. The bridegroom and his four brothers were a prime example of that, at least where Tony and James were concerned.

It was James who had been at complete odds with them because of his unorthodox courtship of their sister Georgina — and that he had previously disabled a couple of their Skylark ships when he'd been known as the Hawk didn't help. They'd beat James soundly and were going to turn him over for hanging, but he'd escaped and stole Georgina right out from under their noses.

However, tenacious Americans that they were, they'd followed him back to England to retrieve their sister, only to find that she was quite in love with him by then. But it had been an uncomfortable beginning. When the two families had finally met socially every one of the Malorys had stood firm behind James until he himself had made an overture of welcome to the American Andersons — albeit grudgingly and at Georgina's prompting.

Reggie's cousins got along well with the Americans. Derek and Jeremy had, in fact, taken the younger two Andersons under their wing, but Drew Anderson, the fourth youngest brother, was a devil-may-care flirt just like Jeremy, and Boyd, the youngest and much more serious, was still more inclined toward frivolous pursuits, so he enjoyed himself with them as well.

Reggie sighed. Now that it had been decided that Warren would remain in England to run the Skylark Lines shipping office, for the large fleet of merchant ships owned by the Anderson family, Reggie didn't doubt that her husband would become quite chummy with Warren. They had so much in common, after all, both disliking James Malory so intensely. And Reggie would have worried about Nicholas's becoming friends with the Yank if Anderson hadn't changed so drastically after he'd finally asked Amy to marry him.

Before that, Reggie had never met a man with such a chip on his shoulder. It was as if Warren carried a grudge against the entire world. And that grudge came part and parcel with a very explosive temper. But you'd never guess that to look at the man now. Happy was what he was, and Amy Malory was responsible for that.

Reggie became uneasy when she noticed that Derek had left her husband alone with her uncles. Nicholas usually always ended up quite annoyed whenever he crossed words with those two, always coming out the loser under Uncle James's sardonic barbs. She was about to go rescue him when he walked away himself, and he was smiling.

She smiled herself. Much as she loved her two youngest uncles, they having always been her favorites, she loved her husband even more. And if he had just managed to come out ahead in one of their many verbal spats, she was pleased for him. But, then, the very reason they were all gathered together that day gave him all the ammunition he needed to annoy James. After all, James couldn't be very pleased that another of his prime adversaries had just become a member of the family.

No, not very pleased at all.

"This makes it official," Anthony Malory remarked to his brother as they both gazed at the newly married couple. "He's definitely part of the family now. 'Course, he was already *your* brother-in-law, more's the pity, but at least he wasn't related to the rest of us — until now."

"Brother-in-laws can be ignored. My George does a good job of ignoring you, don't she?" James replied.

Anthony chuckled. "That dear girl is quite fond of me and you know it."

James snorted. " 'Bout as fond of you, Tony, as I am of her family."

Anthony grinned. "When are you going to stop blaming the Yank for trying to hang you, when *you* instigated the whole silly debacle?"

"Don't blame him for that a'tall," James admitted. "It was threatening to hang my crew along with me that earned him my everlasting ire."

"Yes, I suppose that would do it." Anthony nodded.

James had captained the *Maiden Anne* for a good ten years, and during that time his crew had become like a second family to him — or a first family, as it were, since back then his own family had disowned him. But he was reinstated into the Malory fold now, having retired from his unsavory career of gentleman pirate years before, when he'd discovered he had a sixteen-year-old son who needed taking in hand.

"You think he'll make her happy?" Anthony asked, still staring at the newlyweds.

"I'll wait patiently for the day he don't."

Anthony laughed. "Hate to admit it, but ol' Nick was right. Being so fond of our nieces does tie our hands where their husbands are concerned."

"Doesn't it though?" James sighed. "Although I tend to adhere to 'What one don't know don't hurt 'em.' Leaves a bit of lee-way."

"Hmmm, it does, don't it? I wonder if the Yank would like to continue his lessons in the ring."

"Was thinking of asking him that myself."

Anthony chuckled, but then he caught sight of a new arrival and nudged his brother. "Will you look at that? Frances actually showed up."

James followed his brother's gaze to the small, painfully thin woman standing in the doorway. "That surprises you?" he asked his brother, then, "Good God, you don't mean to say Jason and Frances *still* don't live together?"

"You thought that fence might've mended while you were away to sea?" Anthony shook his head. "If anything, it toppled the rest of the way down and got burned for kindling. They don't even bother to make excuses anymore, and the family wisely stopped asking. She lives the year 'round now in that cottage she bought in Bath, and he stays out at Haverston. Actually, I believe this is the first time I've seen them in the same room in more'n five years."

James gave a look of disgust. "Always thought it was stupid of Jason to marry her for the reason he did."

Anthony raised a black brow. "Really? Thought it was rather noble m'self. Self-sacrificing and all that, typical of something one of the elders would do."

"The elders" was how these two younger Malory brothers referred to the older two, there being such a wide difference in their ages, Anthony and James only a year apart, Jason and Edward only a year apart, but nine years separating James and Edward. Melissa, their only sister, who had died when her daughter, Regina, was only two, had come along in the middle.

"The children weren't desperate for a mother, not when the four of us each had a hand in raising them. Besides, Frances was never around to be a mother for them."

"True," Anthony agreed. "The plan did backfire on Jason. Makes you feel sorry for him, don't it?"

"Sorry for Jason?" James snorted. "Not bloody likely."

"Oh, come now, old chap. You know you love the elders just as I do. Jason might be a stiff-necked, hot-tempered tyrant, but he means well. And he's made such a muck of his personal life, you *have* to feel sorry for him — especially when you and I've got two of the most charming, adorable, wonderful wives this side of creation."

"Hmmm, when you put it that way, I suppose I can dredge up a wee bit of pity. But if you ever tell that blockhead I said so —"

"Not to worry." Anthony grinned. "Ros likes my face just the way it is. Claims your fists ain't healthy for it. By the by, what was Derek chewing your ear off about?"

James shrugged. "Said he needed some advice, but this wasn't the place to discuss it."

"You think he's got himself into some kind of trouble?" Anthony speculated. "Wouldn't be surprised, with him following in our footsteps."

"And dragging Jeremy down the same path," James grumbled.

Anthony hooted. "That's rich. That youngun of yours was out wenching with your crew when he was but sixteen, prob'ly sooner. If Derek's doing anything, he's teaching him the proper way to go about it."

"Or Jeremy's teaching him the improper way — bloody hell, now you've got me spouting that drivel. There *ain't* no such thing as an improper way to go about wenching."

14

Across the room, Lady Frances approached her husband. She was so nervous she was nearly trembling, but she didn't hesitate. She'd made the decision, with her dear Oscar's help, to finally make a full confession to Jason — or, at least, fess up to what he hadn't already guessed on his own.

It was high time their farce of a marriage came to an end. She had never wanted to marry him to begin with, had been horrified at the very idea of it, and originally had flatly refused. He was a great bull of a man, after all, austere, hot-tempered, disgustingly physical — frightening. And she'd known very well they wouldn't suit. But her father had forced her to marry him anyway. He'd wanted the connection with the Malorys, then he hadn't lived long enough to enjoy it.

It had been intolerable though, the eighteen years of their marriage, just as she'd known it would be. Whenever Frances was around her husband, she lived in a constant state of apprehension. Not that he'd ever physically hurt her. It was just that she knew how capable of violence he was, that he was actually prone to it, and that was enough to keep her nerves raw. And he was always blustering about something that had displeased him, whether it was one of his brothers, or some political issue he didn't agree with, or just the weather. Little wonder she'd invented excuses to avoid him.

Her main excuse had been ill health, which had led Jason to believe she was sickly. In fact, his whole family thought so. That she was on the thin side helped, as did the color of her very fair skin, which could easily be mistaken for paleness. But in actuality, she enjoyed perfect health. You could even go so far as to say she had the constitution of a horse. She'd just never let Jason know that.

But she was done with hiding the truth. She was tired of being married to a man she couldn't tolerate, especially now that she'd found one whom she could.

Oscar Adams was the exact opposite of Jason Malory. He wasn't very tall — was short, actually — and he wasn't the least bit muscular. He was a dear, sweet, soft-spoken man who enjoyed scholarly pursuits rather than things of a physical nature.

They had so very much in common, and they had discovered their love for each other nearly three years before. It had taken that long for Frances to finally gather the nerve to face Jason with that truth. And what better time to end a bad marriage than on the very day that another, happier marriage was just beginning?

"Jason?"

He hadn't noticed her arrival, was talking with his son, Derek. They both turned to her, both smiled as they offered her a greeting. Derek's smile was genuine. She had little doubt that Jason's was not. In fact, she had no doubt at all that he desired her company about as much as she did his. He ought to be damned pleased with what she'd come here to tell him. And she wasn't going to put it off with idle chitchat first.

"Might I have a word with you, Jason — in private?"

"Certainly, Frances. Will Edward's study do?"

She nodded and allowed him to escort her from the room. Her nervousness increased. Actually, that had been a foolish suggestion on her part. She should have just asked him to step aside. They could have discussed the matter in whispers. No one would have been the wiser, and at least others would have been about, to keep Jason from losing his temper.

But it was too late now. He was already closing the door to his brother's study. The best Frances could do was hurry across the room and put one of the large stuffed chairs between them. However, when she faced him, the words stuck in her throat because he was lifting a sardonic brow. And although he *ought* to be pleased by what she was going to say, Jason Malory's reactions were never predictable.

She had to take a deep breath before she could get the words out. "I want a divorce."

"A *what?*"

She stiffened. "Your hearing is excellent, Jason. Don't make me repeat it just because I have managed to surprise you, though heaven knows you shouldn't be surprised. It's not as if we ever had a real marriage."

"What we have, madam, is redundant. What I am feeling is not surprise, but pure disbelief that you would even suggest such a thing."

At least he wasn't shouting — yet. And his face was only slightly red.

"It wasn't a suggestion," she told him, and braced herself for the fireworks. "It was a demand."

She caught him off guard again. He just stared for a moment, incredulous. And then the frown came, the stern one that usually twisted her stomach into knots. This time was no different.

"You know as well as I that divorce is out of the question. You come from good family, Frances. You know bloody well that divorce is unheard of in our circle —"

"Not unheard of," she corrected. "Merely scandalous. And scandal is nothing new to your family. Your younger brothers used to create one after another, year after year, when they first descended upon London. You even set the tongues wagging yourself when you announced that your illegitimate son was going to be your heir."

His face was now much redder. He didn't take well to criticism about his family, he never had. And saying that the Malorys had been embroiled in so many scandals could be considered criticism.

"There will be no divorce, Frances. You may continue to hide yourself in Bath away from me, if that is your preference, but you will remain my wife."

That infuriated her, because it was so typical of him. "You are the most inconsiderate brute I have ever had the misfortune of knowing, Jason Malory. I wish to get on with my life! But what do you care? You have your mistress living under your roof, a woman of low birth whom you couldn't marry, even if you were free to do so, without causing an even bigger scandal than a divorce would. So it doesn't matter to you if nothing changes . . . and what is that look for? Did you honestly think I didn't know about Molly?"

"Did you expect me to remain celibate when you have never once shared my bed?"

Frances's face was now glowing hotly, but she wasn't going to let him put the blame for their disastrous marriage on her shoulders alone. "There's no need for excuses, Jason. Molly was your mistress before you married me, and you had every intention of keeping her afterwards, which is just what you did. And that certainly never bothered me, if that is what you are thinking. Far from it. She was more than welcome to you as far as I was concerned."

"How generous of you, m'dear."

"There's no need for sarcasm either. I don't love you. I never have. And you know that full well."

"That was not an expectation or requirement of our arrangement."

"No, of course it wasn't," she agreed. "And that's all our marriage ever was to you, an arrangement. Well, I want out of it. I've met someone whom I do love and whom I wish to marry. And never mind asking who he is. Suffice it to say, he's nothing like you."

She'd managed to surprise him yet again. She wished she could have kept Oscar out of it, but mentioning him told Jason just how serious she was. He still didn't look inclined to be reasonable. Of course, when was he ever, stubborn, bullheaded man that he was? And she did still have one piece of information left to sway him with. She'd really been hoping she wouldn't have to use it. Blackmail was so unsavory, after all. But she should have known better. And she wanted out of this marriage bad enough to resort to any means — blackmail included.

"I have just given you an excellent reason to divorce me, Jason," she pointed out reasonably.

"You haven't been listening —"

"No! *You* haven't been listening. I didn't want to get nasty about this, but you force my hand. Give me a divorce — or Derek is going to learn that his mother isn't dead. He'll learn that she's very much alive and has been at Haverston all these years — and in your bed. Your well-kept secret will be known to all, Jason, if you won't be reasonable about this. So which scandal do you find preferable?"

15

The town house was lovely, but Kelsey didn't assume it would be her new home. She was done with making assumptions. And if it was to be hers, the fact that it was very nice and tastefully furnished didn't mollify her. She wasn't sure anything could mollify her, after the horrid five days she had just endured.

Derek's driver had shown up bright and early that morning, just as Kelsey was about to leave for her daily walk to town. She'd thought he was bringing her word from Derek, but no, the man said he was there to take her back to London. No message from Derek. No explanation as to why she'd been left to fend for herself for five long days. And the driver had no other information to impart. He'd only been told to fetch her and where to take her.

She packed up quickly, everything, including the few essentials she'd been forced to buy herself, just in case where she was being taken was as spartan as the cottage had been. But she had the driver take her to Bridgewater first so she could turn over the last of the dresses she'd contracted to sew, which she had fortunately finished late the night before.

She had finished the first five dresses in only three days, despite catching a miserable cold. She knew she wouldn't be getting any more money until the dresses were done. But the seamstress had liked her work so well that she'd given her the rest of the lady's order to complete, another three dresses for two more pounds.

So at least she wasn't penniless now. She'd even bought her own lunch at the inn the driver stopped at around noon — and some extra food to take with her, just in case. After having experienced such panic that first day she'd been left alone, it was going to take a while for her to stop worrying about where her next meal was going to come from.

Derek Malory had a lot of explaining to do, and Kelsey hoped she could keep her temper under control long enough to listen to what he had to say for himself. But all the way to London she had simmered, and she had been so tense that by the time she arrived late that afternoon, her whole body ached. Added to the cold and the fever she was still running, *and* the fact that neither Derek nor anyone else was there to greet her, it just made her more irritable.

There was about an hour of daylight left for her to explore the town house. The driver had stayed long enough to get the fireplaces lit before he departed. And there were ample lamps and candles about for the evening.

It wasn't a large town house by lordly standards, though each of the seven rooms was a nice, comfortable size, and it was in a nice neighborhood with a small park in the center of the square. There was a separate kitchen with one bedroom for a servant or two next to it — it contained two narrow beds — a dining room with a table large enough to seat six, a parlor, a small study, and two bedrooms upstairs.

The fact that it was so completely furnished, even to having a wall of books in the study, finely framed paintings on the walls, knickknacks on tables, ample bedding and linens, and basic long-lasting staples in the kitchen, led her to believe it was someone's home. Many lords were in the habit of renting out their town houses for long periods of time while they were off on the Continent or firmly entrenched in their country estates. But she was assuming again, which she had told herself she wouldn't do anymore.

There was a full modern bath off the larger bedroom, which Kelsey decided would be hers — if she was to stay there. As she ended her exploring she took a bath. The uncomfortable tub at the cottage — with barely warm water, since she'd had to heat and carry her own — had not been at all satisfying. This one was, though she didn't linger, not knowing when Derek might show up.

There was no fresh food to be found in the kitchen, so she made do with what she had brought along from the inn. She could have fixed up something from the staples, but she didn't really feel like cooking, her fever having increased a few degrees, as it did each evening. She hoped she'd be able to shake the cold now that she was back in London. Those long walks to Bridgewater each day in the frigid air, once in the rain, hadn't allowed her condition to improve.

It was the fever that put her to sleep on the couch in the parlor, that and the plentiful meal and hot bath, and the nice cozy fire. But when the front door opened she woke, giving her enough time to sit up before Derek was standing in the doorway. It didn't give her enough time to look awake.

Her eyes were barely open; the pins had come loose from her hair, letting it spill over her shoulders; her nose had been running, as usual; and she was just giving it a loud blow into the hanky she kept constantly in hand when there he was. And good grief, she had forgotten how truly handsome he was, especially done up all formal as he was. Whatever gathering he'd just come from or was soon going to was a special one, to have him looking so fine.

"Hullo, Kelsey, m'dear," he said with a tender smile. "It's a bit early to be sleeping. Was the trip that tiring?"

She nodded, then shook her head. Damn, this was no time to have her mind muddled with sleep.

"I would've been here sooner," he continued as he started forward. "But the wedding reception I just came from had all my family present, and it's deuced hard getting away from family. By the by, what's happened to your nose?"

She blinked. But her fingers came up automatically to touch her nose, and the rawness she felt there gave her an inkling of what he was referring to. She'd gotten so used to not having a mirror at the cottage that she hadn't even thought to look in one at the town house, but she could imagine the damage all that nose blowing had done.

"I have a cold," she began, but the very mention of it cleared her muddled state and brought her anger surging forth. "Imagine that. A cold I caught while walking to Bridgewater. Why would I do something so silly, with the weather as cold as it was, you might ask? Well, I was starving, you see, and with there being no food in the cottage, and none miraculously appearing, I was forced to use the only transportation I had, my feet, to go and get some. Of course, I had no money to do that, so I was also forced to find work just so I could eat."

The heavy sarcasm at the start of her diatribe stopped him cold, but it was that bit at the end about finding work that stuck in his mind. He equated work for someone of her profession as only one thing, what she would find easiest and most familiar, which was selling her favors.

That this is what occurred to him became apparent when he asked sharply, "And just what kind of work did you find in Bridge-water?"

That that was all he was interested in knowing, after everything she'd said, had her hissing, "Not what *you're* thinking! But what if it was? Would my starving have been preferable?"

That she was obviously accusing him of something brought up his defenses. "I'm deuced if I know what you're talking about," he snorted. "How could you have been even close to starving, when I sent you several weeks' worth of food? And my driver was left there at your disposal, so there was no need for you to walk anywhere unless it was your choice to do so."

She stared at him incredulously. Either he was suffering some sort of delusion or he was lying. And what, after all, did she actually know about him to indicate that he wasn't a liar? He had *seemed* nice enough. He had *seemed* kind. But that could have just been some ploy so she wouldn't suspect that he enjoyed making people suffer deprivation, and panic, and fear. And if the latter was true, then she was in a much more horrid position than she had assumed, being bound to him because of the auction until *he* decided to end their relationship.

That so infuriated her, that he actually might be that cruel, she came to her feet and started throwing whatever came to hand at him, stressing with each throw, "There was *no* food delivered! Your driver did *not* show up until today! And if you think you can deceive and confuse me with denials to the contrary, you —"

She didn't get any further because he didn't just stand there letting her aim missiles at him. He easily dodged the first one, and the second went over his head as he dived at her, pushing her back down onto the couch with himself landing on top of her.

After she got her breath back from the impact, she shrieked, "Get off of me, you clumsy clod!"

"My dear girl, there was nothing clumsy involved in the position you now find yourself. It was quite intentional, I do assure you."

"Get off of me anyway!"

"So you can resume your spat of violence?

No, no. Violence is *not* going to be part of our relationship. I could've sworn I already mentioned that."

"And what do you call squashing me like this?"

"Prudence, actually." And then he paused, his eyes getting greener by the second as he stared down at her. "On the other hand, I'd also call it quite nice."

Her eyes narrowed. "If you're thinking about kissing me, I wouldn't advise it," she warned.

"No?"

"No."

He sighed. "Ah, well." But then a half grin formed as he added, "I don't always take good advice."

There was no way to stop him from kissing her, in the position she was in, especially when his hand came to her chin to keep her from even turning her head to the side. But his lips brushed hers for no more than a second before he jerked back as if he'd been burned, and in fact, it was the heat of her fever that he'd felt.

"Good God, you *are* ill, aren't you? You're bloody well burning up. Have you seen a doctor?"

"What, pray tell, would I have paid a doctor with," she asked tiredly, "when I only earned enough coins with my sewing to feed myself?"

At that his face flushed angrily, and he shot to his feet to growl down at her, "Explain yourself. Were you robbed? Did the cottage and everything in it burn down? Why didn't you have any food, when I sent down plenty?"

"So you say, but as nothing arrived, I would say you didn't."

He stiffened. "Do *not* accuse me of lying, Kelsey. I don't know what happened to the provisions I arranged to be brought to the cottage, though I *will* find out. And I *did* make those arrangements. I also left the coach and driver there for your disposal."

He sounded sincere, he really did. She wished she could know for certain that he was. But she allowed it might be prudent now to give him the benefit of the doubt until she had proof to the contrary.

"If you did," she said as she slowly sat up, "I certainly didn't see hide nor hair of him, at least not until this morning."

"He was to check with you daily, to see if you would need him. You're saying he never did?"

"How would I know if he did or not, when I was rarely there? Or didn't you hear me say I had to walk to town each day just to buy my food?"

It finally dawned on him just what she had faced — alone. "Good God, no wonder you jumped down my — that is to say —

oh, Kelsey, I am *so* sorry. Believe me, if I'd had any idea that you weren't comfortably settled in the cottage, I would have returned immediately."

He looked so appalled that she felt like reassuring him. Actually, aside from the panic and worry, it wouldn't have been so bad if it weren't winter, and if she hadn't caught a cold. And now that the anger was leaving her, the symptoms of that cold were becoming overly noticeable again.

She leaned back against the couch, feeling weak after expending all that angry energy. "I believe I could do with some rest —"

"And a doctor," he cut in as he scooped her up and started to carry her from the room.

"I can walk," she protested. "And a little rest is likely all I need, now that I can stay out of the cold."

He winced, though she didn't notice. She was getting dizzy as the walls passed by her at what seemed an alarming rate of speed. Was he running up the stairs? No, she was merely fainting, which she promptly did.

16

"Molly?"

She awoke slowly, but smiled at Jason when she turned to find him sitting on the side of her bed. She hadn't expected him to return to Haverston that night. He had planned to stay over in the London house since Amy's wedding reception would likely go on so late. But that he was suddenly there in the middle of the night, and in her bedroom, was a normal occurrence, not one to give any alarm.

"Welcome home, my love."

He was that. Jason Malory had been her love for more than half of her life. Molly had always been a little bit incredulous that a man of such consequence as the Marquis of Haverston could fall in love with her. But she no longer doubted his feelings for her.

In the beginning, he had dallied with her as a young lord would with any pretty maid he suddenly discovered living under his roof. He'd been twenty-two and unmarried. She'd just turned eighteen, and had been dazzled by his handsomeness and the charm that very few people ever witnessed.

They had been discreet, of course — very secretive, in fact — because he still had younger brothers living with him, and he felt he must set a good example. He'd even tried to end their affair once when they'd nearly been discovered by one of his brothers. He'd tried to end it again when he felt duty bound to marry. He should have sent her away, but of course he couldn't, not after the promises he had made to her.

He actually managed to stay away from Molly for almost a year, though. But then he'd come upon her one day when she was alone, and in an instant their passion had flared as if it hadn't lain dormant for all those months, and of course, it hadn't. It was almost a physical pain for them both if they couldn't touch when they needed to touch. They suffered too much, each of them, during those separations. And after he'd ended the last one he'd sworn, never again.

And he'd kept his word. She was nearly a wife to him in every way but one, the one that would actually make her a wife. He discussed his decisions and concerns with her. He cherished her when they were alone. And he spent every night with her when he was at home, with no fear of discovery, since he had installed a secret panel in her room that led to the one that had already existed in his room.

Old as Haverston was, there were numerous secret exits from the house that had been needed in years of political and religious turmoil. The concealed exit in the master's bedroom led to stairs and passages that ended in the cellar, where there were two other hidden exits, one led outside, and one led directly into the stable. But the passage to the cellar passed behind the servants' quarters as well, and it had been a simple thing for Jason to put in another hidden opening right into her room, which they had both been using ever since.

Jason had brought a lamp with him as he always did, but it still took Molly a few moments to discern that something was wrong.

She brought a gentle hand to his clenched jaw. "What is it?"

"Frances wants a divorce."

Molly grasped the complications of that immediately. Divorce might be quite common among the lower classes, but it was next to unheard of among the gentry. That Lady Frances, an earl's daughter, a marquis's wife, would even consider such a thing . . .

"Has she lost her senses?"

"No, she's having an affair with some little twit she met in Bath and now wants to marry him."

Molly blinked. "Frances has a lover? *Your* Frances?"

He nodded with a growl.

Molly still couldn't quite believe it. Frances Malory was such a timid little woman. It was quite possible that Molly knew her much better than her husband ever had, because they had spent so much time together whenever Frances was at Haverston. She knew that Frances was intimidated by Jason. One of his tirades could bring the poor woman nearly to tears, even when his wrath wasn't directed at her. She also knew that Frances detested Jason's size — huge, strapping male that he was — because it added to her fear.

Molly had always been in an awkward position, having to deal with Frances as the lady of the house, and listen to her female confidences, when she was Jason's lover. On the one hand, she was grateful that Frances didn't love Jason, because she wasn't sure if she could ever have handled the guilt that would have caused. On the other hand, it had always annoyed her whenever Frances would ridicule or demean Jason for no good reason. Molly could find no fault with him. Frances found nothing *but* fault.

"I find this quite . . . amazing," Molly said thoughtfully. "Don't you?"

"That she wants a divorce?"

"Well, that too, but more that she has a lover. It's just so — well, it's not her, if you know what I mean. An idiot could figure out that she doesn't like men in general, at least that's the impression she gives when she's around them. And we've spoken of it before, if you'll recall. We even concluded that her aversion stemmed from a fear of sex. But obviously, we were wrong — or she got over her fear."

"She got over it, all right," he fairly snarled. "And this has been going on behind my back for I don't know how long!"

"Jason Malory, you are *not* going to get up in arms because she's been having an affair with another man, when you have never touched her yourself, and while you have been —"

He cut in, "It's the principle of the thing —"

She cut back in, "So?"

He sighed, the angry stiffness leaving his body. "You're right, of course. I suppose I should be glad that Frances has found someone else, but blister it, she doesn't have to marry him."

She smiled at him. "I assume you have no intention of agreeing to a divorce, because of the scandal. So what's actually got you so upset?"

"She knows, Molly."

She became very still. She didn't have to ask for an explanation. Just by his expression, she knew it wasn't their affair he was referring to, which she had always suspected Frances was aware of and was even relieved about, because it kept Jason out of her own bed. No, this was about their other secret.

"She can't know. She's just guessing."

"It makes no difference, Molly. She's still threatening to tell Derek *and* the rest of the family. And if the lad asks me outright, you know I won't lie to him. We thought only Amy knew about us, from that time she walked into my study and found me kissing you that Christmas several years ago. Blasted punch, that I know damn well Anthony spiked, didn't give me sense enough to keep my hands off of you."

"But you spoke to Amy, and said she swore she would never tell."

"And I'm sure she hasn't."

Molly was beginning to panic. *She* was the one who had wanted the secret kept, and Jason had given in to her insistence because he loved her. But from the day he had decided to make Derek his official heir, she had been horrified that the future Marquis of Haverston would be embarrassed if he knew that his mother had been a mere parlor maid. She didn't want him to know. It was bad enough that he was illegitimate. But at least he assumed his mother had been a member of the gentry, if a promiscuous one, and that she had died shortly after his birth.

In not telling Derek, she had given up her

right to be a mother to him. That hadn't been easy, but at least she had always been nearby, had been there to watch him grow and knew she always would be. Jason had sworn to her that she would never be sent away where she might never see Derek again.

Derek was grown now, was rarely at home anymore, but her feelings still hadn't changed. She still didn't want her son to be ashamed of his mother. And he would be. How could he not be? After all this time, for him to learn she wasn't even dead, and worse, that she'd been his father's mistress all these years . . .

"You told her she could have a divorce."

It wasn't even a question. With this hanging in the balance, of course he would agree to the divorce.

"No," he admitted.

"Jason!"

"Molly, listen to me, please. Derek is a full-grown man. I have every faith that he could deal with this now with little difficulty. I never wanted it kept from him to begin with, but I let you talk me into it. Once done, it was too late to change the story, at least while he was young. But he's not young and impressionable anymore. You don't think he would be *happy*, at this point, to know his mother is alive?"

"No, and you said it yourself. It was too

late before to tell, and it's still too late. I may not know him quite as well as you do, Jason, but I know him well enough to know he'll be furious, not just with me, but with you, for lying to him."

"Nonsense."

"Think about it, Jason. He's never felt deprived. He's always had a huge family. He always had dozens of shoulders to cry on when he was a child. He was never lonely. He even had his cousin Regina here for a playmate after your sister died. But if he finds out the truth, he'll *think* he was deprived, don't you see? At least, that will probably be his first reaction. Then the shame will set in —"

"Stop it! That drivel might've washed twenty-five years ago, but times are changing, Molly. The common man is making his mark in the world, in literature, in the arts — in politics. You have nothing to be ashamed of —"

"*I'm* not ashamed of who I am, Jason Malory. But you gentry have a different way of looking at things. Lords always have and probably always will. And they don't want their fine, aristocratic blood mixing with the common man's, not for their heirs, anyway. And you're a prime example yourself. Or did you not go out and find 'yourself an earl's daughter to marry, a woman you could barely tolerate, just to give Derek a mother, when his real mother was sleeping in your bed?"

She regretted saying that the moment it was out. She knew he couldn't marry her. It simply wasn't done. And she had never, ever complained to him about it, accepting what he could give her of himself, accepting her place in his life. That she had been hurt when he married Frances, she had vowed he would never know. That she might have felt some resentment occasionally that she couldn't be his wife, she had hoped he would never know. But after a stupid, thoughtless remark like that . . .

Before he could address it, she continued, hoping to distract him. "Frances is apparently determined to give you a scandal either way, Jason, and one isn't much worse than the other, so let sleeping dogs lie, please. You and Frances have lived separately for most of your marriage. Everyone knows that. So do you really think anyone will raise too much of an eyebrow if you divorce? I would imagine most of your friends will merely remark, 'Surprised you didn't do it sooner.' Tell her you've changed your mind."

"I gave her no definite answer," he grouched. "A matter like this needs thinking upon."

Molly sighed in relief. She knew her love very well. Just by his tone, she knew he'd been swayed to her reasoning. She didn't know which point had done the trick. She didn't want to know — as long as her secret remained safe.

17

She looked so fragile lying there, her hair stringy with sweat, moisture on her pale brow and cheeks, her breathing shallow. But Derek knew there wasn't much that was fragile about Kelsey Langton. Quite a temper she had, even when ill. He could just imagine what it could be like when she was feeling up to snuff.

He couldn't blame her for trying to brain him with a candle holder, after what she had endured. He'd sent his driver back to Bridgewater to find out what had happened, and had the story from him the previous night. He'd had no way of knowing that the maid he'd instructed to deliver what was needed to the cottage had already been fired by his housekeeper and so had no reason to comply or even to give those instructions to someone else. She had simply packed up her things and left. And Kelsey had had no way of knowing that either.

Derek hadn't been able to tell her yet. She hadn't been lucid enough since the evening before, the doctor's medicines finally working to free her cold, and as the doctor had warned, her illness had gotten much worse before it improved. But she had just broken her fever and was sleeping peacefully at last. It had been a long night. It had been an even longer two days, because he'd barely left her side since she had fainted in his arms three nights before.

She made a terrible patient, grumpy, argumentative. She hadn't wanted him to do anything for her, had wanted to get up and do for herself. But he had insisted, wiping her down with cool wet cloths, at least those limbs she would reveal to him, bringing her meals to her, unappetizing as they were. He was bloody well all thumbs in the kitchen.

A cook was to show up today for an interview. He had sent his driver to the employment agency to arrange for some help before he returned to Bridgewater. Whoever showed would be hired on the spot, because if Derek never stepped into a kitchen again, it would be too soon. The other servants could wait until Kelsey was feeling up to hiring them.

The night of passion that he had envisioned upon her return to London certainly hadn't worked out as he'd hoped. And he'd left Amy's reception early that evening only to be met with passionate fury instead of what he'd been so looking forward to. But there would be ample time for that now that he had her installed in London.

It was the sunlight streaming into the room that woke Kelsey. Derek had forgotten to close the curtains again the night before. But then he overlooked many little things like that, things that servants usually tended to. Not that it mattered, as helpful as he'd been trying to be. He was feeling remorse, when quite possibly he had no reason to be remorseful. But he was still trying to make amends, and that said a lot for him.

It was the second morning she had awakened to find him still in the room with her. The day before he'd greeted her with tea, broth, and medicine. This day he wasn't just there, he was also in her bed.

It was quite a surprise waking to find him there beside her. And quite a chore trying to rack her sluggish mind to find if there was a reason for him to be there other than that he'd just been too tired to find somewhere else to sleep. But she couldn't recall anything beyond the light meal she'd had the night before and that she had barely kept down, and her raging fever.

She felt much better this morning though, a little weak, a bit bedsore after being confined for two days, but the constant heat that she had been living with was gone. In fact, for the first time in days she was a bit chilled. She noticed that the fire in the room had burned down to a few embers, and that her sleeping gown was damp from the night sweats.

The large body next to her was quite a temptation as a source of immediate warmth, but she didn't have the nerve to snuggle close to Derek, even while he was sleeping. He might have tended her these last days, might be her soon-to-be lover, but she still barely knew him — and she wished she hadn't remembered that he *was* going to be her lover. The very thought made her uncomfortable, with him so close. Well, not so much uncomfortable as . . . physically disturbed. She was suddenly too aware that he was a large, handsome male, and with him sleeping, there was nothing to stop her from taking her fill of looking at him.

He was lying on his back on top of the covers, one arm thrown up above his head, the other slack at his side. The long sleeves of his white shirt were rolled up to his elbows, revealing the same golden hair on his arms that was atop his head. The muscles were rather thick on his forearms too, his wrists wide, his hands large.

Another thatch of golden hair was revealed on his upper chest, where his shirt lay open. With the one arm raised, the shirt was also stretched taut, showing just how wide his chest was, how hard and flat his waist. And his legs, so long that his feet reached the end of the bed, shoeless just now, though he'd left his stockings on.

His jaw was slack in sleep, his firm lips just barely parted. He wasn't snoring, but she wondered if he sometimes did. She supposed she would find out eventually.

She saw long, golden eyelashes that she hadn't noticed before because those changeable green eyes of his tended to capture her complete attention. He was frowning, apparently not liking whatever dream he was having. Her fingers almost itched to smooth his brow, but she didn't dare.

She didn't *want* him waking up beside her. Absolutely not. Their position was just too intimate at the moment, and there was no telling what ideas that might give him — though maybe not. She did probably look a fright, after all. Two days of only bed baths, and her hair had gone through several night sweats without being washed. Undoubtedly a definite fright.

Actually, a bath sounded heavenly at the moment, a nice hot soak to ease those sore muscles she was feeling and get rid of the itch on her scalp. And she might be able to accomplish it before Derek even woke, so that she could look halfway decent again when she got around to thanking him for his tender, if somewhat bossy, care.

It amazed her, now that she thought about it, that he'd stayed to tend to her himself when he didn't have to. He could have arranged for a nurse. But she supposed it was his remorse that had kept him there. Although whatever the reason, she was glad that he'd stayed, glad that he'd shown her again that he wasn't as callous and thoughtless as she'd begun to think.

She eased her way out of the bed without disturbing him and gathered up some clothes. And a last glance his way before she closed the bathroom door showed him still fast asleep — at least she hadn't been able to discern his eyes slightly cracked and watching her. And the bath did wonders, ridding her of any lingering feelings of illness. She even took the time to dry her hair before she dressed for the day, though she was still brushing it when she reentered the bedroom.

She'd taken so long, Derek was no longer there. A fire was now burning in the grate again, chasing the chill from the room. Though truthfully she'd barely noticed that chill when she'd left the bed, after staring at Derek for so long. She smiled now, noting that even the bed had been made, and truly, she wished she could have seen him manage that on his own.

She took a few moments more to fix her

hair into her usual coiffure, then went down to see if Derek had left the flat completely. He hadn't. She found him in the kitchen brewing a pot of fresh tea, and on a tray next to him was a plate filled with a half dozen fat pastries. He hadn't changed clothes yet. It was possible he didn't have any clothes there yet to change into.

She smiled when he looked up and noticed her in the doorway. "I won't believe you've had time to bake those," she said, nodding toward the pastries.

He snorted. "Not bloody likely, and never again will I even try. No, I heard a hawker passing and ran down to see what he was selling. Just pastries, but welcome this time of the morning, and actually still warm."

His "never again will I even try" made sense as she noticed the disastrous mess the kitchen had become. Seeing her expression as she gazed about the room, he told her, "A cook will be showing up today — What?" he added, when she looked even more appalled.

"She will poke her head in here and head straight for the front door," she predicted.

He frowned. "Nonsense," he said, but then, "You think so? Very well, I'll make it worth her while to stay. But if you don't like this cook, please don't let her go until you have a replacement ready to take over

— that is, unless you can cook. As for your other servants, they will be showing up this week for you to interview."

"So I *am* to stay here?"

"Don't you like it?"

He looked so disappointed, she was very quick to reassure him, "Of course I like it, I just wasn't sure this was where you were putting me."

"Gad, didn't I mention that? No? Well, I've signed a six-month lease, which can be easily extended. So if there's something you don't like, any of the furniture or whatever, we can change it. This will be your home, Kelsey. I want you to feel comfortable in it."

She blushed slightly at the permanence of that statement and how it related to their relationship — which had yet to really start. "That's very kind of you. I'm sure I will be most comfortable here."

"Excellent. Now, shall we partake of this meager fare in the dining room, where it's not so cluttered?"

She smiled and left the kitchen. The dining room was very cheerful at that time of day, catching the early sun, which hadn't disappeared yet under a bank of clouds, a rare occurrence that time of year.

"How many servants am I to hire?" she asked as she took a seat across from him and poured their tea.

"As many as you need."

"Will you be paying their wages, or do you wish me to see to that?"

"Hmmm, hadn't thought of that. I suppose it will be easiest if I just leave you an allowance for the household, as well as for yourself. And by the by, as soon as you're feeling up to it, we need to take you shopping. You can't have very many clothes stuffed into that small valise of yours."

She supposed she could save him the cost of that by sending for the rest of her own wardrobe. But how would she explain that to Aunt Elizabeth, when she was supposed to only be visiting her friend in Kettering for a short time? It was bad enough that she would have to continue to invent excuses for extending her visit. Besides, her clothes likely weren't in the style of the kind he had in mind buying for her, though she sincerely hoped there wouldn't be any other atrocious red gowns.

So she said, "As you wish."

"And you *are* feeling better this morning?" he asked somewhat hesitantly. "Fever all gone?"

"Yes, I'm quite well finally."

His smile suddenly turned sensual. "Excellent. Then I will leave you to your own devices today, but will return to spend this evening with you."

Kelsey could have kicked herself for not realizing why he was asking after her health. And she had no doubt at all what he meant by "spend this evening with you." She could have postponed it further with just a complaint or two. Now, blushing, she could only nod her concurrence.

18

The cook arrived that morning just after Derek left. And just with the little time that Kelsey spent with the woman, she knew they were going to get along splendidly. Alicia Whipple didn't put on airs, claimed she minded her own business, and after Kelsey got through the embarrassing part of having to explain that she would be receiving a gentleman caller in the evenings, the only polite way to put it, Alicia assured her that whomever she entertained was Kelsey's own affair and none of hers.

Her situation was a problem. She didn't doubt that there were people of the servant class who would refuse to work for someone like her, figuring they would be tarred with the same brush.

For some servants, who they worked for was a matter of pride, and working for a lord's mistress was definitely nothing to be proud about. But there would be others who wouldn't care, who just needed the work, and she would find her people from these.

A carriage and driver showed up around noon. The driver, not Derek's, informed her that he was now in her employ. He explained where he would house the carriage and horses — the town house didn't come with its own stable — and where he could be reached whenever he was needed. And that made her realize that she would need at least one footman, when she had thought she could make do with a smaller staff.

She made her first use of the carriage that afternoon. After giving it some thought, and after the sweet kiss that Derek had left her with, she decided to try to make the evening somewhat romantic, rather than the sordid affair it was. To that end, she arranged with Alicia a nice dinner with wine, and gave her ample money to supply it.

Thankfully, Derek had left her with more than that kiss. The wad of pound notes he'd handed her had added up to nearly one hundred, and he had merely said, "This should tide you over for a bit." Indeed. Large households could be run on much less, and her household was small.

She left Alicia to shop for the food, but she did some shopping of her own. It took quite a while to find what she was looking for, because she wasn't familiar with London. Finally, she'd had to explain her needs to the driver. She did finally find a shop that supplied negligees of the fancy sort — or rather, her driver did. And although she'd never owned anything even remotely similar — her sleeping gowns were all of the warm, serviceable kind — the woman who sold her the ensemble, which came with a matching robe and slippers, assured her that all new brides were wearing negligees on their wedding nights these days.

Whether that was true, or whether the woman had sensed Kelsey's hesitancy and had just been determined to make the sale, she didn't know, nor did she care. The negligee was exactly what Kelsey had envisioned when she'd gone hunting for it, so she was quite satisfied with her purchase. Now, if she would just have the nerve to wear it when the time came. . . .

Derek hadn't told her what time he would be returning that evening. She should have asked him, but not knowing wasn't too much of a problem, or at least Alicia didn't think so. The gentry were accustomed to eating at unusual hours, after all, depending on which party they were attending, and food could be kept warm.

As it happened, he arrived earlier than anticipated, just after sunset. She didn't know it, but he'd had to force himself to stay away even that long, to give her some time to herself, he was so eager to commence their relationship. And he didn't mention it, which was fortunate. She was nervous enough. Knowing that he would have preferred to take her straight up to bed would have undone her.

He was quite the gentleman, however, giving her no indication by look or word what was on his mind. And he arrived with flowers in hand — unnecessary, but very thoughtful. Arranging them helped to put Kelsey at ease during those awkward first moments.

He was dressed rather formally, but then she imagined his valet didn't let him out of the house of an evening dressed any other way. His cravat was perfectly tied, and a bit of white lace showed at the cuffs of his dark brown coat, which stretched so tautly across his wide shoulders. It was sinful, how handsome he was, and she felt so dowdy in comparison.

She had arranged her hair only a bit more fancy tonight, but it was the best she could do. She had brought no formal clothes with her, just a few day dresses for traveling and one gown, which she was wearing now, that could be used for an informal evening. But it was nothing fancy.

It was plain rose taffeta with the short puffed sleeves favored for evening wear, in the empire style, but very unsophisticated for London in that the scooped neckline wasn't the least bit low, as was fashionable. There was nothing provocative about it, no lace or fancy trims to make it a bit more elegant, but Derek still couldn't seem to keep his eyes off her.

They shared aperitifs in the parlor before dinner. Kelsey hadn't thought beyond a little wine, but Alicia had taken stock of what was in the house before going to the market, and fortunately, she'd made a few extra purchases.

Derek kept the conversation light even after they adjourned to the dining room. He mentioned a stallion that his friend Percy had bought that week that was expected to do well at the races. He spoke of his school days and told her about his best friend, Nicholas Eden, and how they'd met. Some of his family was then mentioned, at least his cousin Regina, who had married Nicholas, and his Uncle Anthony, whom he had gone to watch demolish some contender today at Knighton's Hall, whatever that was.

Fortunately, he kept the conversation going with anecdotes about himself, because there was not much she could tell him about herself without lying or giving away the truth. They had no history yet that would lend to discussions about things they had done together — nothing that wasn't disturbing in some way, at any rate.

Over dessert, he finally cleared up the mystery of what had happened in Bridgewater. "The girl I instructed to deliver the supplies to the cottage was let go."

"Because she didn't deliver them?"

"No, she was let go before I gave her the instructions, which is why she didn't bother to carry them out or turn them over to someone else to do. Would have been nice if she'd told me that at the time, but she didn't. She was miffed with the house-keeper for discharging her, and simply packed up her things and left."

"Then I owe you an apology."

"No, you don't," he assured her.

She shook her head. "Yes, I do, for think-ing you were thoughtless and inconsiderate — and for tossing that note you left me in the fire and wishing it were you instead."

He stared at her incredulously for about two seconds before he burst out laughing. Kelsey blushed. She wasn't sure why she'd made that confession, except it went hand in hand with her apology, to explain it anyway.

But she had no idea why he found it so funny until he remarked, "That's quite a temper you keep under wraps. Would never guess it was there, listening to you."

"I suppose I do have a bit of one, though it's rarely had occasion to be provoked," she admitted. "It runs in my family, I guess, at least on my mother's side."

Which was an understatement. In fact, folks would say her mother's temper was a bit too hot, considering she'd killed her husband during one of her tantrums, un-intentionally, but final all the same.

She peeked at him under her lashes. "You don't mind?"

"Hardly. Tempers run high in my own family, so I'm used to it." Then he smiled. "And I don't believe I'll be provoking yours often."

She smiled back at him. What a nice roundabout way to say that he'd be giving her no reason to find fault with him. She was glad then that she'd gone to a little extra effort to make their evening special. Although looking at him, how she could have thought that anything to do with him would be sordid, she didn't know.

It was just the sinful aspect of what they were going to do, she supposed, but she really ought to get over thinking of it that way. She'd made a bargain. She'd kept her family off the streets by doing so. She ought to be infinitely grateful that Derek Malory was the one who'd bought her.

She imagined that many women would consider her lucky. Maybe after that night, she would too. But there was still the night to get through — or rather, what was going to happen upstairs. And it was time. They had enjoyed a very nice dinner. She had even bolstered herself with the wine. She could delay it a bit more, but that wasn't going to make it easier, was only going to increase her nervousness.

So, blushing, she said, "If you don't mind, I will retire now to change into something — cooler — to sleep."

"Good God, yes! That is, please do."

She blinked, unaware until that moment just how eager he was to bed her. Knowing that he was so eager caused a warmth inside her that was actually pleasant — and had her blushing even more furiously.

She stood up to leave. "I will see you shortly, then — upstairs."

He caught her hand as she passed and brought it to his lips. "You're nervous, m'dear. You needn't be. We're going to have fun together, you and I, I promise you."

Fun? He thought of lovemaking as fun? Imagine that. But she could only nod. Words wouldn't escape her tight throat. She wanted to cry for what she was about to lose. She wanted to get it over with. She wanted to shoot her Uncle Elliott for putting her in this house, where she was about to have a wedding night — without the wedding. And deep down, she wanted to taste Derek Malory's kisses again. Good God, she didn't know what she wanted anymore.

19

Kelsey donned the negligee with trembling fingers. She had known she wouldn't feel comfortable in it, and she didn't, but she stubbornly refused to take it off.

It was indecent by itself, not due to any transparency but because the sides were split clear to her hips, revealing more leg than she'd ever shown to anyone. It was made of soft pale blue silk, sleeveless, the bodice in a deep V, the straps mere ties that could be undone easily.

If not for the robe in the same soft silk, she wouldn't have dared to wear it. But the robe covered her legs and arms. There was still a bit of her breasts showing, even with the robe belted closed, but under the circumstances, she supposed that was appropriate.

She was standing by the fire, combing her hair, when the knock came at the door. The words wouldn't come to tell Derek to enter. He obviously felt he didn't need them, because the door opened, and there he stood, his eyes coming directly to her, widening a bit, darkening . . .

"We *really* have to work on those blushes, Kelsey," he said in an amused tone.

She lowered her eyes, the heat in her

cheeks feeling hotter than the fire behind her. "I know."

"You look — beautiful."

He said it as if that wasn't quite the word he wanted to use, as if he were a bit in awe. And he was standing in front of her within moments, taking the comb from her hand, setting it aside, lifting a lock of her long hair to his cheek, then letting it drift back to her waist.

"Absolutely beautiful," he repeated.

That drew her gaze up to him, and the look in his green eyes, so admiring, warmed her even more. His being so close, though, was causing her to feel other things, a tickling in her belly, a tightening in her breasts. Even the smell of him, spicy, was thrilling her senses. And she found herself staring at his mouth, almost willing him to kiss her, re-membering how much nicer it had been before when he was kissing her, how she wasn't self-conscious then, how her thoughts had scattered, giving her some peace.

The belt of her robe came undone — with his assistance. Her blush started again as the thin silk pooled at her feet. But she heard his indrawn breath, felt his eyes slowly traveling the length of her.

His voice was exceedingly husky when he said, "We will have to buy you more of — those," and a hand indicated the negligee. "Many more."

Must we? She thought she'd said it aloud, but the words hadn't come out. And she was too tense now, waiting . . . waiting.

And then his hands were gently cupping her cheeks. "Do you know how much I've been looking forward to this?" he asked her softly.

She had no answer for him. She didn't need one, because he'd no sooner said it than he was kissing her, seriously kissing her, parting her lips, his tongue delving, tasting, dueling with hers. He'd moved closer. Her breasts now touched his chest. And she was getting weak with the need to lean against him, until she finally gave in to the urge.

He groaned at that sign of yielding and lifted her in his arms, carried her to the bed and laid her gently there, then leaned back to gaze at her while he removed his coat and cravat. Her eyes met his and went no further. Her lips parted, trembled, but she couldn't look away, so intensely sensual was his gaze, so mesmerizing.

She hadn't extinguished the lamps in the room. She wished she had, she was so self-conscious. She wanted to dive under the covers too, but didn't, remembering what May had said about men liking to gaze at a woman's body, and she might as well have been naked already, the soft silk molded so clearly to her skin in her prone position. But it was so hard lying there, waiting for him to join her.

She couldn't know how enticing she was, with her black hair spread out over the pillows, her knees bent just so, so that one slim leg peeked out of the blue silk. With her full lips parted, she seemed to be begging for the return of his mouth. And those black-lashed, turbulent gray eyes, fearful — surely not. But they somehow made Derek feel like a bloody Spartan about to ravish a village maid. Strange feeling, and it did absolutely nothing to tamp down his raging desire.

From the moment he entered the room and saw her in that skimpy ensemble, he became thick and turgid. He tried to think of other things, but nothing helped. He wanted her too much, that was the problem. And he wasn't even sure why.

He'd bedded other women more beautiful. But there was just something about Kelsey, the feigned innocence perhaps, those silly, ridiculous blushes that she could summon at whim, maybe the fact that he'd bought her . . . he didn't know, but he wanted to jump on her and savor her simultaneously, which of course was impossible.

It was a hard choice to make, and didn't get any easier when he joined her on the bed and touched her again. Silken smooth she was, and soft in all the right places. And he was nearly undone when he released her shoulder ties and slowly peeled down the blue silk to reveal her breasts, which puckered immediately under his hot gaze. Again, he felt the urge to bury himself in her then and there, and he simply couldn't think of anything to cool his ardor short of a cold bath, which would be ridiculous under the circumstances.

He should have had more wine with dinner. No, she should have had more, then she might not mind if he simply pounced on her. Maybe she wouldn't mind anyway? Damnit, *he* minded. He wasn't some untried, wet-behind-the-ears youth with no control to speak of. He would take his time, even if it killed him.

He began kissing her again, deliberately, concentrating. But he couldn't keep his hands from wandering. Her breasts were plump and firm, quite the handful. It wasn't long before his mouth worked its way there, and her gasp of pleasure was the sweetest music.

He was touching her all over. Kelsey had to repeatedly remind herself that he had that right. And his mouth, the things it was making her feel. She was afraid her fever was coming back.

His hand tried to part her legs. She held them tightly closed. He chuckled, just before he kissed her again, so passionately that she quickly forgot about her legs — and his hand slipped between them. She nearly arched off the bed. Never could she have imagined anything so shocking — and so wildly thrilling — as what he was doing with his fingers.

All thoughts gave way to sensation that was so intensely pleasant that the ache steadily building inside her wasn't noticed until it fully caught up with her, overwhelming her. She moaned deep in her throat. She arched toward him. She pulled at him. She didn't understand.

And all semblance of control deserted Derek in that moment. He moved between her legs. He lifted them. And in the next second, he was deep inside her, his penetration so swift that there was no time to stop for any barriers. He vaguely noted there had been one, but what it was didn't quite register, not when he was surrounded by such tightness, such exquisite heat, such primitive pleasure. It was so sweet he nearly came with that single thrust, but a moot point, since the next thrust sent him over the edge.

When clear thought managed to work its way back into his pleasure-dazed mind, Derek sighed. Had he thought he'd gotten far beyond his first pathetically eager experiences of lovemaking as a lad, when he'd been concerned only with his own pleasure and had no control whatsoever over his responses? He gave himself a mental snort. A fine demonstration he'd given of control this night.

He didn't even know if the dear girl had come to her own pleasure, he had been so consumed with his, but it was considered quite tactless to ask. Of course, if she hadn't, he was more than game to rectify that. In fact, the very thought hardened him to fullness again. Amazing. But then she did have an incredibly tight sheath gripping him . . .

"Can you — move to the side — please?"

His weight. What a dolt, lying there savoring his pleasure while he was crushing the poor girl. He leaned up to apologize, taking his weight from her chest, if not the rest of her, but the words didn't make it past the shock of seeing her tears, her woebegone expression, and the realization that he *had* come upon a barrier that had prevented full access. It had been there less than a second, but it had been there.

"Good God, you *were* a virgin!" he blurted out.

Her blush was immediate. "I believe that was mentioned at the auction."

He stared at her incredulously. "My dear girl, nobody bloody well believed that. Purveyors of flesh are notorious liars, after all.

And besides, you were sold in a whore-house. What in the bloody hell would a virgin be doing in a whorehouse?"

"Obviously being sold outright, and as stipulated," she said quite stiffly. "And I'm sorry I didn't have Lonny rid me of my virginity before the sale. I wasn't aware that it would be a liability."

"Don't be absurd," he replied gruffly. "It's just a — surprise — that needs a bit of adjusting to."

A bit? All those blushes had been real, not contrived. All those innocent looks quite appropriate.

A virgin, and his first, if he didn't count the kitchen maid at Haverston who had gone on to spread her favors with every footman in the house. No wonder Ashford had wanted her so much and had been so furious when he didn't get her — more blood to add to his sick pleasures.

A virgin. And the full implication suddenly hit him with a wave of possessiveness the likes of which he'd never felt before. He was her first lover, the only man to have touched her, and not only that, he *owned* her. She belonged to him.

He smiled at her suddenly, brilliantly. "There, you see? Already adjusted." He was hard and aching to have her again, but he carefully, slowly eased out of her instead. "I've made quite a muck of it, your first

189

time. Acted like an untried youth m'self, wanting you so much, but that can only have made it worse for you. When you've recovered, I'll see to giving you the same pleasure that you gave me. But just now, we'll see to your wounds."

Before she could protest, he was lifting her in his arms again and carrying her into the bathroom. He set her down there and wrapped a large towel around her while he drew her bathwater and adjusted it, adding salts and suds and perfumes as the tub filled. It was all she could do to keep her eyes off him, because he hadn't covered himself, was still completely and unself-consciously naked.

When he moved to put her in the water, she held up a hand. "I can manage from here —"

"Nonsense." And he flicked the towel aside and lifted her again, lowering her carefully into the steaming tub. "I've gotten in the habit of bathing you, after all, and it's rather a nice habit to get into."

Kneeling there at the side of the tub, he washed her, *everywhere*. Her skin remained pink the entire time, and not from the steamy heat. And then he was lifting her out again, drying her, and carrying her back to the bed, where he put her under the covers this time and, joining her there, drew her snugly into his arms.

She was able to relax then, realizing that there would be no more pain — or pleasure — that night. Even their nakedness didn't disturb her, merely added to the warmth that was putting her to sleep.

She'd almost nodded off when she heard, "Thank you, Kelsey Langton, for gifting me with your virginity."

She didn't point out that she'd had little choice in the matter. And it hadn't been as bad as it could have been with anyone else. There had even been a great deal of pleasure — before the pain.

So in the same formal tone, though with a half yawn, she replied, "You're quite welcome, Derek Malory."

She didn't see his smile, though she felt him pull her just a tad closer. Her hand drifted up to rest on his chest, hesitantly at first, then without worry. She *could* touch him now, whenever she liked. After this night, she had that right — just as he had the right to touch her — and amazingly, she was pleased by it.

Imagine that.

20

Kelsey awoke the next morning alone, Derek having left sometime in the middle of the night. He was quite thoughtful, sparing her the embarrassment of facing him bright and early, still in bed, still naked. She wondered if that was going to be his habit. Quite possibly, to be discreet. It was a nice neighborhood, after all, that he'd put her in. And he did seem to be concerned with discretion.

Of course, he could be married, and that was why he wanted secrecy. What a horrid thought. But it was possible, and even something she'd been advised to expect. She'd have to ask him. She'd rather know, even if it were so, than constantly wonder.

She found Derek's note on the pillow next to her. His scent was still there too, which made her smile for some reason. The note informed her that he'd be picking her up that afternoon for shopping and then dinner. She smiled again. That actually sounded like fun. She had always enjoyed shopping, at any rate. As long as he didn't intend buying her gaudy, mistresslike clothes. She sighed. That was probably exactly his intention. But if she must wear them, then she must.

It was amazing, the burden that had been lifted from her now that she was no longer a virgin. She might regret that fact, but there was no changing it. She was well and truly a mistress. No more agonizing, no more fear of the unknown. The pain was behind her. It hadn't been pleasant. But there was pleasure to look forward to. She had experienced some of it, had been promised more. And Derek was not only handsome but so very considerate of her. What more could she ask for under the circumstances?

"Well, don't you look full of it," Nicholas Eden remarked as he came into his dining room to find Derek there already, just as used to be the case so often before he'd married.

The grin that Derek had been wearing as he sat there absently moving food around on his plate altered slightly. "Full of what? Only just sat down to eat."

Nicholas chuckled. "Wasn't referring to food, dear boy, but satisfaction. It's fairly oozing out of you. You remind me of a randy rooster that's finally located the henhouse. That good, was she?"

It wasn't often that Derek blushed, but this was one of those times. And that was unusual, because ribbing about his peccadilloes from his friends tended to amuse rather than embarrass him. It was possibly because he'd sworn off mistresses and Nicholas knew that, yet he was about to admit he had a new one.

He'd had a note yesterday from Nicholas when he returned home for a change of clothes. The note said that Nicholas and the wife were staying in town for the week for some shopping and visiting, which really meant that Reggie wanted to do some shopping and visiting and old Nick had been wheedled into keeping her company. These days, Derek didn't often get out to Silverley, which was Nick's country estate where he and Reggie tended to hibernate, at least during the hectic London social seasons. And he'd been too absentminded at Amy and Warren's wedding, thinking about excuses to leave early so he could see Kelsey again, to talk much with his friend.

Strangest thing was, he wanted to discuss Kelsey with Nick, and yet he didn't want to.

They were much alike, Nicholas a few years older, a tad taller, his hair a bit darker, though streaked with gold, and his eyes more amber than brown. Nick was a viscount. Derek was too, for that matter, a title that had come with one of the estates turned over to him, though one day he would also become the fourth

Marquis of Haverston.

They were also both illegitimate, which was why Nick had befriended Derek in their school days, it being a known fact in Derek's case, a secret in Nick's. Even Derek hadn't known until after Nick's marriage to his cousin Regina.

But at least Nicholas knew who his mother was, or at least he did now. The woman whom everyone thought was his mother, his father's wife, despised him, just as he did her, and had made his life miserable. It was her sister, whom Nick had always thought was his aunt, who was his real mother. She'd always been there for him, but he hadn't discovered her true identity until a few years before.

They each felt differently about their illegitimacy. When Nicholas had discovered the fact he'd been bitter, until he married Reggie, who didn't give a fig about it. Derek had always known but hadn't let it bother him — much. He had a large family, after all, who accepted him as he was. Nicholas hadn't had that type of support. But Derek did regret never having known his mother, or even known who she was. The few times he'd asked his father many years ago, he'd simply been told that she was dead, so it wasn't important.

As for Nicholas's remark, Derek admitted, "Actually, she's my new mistress."

Nicholas raised a brow. "Correct me if I'm wrong, but didn't you swear off keeping any more of those?"

"Yes, but these circumstances are different," Derek assured him.

"So we all tend to think — for a time," Nicholas said with a touch of his old cynicism, but then he shrugged. "Well, enjoy her while you can, because the newness will wear thin soon enough and you'll be sniffing around for a replacement. Happened to me every bloody time — well, at least until I met your cousin. Should have known I was in love when I couldn't get that little minx out of my mind no matter what I did."

"No, Nick, these circumstances are *really* different. Fact is, I'm not just keeping her, I — er — bought her."

Up went that brow again. "I beg your pardon?"

"Bought her," Derek repeated, then clarified. "As in found her being sold at an auction and — bought her.".

"Just how much blunt are we talking about here?" Nicholas asked.

"You don't want to know."

"Good God, you better hope your father doesn't learn about it."

Derek cringed at the very thought. "I know, and there's no reason he should."

Nicholas shook his head. "I assume she

was just so beautiful you couldn't resist the impulse?"

"Actually, that was Jeremy's reaction rather than mine. That scamp wanted to *borrow* the money from me to bid on her. He was bloody well determined till I reminded him he ain't got no place to keep a mistress."

"So Jeremy was there?"

"And Percy."

"Where was this unusual occurrence? One of our — er — your usual haunts?"

Derek grinned. Their threesome had previously been Nick, Percy, and himself, but that was before James moved back to England with Jeremy — and before old Nick got himself thoroughly leg-shackled.

"No," Derek said. "It was at the new House of Eros that's opened up since you retired from availability, a place that caters more to perversion than not, though we didn't know that at the time. Just stopped by because one of Jeremy's favorite light o' loves had moved there."

Nicholas chuckled. "So the lad asked to borrow money from you when you outbid him? That takes gall, but then gall runs in that side of your family."

"Now, now, let's not get into bashing my Uncle James, whom we all know you are so fond of." Derek waited for the expected snort to that remark and got it. "And I wasn't bidding, had no intention of doing so."

"No? Then why did you?"

"Because of who else was bidding on her. Ever have any dealings with Lord David Ashford?"

"Can't say as I have. Why?"

"We had a run-in with him not so long ago, one night when we were slumming down by the waterfront. Found him severely whipping a tavern wench he'd tied to a bed, so badly she'll likely be scarred for life, and this was to — prepare himself — to have sex with her. If she hadn't worked the gag out of her mouth, we never would have heard her screams."

Nicholas made a sound of disgust. "Sounds like he belongs in Bedlam."

"I couldn't agree more, but apparently he's kept his despicable habit quiet. Very few know about it, and he pays his victims too handsomely for them to file any charges. I beat him senseless that night — damn near killed him, actually. Thought that would be the end of it, until the other night, when I saw him bidding on this girl and knew damn well what her fate was going to be if he got her. Couldn't let that happen, now, could I?"

"I'd have taken him out and beaten him senseless again. Much less costly, particularly since you didn't really want the girl for yourself."

"But he'd have still got her. His bid was the last one. The proprietor would merely have collected from him and turned the girl over to him later. And besides, I'm not displeased that I won her."

Nicholas laughed. "That's right, I was forgetting that look you were wearing when I walked in."

Again, Derek felt himself blushing. Bloody hell, it must be catching from Kelsey.

"She's not at all what you'd figure you'd get from an auction in a place like that. She's had a superior education, what with her mother being a governess, possibly better than some ladies we know. Her manners are impeccable. And although it was stated at the auction that she was a virgin, which no one in his right mind would have believed, turns out she actually was."

"Was? As in no longer is?"

Derek hesitated a tad before nodding because he felt that blush coming up again. He groaned mentally. And finally realized that the problem might be that he simply didn't want to discuss Kelsey in this vein, even with his best friend. Which was silly, of course. She was just another chit he'd enjoyed bedding, and Nick was undoubtedly right. The newness would wear off soon enough, and he'd be back in the social whirl searching for the next lady to catch his interest.

"At any rate, I'm not displeased that I have her. The extra cost wasn't even for her but to thwart Ashford, which I'm very pleased to have done. Trouble is, it turns my blood cold, knowing that I only stopped Ashford this one time, that he's still out there finding penny whores to scar up and pay off, and God knows who else he's put through the pain and horror of his sexual habits. He's no doubt a regular at that house that caters to his sort, though unlikely to his degree of brutality. I'd bloody well like to see him stopped — for good. Any ideas?"

"Short of killing him?"

"Well, yes, short of that."

"Castrate him?"

"Hmmm, do you really think that would work," Derek wondered, "when he apparently derives so much pleasure from inflicting pain?"

"Maybe, maybe not, but it'd be bloody well deserved, if everything you've said about him is true."

"Oh, it's true all right. I might have been a bit foxed that night we found him with that poor girl, but I didn't imagine anything. Percy and Jeremy were there and just as sickened as I was."

Nicholas frowned thoughtfully. "I take it the girl won't help if he's taken to court?"

"No, she was in too much pain that night

to even talk coherently, but I went back to find her a week later, when she was beginning to mend, and she flatly refused to point a legal finger at him."

"Because he's a lord?"

"That might have influenced her, but it was more that he'd paid her handsomely up front, more money than she could have made in two or three years doing what she does, and she was afraid she'd have to give it back. And the amount was negligible to Ashford. I checked. He comes from enough wealth that he could be doing this several times a week and it wouldn't dent his pockets."

"I assume you offered her a like sum or more to press charges?"

"Oh, yes, that occurred to me immediately," Derek admitted. "Unfortunately, that was when she admitted she *knew* what he was going to do and had agreed. Doesn't matter that she couldn't have known just how bad it would be or that she'd end up physically scarred from it. And ironically, she hasn't realized yet that those scars are going to damage her future trade, nor did I have the heart to point that out to her."

Nicholas sighed. "You've taken on quite a dilemma here, dear boy. I'll give it more thought, but at the moment, I can't think of anything to help you solve it, not when he's covering his arse in being honest, or at least partially honest with these girls in explaining up front what he wants. And unfortunately, he'll find an endless supply of cheap whores in this town who will jump at the chance for the extra blunt without thinking the thing through before it's too late and done."

"My thoughts exactly," Derek said.

"I hate to say it, but you know, you ought to be asking your Uncle James for advice. It's right up his — er — area of expertise, wouldn't you say?"

Derek grinned. "Already thought of that. I'm meeting with him tomorrow morning."

"Good. Associating with the scum of the earth, as he's done, tends to give one a different perspective. Now, enough of this seriousness. Glad you stopped by. You can keep me company today while Reggie gads about."

"Delighted to — this morning anyway. Have plans for this afternoon myself, though."

"That's quite all right, old chap. I'll commandeer what time of yours that I can. Miss you, you know, since I've moved out to the country. You don't visit often enough. And by the by, I've picked up a new racer I want you to see."

"Percy did, too," Derek replied. "You'll be drooling when you see his."

Nicholas chuckled. "Already did that yesterday. Who d'you think I got my new racer from? Managed to talk the dear boy out of another one."

21

"Are you married?"

Derek blinked. They'd no sooner sat down in the carriage when Kelsey dropped that question on him. But it had been on her mind ever since she woke up that morning. And although she should have led into asking more tactfully, she didn't know how much time they'd have before they reached their destination, and she did want an answer. Today. And she got just what she was hoping for.

"Gads, no!" he exclaimed. "And I don't intend to be for a very long time." Her relief was immediate and obvious, making him add, "No, no, dear girl, you're not stealing me away from anyone."

"Not even from another mistress?"

He snorted. "Especially not — that is to say — dash it all, tried having a mistress once and it bloody well didn't work out. Wasn't going to have another, but, well, circumstances changed my mind."

"Circumstances? Are you saying you bought me for other than the obvious reasons?"

"Well, yes, actually," he replied a bit hesitantly. "I couldn't let Lord Ashford have you, now, could I, when I know what sick perversions he's capable of."

Kelsey shuddered mentally, realizing who he was talking about. She'd thought Ashford looked cruel. She really had been saved from a fate worse than she could imagine. And she had this man to thank.

"I'm grateful, very, very grateful, that you felt so disposed."

"Think nothing of it, m'dear. I consider it money well spent — now."

That brought on the expected blush. Derek smiled.

But Kelsey's curiosity still wasn't completely satisfied, so she said, "I've noticed that you don't want to call attention to our — association. At least, that was the impression you gave in Bridgewater. But since you don't have a wife, is that just a matter of preference?"

"Not just that, no," he replied. "My youngest two uncles, you see, were rather scandalous. Drove m'father through the roof, the scandals they got into one after the other. I grew up with his tirades over his brothers. Tends to lead to caution, or at least a desire not to cause him any more grief as far as scandals go."

"And I'd be a scandal?"

"No, not a'tall — at least, not out of the ordinary. It's more a desire to keep my name out of the gossip mill for any reason. M'father objects to giving even our own servants food for that mill, you under-stand."

She nodded and smiled, because she did understand. She'd been raised the same way, to be circumspect. In fact, she couldn't count the times her parents had gone com-pletely silent, whether in the middle of a heated debate or not, if a servant happened to walk into the room.

"I'm sorry to be so nosy. It was just that I had been wondering if this might affect the times you might be visiting me."

He frowned, having forgot that he would need to be cautious in that regard, as he had been with his previous mistress. Show-ing up in the daytime to pick her up was nothing. Showing up repeatedly to visit for long hours at a time would definitely begin to raise brows. But damned if he wanted to restrict his time with Kelsey to a few stolen hours.

So he replied evasively, "Can't say right now. Don't know anyone offhand who lives in this area, so we'll have to wait and see. But you needn't be sorry for asking, dear girl. How else are we to learn about each other, eh? I have a few questions m'self, actually."

"I will be glad to answer them — if I can."

"Splendid. Then tell me, with your excep-tional education, why didn't you follow in your mother's footsteps and become a governess? Not that I'm sorry you chose the path you did, but why did you?"

Kelsey sighed mentally. In questioning him, she'd left herself wide open for questions like that. But, then, she'd figured he'd ask something like this eventually, and she was somewhat prepared.

"I'm too young, really, to be a governess. Most parents want a mature woman to trust their children to."

"You had no other options?"

"None that would supply me with a large sum of money to pay off debts."

He frowned. "How the deuce does anyone as young as you run up twenty-five thousand pounds in debts?"

She smiled slightly. "I have no idea. The debts weren't mine and weren't even half that amount."

"Ah, then you made a tidy profit."

"No, none of the money came to me. The proprietor of that place gained a large portion of it for arranging the auction, but the rest, well, as I said, there were debts that needed taking care of."

She hoped he'd leave it at that, but of course he didn't. "Whose debts did you feel obliged to pay off?"

She could lie or avoid the question as she'd done before. But she really didn't want to lie to him any more than she already had, so she fell back on the excuse she'd used previously.

"That's a private matter I don't feel comfortable discussing, if you don't mind."

His expression said he did mind, nor was he dropping it completely. "Is your mother still alive?"

"No."

"Your father?"

"No."

"You've no other relatives?"

She knew what he was doing, trying to figure out for himself who she might have given the money to, but that was information she couldn't afford for him to ever find out, so she said, "Derek, please, this subject is very unpleasant for me. I'd as soon not discuss it."

At that point he sighed, giving up — for the time being anyway. But then he leaned over and patted her hand. Only that must not have been enough for him, if it was comfort he was trying to offer her, which it seemed to be, because he then pulled her over into his lap.

Kelsey stiffened slightly, remembering what had happened the last time she had sat thusly. But Derek merely put his arms around her and rested his cheek against her forehead, surrounding her with his pleasant scent and the soothing, steady beat of his heart.

"I have a feeling, m'dear, that you and I

are going to become very close," he said so softly it was almost a whisper. "So the day will come when you will feel comfortable telling me anything. I'm quite patient, you know. But you'll find I can also be quite determined."

In other words, this discussion would come up again in the near future?

"Did I thank you for the carriage you sent me?" she asked him.

He burst out laughing at her so obvious change of subject.

22

The dressmaker Derek took Kelsey to was certainly not what she'd been expecting. The woman's establishment was very elegant. Satin couches and chairs filled the front room, where several of her more magnificent formal creations were on display, as well as dozens of books featuring the latest in fashions. It was a comfortable room for the gentlemen to wait, if they were so inclined, while their ladies made their selections.

And ladies did frequent this shop. But then Kelsey found that Mrs. Westerbury had many private fitting rooms, so she had little problem keeping her affluent customers separated from her less savory ones. She was in the business of making money, not casting judgments. She didn't turn down customers just because she might frown on their professions, though she did probably suggest to some that they use the back door rather than the front for their visits.

But considering that the establishment appeared to cater to the upper crust of London society, Kelsey was no longer sure how Derek would like her to be outfitted. Of course, his bringing her there could simply be because he knew of no other dressmakers.

She decided to leave the matter entirely in his hands and told him so. He hadn't been expecting that, but accepted the responsibility and went off to have a few private words with Mrs. Westerbury. When he came back, it was to tell her he was leaving her in capable hands and would return for her in several hours.

Which told Kelsey absolutely nothing about what she was to order, how much she was to order, or anything else. But hopefully the dressmaker had those answers, and hopefully Kelsey wouldn't be too appalled by them. Derek had only looked slightly embarrassed from the encounter, after all, a bit of color riding his cheeks. But he'd quickly escaped any further embarrassment, too.

Mrs. Westerbury soon returned and led Kelsey into the back of her shop for measurements and selections. Not by a single look did the woman reveal that she'd been told Kelsey was Derek's mistress and she should be dressed accordingly.

The measuring didn't take long, with one of the shop assistants whisking her tape around and along Kelsey's limbs and quickly jotting down notes, chatting amiably all the while. The selection of materials, designs, and accessories, though, could have taken all day, Mrs. Westerbury had so much on hand to choose from.

But there wasn't really a choice. The woman made suggestions, and Kelsey merely nodded or shook her head. And it wasn't as bad as it could have been. The suggestions were mostly in vibrant colors and combinations that Kelsey would never have chosen for herself, but at least the actual finished gowns weren't going to be anywhere near as gaudy as that red gown had been.

They weren't quite finished when another customer arrived, a beautiful young lady who declined Mrs. Westerbury's assistance, claiming she was only changing the material of the ball gown she'd just ordered. However, she was friendly enough to introduce herself to Kelsey, who would have been extremely rude not to do likewise, uncomfortable as it made the dressmaker.

The young woman made her selection within moments, but she didn't leave immediately. Kelsey didn't realize the lady was watching her until she spoke up again.

"No, no, that color isn't you a'tall. It's much too — well, too green, don't you think? These silvers and blues over here, even the sapphire, would do wonders for your eyes."

Kelsey smiled, agreeing wholeheartedly. She had been eyeing that stack of blues in varying shades and materials wistfully. And Mrs. Westerbury was forced to concede the point, with the lady still standing there, awaiting a response to her advice.

"Quite right, m'lady," the woman said, and moved to dig out several bolts from the stack, including the bright sapphire velvet, which would make a lovely new spencer and outing dress, and one silver and gray satin brocade for evening wear.

But the lady still didn't leave, waiting to see what trimmings would be offered for each material. And because of that, Kelsey completed her wardrobe with some very elegant creations that even her mother would have been proud to see her wear. She would have liked to have gone back and changed the earlier selections too, but that would have been pushing her luck. Mrs. Westerbury had her instructions, after all, from the one who would be paying the bill.

Derek had also arranged for one completed ensemble that she could leave in, as she discovered when she was almost finished. And that had likely cost him quite a bit extra, the gown having to be taken from another customer's order and altered to fit her while she'd been busy with her selections. And obviously, the customer whose order it had been taken from wasn't the kind who'd ever be required to come in through the back door.

It was a dinner gown in a thick lavender silk with darker, delicate magenta eyelet lace trimming the short puffed sleeves, neckline, high waist, and hem. It came with a matching mantle in the same lavender hue, though of heavy velvet. Wearing it as she returned to the front room, Kelsey felt like her old self again.

Derek wasn't there yet, but a few other gentlemen were lounging on the couches, and each gave her an admiring glance. That young lady who had offered advice in her selections was also there. She was just putting on gloves in preparation of leaving, and gave Kelsey a friendly smile.

"All done then?" the lady asked cheerfully. She too had noticed those admiring glances, which was possibly why she added, "Perhaps you could use a lift some-where? My carriage is just outside."

Kelsey would have loved to say yes. The lady seemed genuinely friendly, and Lord knows, she could use a friend in this large city. But of course she couldn't say yes. Nor could she risk being friends with a member of the *ton,* who would despise her if she knew what Kelsey was.

So she was forced to say, "That's very kind of you, but my escort should be here shortly."

That should have ended the conversation, but the lady was too friendly for that. "Have we met before?" she asked curiously. "You seem vaguely familiar to me."

How discerning. Kelsey had been told numerous times how closely she resembled her mother, and her parents had frequently come to London to enjoy the social whirl.

"A coincidence perhaps," Kelsey offered. "I doubt we have met, though. This is my first time in London."

"You must be quite excited, then."

"Intimidated, to be more exact."

The lady laughed. "Yes, it is a big town, isn't it? And very easy to get lost in, until you've been here a few times. But here" — and she reached into her reticule to pull out a calling card, which she handed to Kelsey — "if you should need any assistance, or just feel like having a chat, do stop by for a visit. I'm not very far from here, just over on Park Lane, and will be for another week or so."

"I'll keep that in mind," Kelsey said.

But of course she wouldn't, and for a brief moment she was heartsick that she couldn't. The young lady could, and obviously did, make friends so easily. A few weeks before, Kelsey could have too, but not anymore.

She shook off her regret. Bemoaning her new lot in life was pointless. She'd walked into it with open eyes. She just had to learn to live with it.

23

"Damned fetching."

Kelsey had smiled, assuming that was a compliment — of sorts. It was all Derek had said when he returned to collect her, and that was after staring at her for a good twenty seconds first without a word. It made her feel quite beautiful, something she'd rarely felt before.

In the carriage again, though, he seemed — well, to be having some sort of dilemma as he continued to stare at her. The frown he was wearing finally made her uncomfortable enough to ask, "Is something wrong?"

"Do you realize you look like a bloody debutante in them togs?"

She blushed. She nearly squirmed on her seat. Mostly, she wished he hadn't noticed that. But since he had, it would be prudent to get his mind off it.

"And how did I look that night wearing the red gown?" she asked.

As hoped, his frown smoothed out a bit. He even grinned sheepishly, catching her meaning — or at least she assumed he did. Just to make sure . . .

"There, you see?" she continued. "It's the clothes that give the impression, not the person wearing them. As it happened, this was the only gown available to alter for me on such short notice. I believe Mrs. Westerbury was under the impression that anything would do as long as it was suitable for evening."

"Yes, I did tell her something to that effect. Well, no matter. Just changes my plans somewhat."

"What plans were those?"

"I thought dinner in some quiet, out-of-the-way place would be just the ticket, but damn me, hate to waste you looking so spiffy."

Again she blushed. Compliments from him were really *very* pleasant, making her feel warm all over. But she certainly didn't want to inconvenience him.

Reasonably, she said, "Please, you needn't change your plans just because —"

"Not a'tall, dear girl," he interrupted. "I've been meaning to check out the new chef at the Albany anyway. And then I thought perhaps a visit to Vauxhall Gardens to top off the evening."

Even she had heard of Vauxhall Pleasure Gardens, her parents having mentioned it more than once in one light or another. By day, it was quite respectable, with its shaded lanes, vendors, and concerts. But at night, all those narrow lanes with benches were ideal for lovers, and any lady worth her salt wouldn't be caught there after hours. Which, of course, made it a perfect place for a gentleman to take his mistress, she supposed.

Derek had had other plans as well. It being too early yet for dinner, they visited several more shops, and the carriage became quite full of packages before they were through. Bonnets and shoes, parasols for summer, and he made certain to not forget more negligees, which had been an extremely embarrassing experience, since he wanted to pick each one himself.

Kelsey was feeling a bit exhausted by the time they reached the Albany, which turned out to be a hotel on Piccadilly. The dining room there was lovely, though, and she began to relax with her first glass of wine. The only problem was, Derek was recognized there. But he must have known he would be, because when he introduced her to the two gentlemen who came over, separately, to pay their respects, it was as the widow Langton.

And the second gentleman was surprised enough to say, "Not the Lady Langton who shot her husband?"

Derek was forced to explain that she came from a different family altogether, and the lie sounded much better coming from him than from her. Of course, his not knowing it *was* a lie gave it credence.

She did ask toward the middle of what turned out to be an excellent dinner, "Why a widow?"

"Well, widows tend to do as they please, don't you know, whereas young debutantes, which at the moment you certainly appear to be at first, second, and even third glance, require chaperonage. And I'm deuced if I make a good chaperone. Anyone who knows me would quite agree."

He grinned unrepentantly.

"That wouldn't be because you do more seducing than chaperoning, would it?" she teased him.

"But of course," he said, his eyes turning lambent with sensuality.

But then they were interrupted by a pair he *wasn't* expecting.

As both Jeremy Malory and Percy Alden sat down at their table, uninvited, Derek demanded, "How the devil did you find me?"

It was Percy who answered as he avidly surveyed the food on their plates. "The youngun here had to deliver a note to your Uncle Anthony from his father. That being just down the street, it was rather hard to miss seeing your carriage out front. By the by, how's the food? Good as they say?"

Derek looked disgruntled to say the least. "Haven't you two something better to do this evening?"

"Better than eating?" Percy seemed aghast.

Jeremy chuckled. "Might as well fetch your waiter over, cousin. You don't really want to deny us such lovely company for dinner, when *you* can have her to yourself at any other time. Have a heart."

"He's been pining for the sight of her all week," Percy added in what should have been a whisper but wasn't. "Might as well give in gracefully, old chap."

The table suddenly jumped as someone kicked someone else under it. With Percy and Jeremy now glaring at each other, it was a good guess who did the kicking.

Derek sighed. "If you're going to stay, behave."

Kelsey had to bring a hand up to hide her smile. Jeremy was beaming now that he'd got his way, and he turned that stunning smile on her. She had forgotten how unbelievably handsome this young man was.

For several long moments, she was quite dazzled, staring at him, until he asked her, "So how's this clod been treating you, sweetheart?"

She blushed, and not just because he'd managed to mesmerize her, but because the subject he'd introduced was too personal by half.

But she replied neutrally, "He just today spent an amazing amount of money on me, refurbishing, or rather supplying me with a new wardrobe."

Jeremy dismissed that with a wave of his hand. "He'd have done that in any case, but how's he *treating* you? No need for rescuing?" he asked hopefully. "I'd be glad to, you know."

The table jumped again. Kelsey couldn't help it, this time she laughed aloud, because it was Derek doing the kicking now. And Jeremy wasn't as circumspect as Percy. He howled, drawing dozens of eyes in their direction.

He also mumbled, "Hell's bells, a simple no would have sufficed."

Percy chuckled. "Gads, Jeremy, ain't you learned that if you're going to try to steal someone's lady, you shouldn't do it in front of him?"

Jeremy snorted. "I wouldn't steal from my own cousin. He knows I was just teasing. Don't you, Derek?" At Derek's stony look, the lad hooted, "I don't believe it! Derek jealous? But you *never* get jealous."

"Better protect the other knee, lad," Percy warned, grinning.

Jeremy immediately scooted his chair back, nearly toppling it over, and scowling, said, "Bloody hell, I got the point the first time. I'll be wearing it for a week. No need to make it again."

To that, Derek shook his head, muttering,

"Incorrigible scamp."

Jeremy heard him and grinned. "Well, of course. Any other way is no fun a'tall."

24

Kelsey couldn't remember ever laughing so much, or having so much fun, as she did that evening with Derek and his friends. The teasing and bantering among them had gone on mercilessly. Derek had aptly termed Jeremy an incorrigible scamp. But she could also tell how fond he was of his cousin, and vice versa.

Close familial ties were good. She felt them strongly herself, or she wouldn't be where she was now. Her sister, Jean, was her responsibility. She loved Jean dearly. She loved her Aunt Elizabeth, too. Uncle Elliott — well, she'd lost what respect she had for him, but she would reserve further judgment until he proved he could be responsible again. And if he couldn't be, after what she had sacrificed, well, she just might take a leaf from her mother's book and find herself a pistol.

The laughter hadn't ended with dinner. Kelsey had inadvertently mentioned they were going to Vauxhall afterward, and both Jeremy and Percy swore upside and down that that was exactly where they'd intended on going, too. Which was patently untrue, of course. But Derek finally gave up the idea of trying to get rid of them.

And they had likely regretted their determination to tag along when they were both beset with shivers — though watching their antics to keep warm was hilarious. Derek had brought along a greatcoat, and Kelsey had her velvet mantle, which kept her warm enough with the addition of Derek's arm around her shoulder. But Jeremy and Percy were dressed for going from heated carriage to indoors and back, not for an outdoor excursion late of an evening in the winter.

It had been a very long but very nice day all the way around — and it wasn't over yet. When Derek took her home, he kissed her gently in the foyer while his driver brought in her parcels. He held her hand to walk her upstairs. In her bedroom, they found cheese and fruit with a bottle of wine on the table by her bed that Mrs. Whipple had left before she went home for the night.

"Very thoughtful," Derek remarked, gazing at the arrangement.

"Yes, Mrs. Whipple is very competent in that way," Kelsey agreed. Alicia had also stoked the fire so the room was toasty warm.

"You're keeping her, then?"

"Oh, yes. You've sampled one of her dinners. And she outdoes herself for breakfast, too, as I discovered this morning."

"I'll wait and reserve judgment on that

tomorrow," he said in a deeper tone, glancing at her again.

Her own voice sounded thick as she asked, "You're staying — the entire night, then?"

"Oh, yes."

He put so much more meaning into those words than she had. Kelsey was starting to feel nervous, though not anywhere near as nervous as she had been the night before. In fact, she was looking forward to making love with Derek again, to experiencing the pleasure he'd promised her.

Ever since he had put his arm around her in the gardens, she had started to feel a tingling inside. What had May said about it? That she'd know it if she desired a man, and she could thank her lucky stars if that man happened to be keeping her. Was it desire, then, when she felt all mushy when Derek gave her a certain look, his lips turned up just so? Or when her pulse leapt at just the touch of his hand?

Her heart was pounding now in anticipation, but he made no immediate move toward her. He opened the bottle of wine and poured a bit in each of the two glasses. He picked up a stem of grapes and tore off one with his teeth, then glanced at her again as he slowly chewed.

How quickly she felt overly warm. He must have felt it too, because he shrugged out of his greatcoat and said, "Come, let me remove your wrap."

She approached him hesitantly. His fingers were warm at her neck as he untied the silver cords of her mantle and tossed it with his greatcoat over a nearby chair. His hands then slipped behind her neck, not to pull her closer, merely to massage the muscles there. Heavenly. Her sigh told him so.

She then felt the glass placed in her hand and looked down to see the wine. She gulped it down. He smiled. She was beginning to feel nervous again.

"I really enjoyed this evening — the whole day, actually," she said. "Thank you."

"No need for thanks, m'dear," he replied. "I enjoyed it, too."

Surprisingly, that was quite true. Derek was still very, very eager to make love to her again, he had been all day, and yet he had simply enjoyed her company, too. Which was unusual for him. Typically, he spent very little time with women outside of the bedroom, other than the female members of his large family.

It had also been surprising how much he had at first resented his friends' intrusion at the Albany, and how right on the mark Jeremy had been when he'd accused Derek of being jealous. Seeing Kelsey dazzled by Jeremy had really infuriated him. But it hadn't lasted, and she shared her smiles with him, not with Jeremy. That more than anything had put his jealousy to rest.

"Your friends are very amusing," she remarked.

"Obnoxious is more like it."

She grinned. "You did your share of laughing," she reminded him.

He shrugged. "So I did."

He picked up the stem of grapes again, tore another off, and leaned toward her to offer it with his mouth. She took it, blushing as she did. It was warm and sweet, like the wine.

"Some cheese?" he asked.

"I'd rather have you kiss me."

Her blush spread like wildfire. She couldn't imagine where those words had come from, or the boldness that had allowed her to say them. But he was delighted apparently, if his expression was any indication. He set their glasses down as well as the grapes.

"So much for savoring the moment," he said as he gathered her fully into his arms. "It was killing me anyway."

Killing him? But the thought didn't last any longer than the first touch of his lips on hers. Mush, pure mush inside. Her knees buckled, but she didn't need her legs for support, he was holding her so tightly. Her arms went about his neck anyway, because it felt good to hold him, too.

She was growing accustomed to kissing, but she had an excellent teacher in Derek. When she got up the nerve to make a foray with her tongue as he was doing, it produced a groan from him that was so highly gratifying it encouraged her to even more boldness.

The bed was conveniently next to them. He kneeled on it, laid her down so carefully, she barely noticed. But the loss of her gown was noticeable, then the warmth of his hands as they caressed her from neck to thigh. Her fingers circled the corded muscles on his arms, felt them ripple on his back. His skin was so smooth, but so unyielding.

His lips began to move on her, branding a heated trail across her cheek to her neck. His tongue flicked into her ear, and she trembled with pleasure. Down his lips moved, over her shoulder, along the side of her breast, under it, then up to capture the hard nub and draw it deeply into the heat of his mouth.

Sensation spiraled down to her belly, still farther to her loins, where it gathered and coiled into a nearly unbearable tension. The last of her inhibitions just disappeared. She arched toward his body with silent demands. He pulled her close, belly to belly, but he wouldn't relinquish her breast yet. Her fingers dug into his shoulders, leaving half moons without realizing it.

After what seemed an endless time, he let go of one nipple to capture the other, and even more heat shot down that invisible cord to her belly and loins. She was going up in smoke. He seemed an inferno himself. And then his hand slid between her legs and Kelsey cried out.

It was too much, too intense. But he was kissing her again, deeply, ravenously, his body settling over hers, slowly pressing her down. And then that hard, heated part of him pushing for entrance, finding it easily, sliding smoothly to her depths.

The tension was relieved immediately, pleasure coursing through her, shooting outward, reaching even her toes. And it was repeated with his second slow thrust, then his third, until a new tension began to build, more powerful, racing swiftly toward a pinnacle that suddenly burst on her in a wave of purest sensation, purest ecstasy that held her in its grip for long, blissful moments.

She was smiling when he looked down at her a while later. She couldn't seem to help it. And he was grinning rather smugly himself.

"Better this time?" he asked softly, already knowing the answer.

"An understatement," she replied with a long, languorous sigh.

His grin got wider. "Yes, I must agree. And the nicest part is, we've only just begun."

She blinked. But he went on to prove that remark to her complete satisfaction.

25

Later that week, Derek came by on the spur of the moment to take Kelsey to the races with him. He had planned on going with Percy and Jeremy, but at the last moment he had told them that he'd meet them there.

It wasn't that he'd decided that Kelsey might enjoy the outing. Likely she would, but that wasn't his motive. It was that he'd tried to put their relationship in perspective, to visit her only in the evenings, as was proper with one's mistress. And having done so for several evenings, he'd found that he didn't enjoy behaving properly where she was concerned. Far from it. As he'd gone about his business, or tried to, as if nothing had changed in his life, he'd had to force himself to leave her in the mornings and fight the urge to stay away until the evenings.

On the day of the race, he'd given in to the urge, telling himself that it wouldn't hurt, just this once. The problem seemed to be that he enjoyed her company too much. She made him laugh. She didn't run on with endless chatter. She was intelligent. They had discussed literature one evening over dinner, and he'd been amazed to find himself in a heated debate with her over philosophy, of all things — and he'd enjoyed every minute of it.

Whether this was going to be a serious problem, he couldn't say. In the back of his mind was the notion that a mistress served one purpose and only one purpose. His last mistress had talked him into being her escort as well, and he had resented that intrusion upon his time. Nor had he enjoyed Marjorie's company outside of her bedroom. But Kelsey was different. She didn't make demands. In fact, she'd never asked him for a single thing, other than that one time when she'd asked him to kiss her.

That was an extremely fond memory. It brought a smile to him every time he remembered it. Actually, he'd been smiling much too often lately, for no good reason. Even his valet had remarked on it. But then Kelsey was never very far from his mind. And the truth was, she'd turned out to be a pleasure to him in every way.

Kelsey quickly dressed for the outing. He liked that about her, too, that she didn't spend endless hours over her toilette, fussing and primping and expecting every curl to be just so, and yet she always ended up looking perfect to him, a delight to each one of his senses, and today was no exception.

She had made another visit to the dressmaker's, and had come home this time with several completed dresses, including a bright sapphire velvet with matching spencer. She looked so lovely that it made him wish the weather were warmer so he could take her about in an open carriage to show her off in Hyde Park, a scandalous thought that appalled him even as it occurred to him. Promenading through the park with a lady you were seriously courting was one thing, with your mistress, quite another. That might have been something his younger uncles would have done without a care, but then neither one of them had ever been bothered by what people said or thought about them. They hadn't been called two of London's more notorious rakes for nothing.

The races were to be held just on the outskirts of London. Arriving, they were able to squeeze their coach in between a barouche and a phaeton right next to the track for ideal viewing, despite the large crowd already gathered. Usually, the high bettors would stand right at the track, so they would park their carriages farther away, leaving the circle around the track for those people who preferred to watch with their ladies from the comfort of their vehicles.

Some ladies did attend with either husband or family, though not many ventured out in the winter. So Derek wasn't too concerned about offending anyone with Kelsey's presence. No one other than Percy and Jeremy would even know she was there, as long as she stayed in the coach, which he'd already cautioned her to do.

They had a brazier going in the coach, but the weather wasn't miserable. Chilly it was, certainly, but there was no wind, and the sun was even making periodic appearances.

Refreshments could be bought, but most of the gentry brought their own along, including Derek. He'd had Mrs. Hershal prepare him a basket with an assortment of snacks and sandwiches, enough to feed his friends as well, and several bottles of wine. The races could last half a day or more sometimes, after all, depending on how many challenges were issued after the official races were over.

Percy and Jeremy soon joined them after the first race. Percy was all smiles as usual. He seemed to have a sixth sense about racing. He not only found exceptional horseflesh to buy, and in the oddest places, but he was rarely wrong in picking a winner, despite the odds. He never took betting seriously, though. For him, it was just a pleasure to have his judgment be proven correct.

"I take it you've already collected a few wagers?" Derek remarked as Percy said a mere "How do" before he dug right into the basket of goodies.

Jeremy said drolly, "Need you ask?"

Derek grinned. "Percy isn't *always* right on the mark. I can remember losing a few thousand pounds once when he wasn't, which is why I don't go overboard on his choices anymore."

Percy made a long-suffering face. "And he'll never let me live it down," he said to Jeremy.

The lad chuckled. "I think you enjoyed taking old Nick's wager more'n you did the win on that first race."

Percy suddenly beamed. "Didn't I though. But, then, Nicholas always manages to talk me out of every fine Thoroughbred that comes my way. Don't know how he does it, damn me, but I don't."

"Nicholas is here?"

Percy nodded. "He's entered that stallion he just bought off me. Should be coming up in the fourth race."

"You should have asked him to join us," Derek said.

Jeremy coughed. "No, actually, that wouldn't be a very good —"

He didn't quite finish because the door opened just then and in climbed Regina Eden, Nicholas's wife — and Derek and Jeremy's cousin. Obviously, this was why Jeremy hadn't thought it would be a good idea to invite Nick over, and Derek couldn't have agreed more. He was, in fact, confounded, wondering how the deuce he could avoid introducing his irrepressible cousin to his mistress.

"I thought I recognized your coach, Derek," Reggie said as she leaned forward to kiss his cheek, then plopped down on the seat next to him. And to Jeremy, "And why didn't you tell me he was here?"

Jeremy stuffed his hands into his pockets and slouched down on the seat across from them. "Didn't think of it," he said lamely.

"Reggie, what the deuce are you doing here?" Derek asked. "You don't like the races."

"I know I don't." She shrugged, then grinned. "But somehow I ended up betting with Nicholas that his new stallion wouldn't win today, so I had to be here to see for myself. You don't think I'd take his word for it, d'you? When he *hates* losing to me?"

Derek had turned sideways in an effort to try to block Kelsey, who was sitting on his other side, from Reggie's view, an impossible task, considering how bright the sapphire blue of her dress was.

"You could have asked me," he pointed out reasonably, he thought.

She raised a brow at him. "When I so rarely see you anymore?" she said reproachfully. "And how'd I know you would even be here?" Then she practically shoved Derek back so she could lean around him to say, "How nice to see you again, Kelsey. I had no idea you were acquainted with my cousin."

Kelsey had been horribly embarrassed the moment she recognized Regina Eden entering the coach. It was one thing to talk to a stranger and let her assume what she would, because you never expected to see her again. But when you did see her again . . .

She had immediately turned to face the window near her, like Derek, hoping the lady wouldn't notice her. It had been a slim hope.

"Derek is your cousin, Lady Eden?"

"Oh, my, yes, we were raised together, don't you know. And please, just call me Reggie, as the rest of my family —" She paused to glance at Jeremy. "Well, *almost* the rest of my family does."

Derek was no longer confounded, he was utterly appalled. "Reggie, how do you know Kelsey?"

"We met at the dressmaker's the other day — and hit it off splendidly, if I do say so myself. But goodness, what's she doing here *alone* with you, Derek? You know how vicious gossips can be."

"She's — she's —"

Derek drew a complete blank, at which

point Jeremy supplied helpfully, "Percy's cousin."

Percy blinked. "She is" — a pinch from Jeremy made him add — "my cousin. Yes, distant cousin on m'mother's side, don't you know."

"How delightful," Reggie said. "I knew instinctively when I met her that she and I were going to be good friends, and now I know why. If she's related to Percy, then she's already almost like family, considering that *he* is. You must bring her by for dinner tonight, Percy. And of course, you're invited too, cousins, the both of you."

The three men each went into full-blown panic.

"That wouldn't be —"

"Couldn't possibly —"

"I've got other —"

But Reggie was quick to interrupt, frowning. "You aren't *really* thinking of giving me excuses, are you, when I'm only going to be in town a few more days? Your father and Aunt George are already coming, Jeremy. So's Uncle Tony and Aunt Roslynn, so this will be a nice little family gathering. Whatever plans you might have had aren't as important as a family gathering, now, are they?"

Jeremy rolled his eyes. Derek slumped back, groaning inwardly. Reggie always had been an excellent manipulator. And she went about it so innocently, the little minx.

"Oh, I say, does that mean we're all going?" Percy asked Derek.

Derek could have cheerfully killed his friend just then. Jeremy and Derek might have just been cornered, but Percy could still have made some excuse, since he wasn't really family. But did that half-wit have the sense to realize that? No, not good old Percy.

26

"Well, it was rather strange, if you ask me," Reggie told her husband as she prepared to receive her guests that night. "I mean, all three of them hedging, as if they didn't really want to come. Goodness, it's only a dinner, a few hours of their time. It's not as if they can't go on and do — well, whatever they normally do, afterward."

"Percy's cousin, you say?" was Nicholas's response, and that with a frown.

Reggie sighed. "Have you even heard one word I said after mentioning his cousin?"

Nicholas blinked. He *had* become preoccupied with that, considering that Percy had told him once that he didn't have any other relatives, distant or not, yet here suddenly was a distant cousin. But he had heard what else she'd said — vaguely. It was only just registering.

So he assured her, "Of course I heard you, luv. But what makes you think they were hedging? Perhaps they did have other plans."

She gave an unladylike snort. "If they were important plans, then they would have mentioned them, wouldn't they? But they didn't. And they seemed remarkably uncomfortable with the idea of coming here."

He chuckled. "Percy and Derek used to practically *live* here, they were here so often, so you know that can't be true. It's possible you just caught them with other things on their mind and imagined any hedging."

"I did, did I?" she said skeptically. "Well, we'll see tonight, won't we, if their behavior is normal or not. And if it's not, I want you to find out why. Obviously, they won't confide in me, but they will you."

"Reggie, you're likely making a big to-do over nothing, you know, so do give it a rest for now. If anything is actually amiss, I'm sure it will come to light. And by the by, thank you for inviting Derek and Percy. Don't feel so bloody outnumbered now."

He was, of course, referring to her uncles James and Tony. He had not been looking forward to that night ever since she'd informed him that her uncles were coming.

She poked him in the chest and warned, "No baiting tonight. You promised you'd behave."

He gave her a hug and an innocent grin. "I will if they will."

Reggie sighed, anticipating disaster. After all, when did her uncles *ever* behave?

Anthony pulled Derek aside before they went in to dinner. They had been gathered in the parlor, where Anthony and his brother James had actually been on their best behavior, a rare thing when they were in the same room with Nicholas Eden. But the fact that the children had been present, James holding his little Jack, and Roslynn keeping baby Judith in hand, likely had something to do with it. It was an amazing thing, the change that occurred in Derek's younger uncles when their daughters were around.

But right then Anthony looked rather serious as he waited for the others to go on into the dining room before he said to Derek, "D'you think it's a good idea to be bedding Alden's cousin?"

Derek felt as if he'd just been gut-punched. "What makes you think — ?"

Anthony's chuckle cut him off. "Come now, dear boy, I've been there. It's bloody well obvious with the way you look at her."

Derek blushed. And here he'd thought the evening had been progressing splendidly, all things considered.

Unfortunately, he'd been unable to come up with a reasonable excuse not to attend that wouldn't have Reggie badgering him for the next year and making him feel like the lowest cad. He'd even considered accidents and dire health, but knew his cousin well enough to know she'd be suspicious and insist on sending a doctor.

So after talking it over with Percy and

Jeremy, and having Percy assure him that he could carry off the lie that Kelsey was his cousin, he'd decided to risk it. It was only family, after all, and only one evening. And even if something went wrong and they were found out, no scandal would actually come of it — just one very furious Jason Malory.

Nicholas had known immediately who Kelsey was when Derek had introduced her to him, and had looked daggers at Derek. But Nick had relaxed soon enough when he saw how Kelsey comported herself. In no way did she appear other than what Reggie thought her to be. She looked like a lady. She acted like a lady. And informing Reggie right up front that Kelsey would soon be hieing back to the country had put an end to his cousin's plans for The Great Friendship.

But here Derek had actually given their relationship away himself, because he bloody well couldn't help the way he looked at her. Yet he didn't want Anthony worried about it, which he apparently was.

So he was forced to fess up, admitting, "Kelsey's not Percy's cousin."

"She's not?"

"No, she's no relation to him a'tall. Reggie had met her previously, you see, and mistook her for a member of the *ton,* and then when she found Kelsey with me today, well, we were at a loss to explain that, since she wasn't properly chaperoned, at least as far as Reggie was concerned. It was Jeremy who came up with the idea of making her Percy's cousin, which put proper to it, since he was there, too."

"Who is she, then?"

"My mistress," Derek mumbled.

Anthony raised a black brow. "I do believe I misheard you. You didn't actually say — ?" Derek nodded, and Anthony suddenly hooted with laughter. "Good God, Reggie is going to have your head if she finds out you've let her become chummy with your mistress."

Derek winced. "There's no reason she should ever find out. She's going home to Silverley in a few days. So they won't be seeing each other again."

"You hope. But didn't it occur to you to simply tell your cousin the truth? She's a married woman, you know, though we could wish she'd been a little more particular in her choice of husbands. But the fact is, she wouldn't have been all that shocked."

"True, though I don't believe any of us were thinking very clearly at the time. I know I wasn't. And Jeremy was just trying to spare us all the embarrassment that the truth would have caused, when he related her to Percy."

Anthony grinned. "Gad, what a choice, Percy's cousin or a soiled dove. Can't say I'd choose either."

"Percy is a good friend, Uncle Tony," Derek felt the need to point out. "Loyal, trustworthy —"

"I don't doubt it, dear boy," Anthony cut in. "But he's still a bloody nitwit."

That was hard to dispute, so Derek gave up with a shrug. Anthony put an arm around his nephew's shoulder to lead on to the dining room.

But he had one last remark on the subject. "It's damned hard to believe she's not gentry. You're sure she's not pulling your leg and is?"

Derek stopped cold. Could she be? No, it wasn't possible. No lady would put herself on the auction block as Kelsey had done.

Anthony glanced back at him with his brow raised questioningly, but Derek shook his head with a weak smile. "Yes, I'm sure."

"Glad to hear it, because it's rather prevalent, you know, young lords getting caught by entrapment, of the marriage sort, and quite deliberate on the female's part, usually with the help of her relatives. But then you likely know that, having avoided the shackles this long. Just be careful, puppy. James and I would be the last to censure what you do, but you know how your father is. Actually, you better hope he don't get wind of tonight's little comedy. Damn me, wouldn't want to be in your shoes if he does."

Neither would Derek.

27

"I got a missive from Jason today," Anthony remarked just after the women left the room, leaving the men to enjoy their brandy and cigars. "Said to come by Eddie boy's house tomorrow afternoon, but didn't say why. Any of you know what he's coming to town for?"

"Got the same missive myself," James replied with a thoughtful frown. "Jason don't usually come to town unless he's got business to attend to or he thinks someone needs a tongue-lashing."

Since James happened to glance at Jeremy when he said that, his son sat up stiffly and complained, "Don't look at me. You already chewed me up over getting sent down from school this time. George did too, for that matter. Ain't going to happen again. Gave my word, didn't I?"

"He wouldn't want me there if this is about Jeremy," Anthony pointed out.

Derek was still worrying about Kelsey's leaving the room and being alone with not one but *three* female members of his family. So it took him a moment to realize both his uncles were looking at him.

He shrugged. "I haven't heard anything, and I was just out to Haverston last week.

Nor was anything mentioned at the wedding. But, then, I haven't been home since this morning, so I don't know if I've received a missive as well. And aside from tonight's fol— er, well, I haven't been involved in anything that m'father would want to remark on."

"You're forgetting the auction, old chap," Percy put in helpfully. "He'd have a thing or two to say about that if he found out, public as it was."

While Derek was looking daggers at Percy for mentioning that, James asked, "What auction?"

And Anthony said to Derek, "Good God, you didn't actually *buy* her, did you?"

Before Derek could answer, James deduced for himself, "He bought Kelsey? Damn me, and I thought I'd done everything at least once."

At which point Derek looked at his Uncle Anthony accusingly, demanding, "You *told* him?"

Anthony chuckled. " 'Course not, puppy," he said with obvious amusement. "If I noticed it right off, d'you really think *he* wouldn't? When James was decidedly more lecherous than I ever was?"

James raised a golden brow toward his brother. "I beg your pardon. Lecherous?"

Anthony's brow went up at just about the same angle. "Weren't you?"

"Well, possibly, but I prefer the way Reggie puts it, if it's all the same to you. 'Connoisseur of women' has a much nicer ring to it."

"I'll have to agree there," Anthony replied. "The little darling does have a nice way with words."

"Thought lecherous was rather apropos myself," Nicholas remarked with a smirk.

James's green eyes swung directly toward his nephew by marriage, and he said in one of his drier tones, "Been sleeping on the couch lately, dear boy? If not, I'll be glad to assist you in that direction."

Nicholas immediately flushed. It was a well-known fact — at least among James, Anthony, and himself — that Reggie got rather annoyed with her husband whenever he had words of the battling kind with her favorite uncles. Bloody hell, he should have kept his mouth shut, and Anthony, heard from next, confirmed that.

"You know you shouldn't have started in on him. Just because Reggie ain't here at the moment don't mean she won't hear about it."

"You're all heart, *uncle*," Nicholas mumbled.

Anthony raised his brandy in a silent toast and grinned. "Ain't I though."

If Nicholas was wishing he were somewhere else just then, Derek was wishing he *had* gone and broken a limb or something so he wouldn't be there either. It had been insane to think he could have gotten through the evening without something giving his relationship with Kelsey away.

But as long as Percy had brought it up, he said to James, "I was meaning to talk to you about this, Uncle James. Came by your house twice this week to discuss it, but I missed you each time."

"Yes, George told me. I was going to call on you tomorrow myself, but as long as we're here . . ."

"Yes, well, it's not exactly a pleasant subject for the digestion; it's rather disgusting, actually —"

"Let me worry about my digestion, lad," James said with a smile.

Derek nodded, continuing, "We stumbled upon this auction, you see, and I had no intention of getting involved, certainly didn't want another mistress — that was what the girl was being sold as — but then I saw who was doing the bidding." And he went on to tell them everything he knew about David Ashford, ending with, "So you see, I couldn't let him have Kelsey, knowing what I do about him."

" 'Course you couldn't," Anthony agreed.

James's expression had definitely hardened. "And the reason you were coming to me with this tale?"

Derek sighed. "I find it intolerable that this lord is out there going about his depravities unhindered. I was hoping you might know some way to deal with the man."

"Oh, yes," James said with a dark, ominous smile. "I can think of a few ways."

"Short of killing him, that is," Derek felt it prudent to add.

James said nothing for nearly ten seconds, then, "If you insist."

28

The women had gone upstairs to spend a bit more time with the children. Judith had tuckered out and was sleeping peacefully in a cradle in the corner, but Jacqueline was swinging her arms energetically on her mother's lap, and little Thomas was toddling about the room among the women, proudly showing off one of his prized toys to each of them.

The Malory women had made Kelsey feel so comfortable that she actually forgot for a while what she had become and was able to just enjoy their company. And she adored children herself, just as they seemed to. She'd always looked forward to the day she'd have some of her own, though that didn't seem quite possible now, which was, sadly, something else that she had given up.

Their conversation was quite amusing, too, and it tended to relate to either their children or their husbands, or both, as it did when Reggie remarked with a grin, "I heard Uncle Tony had Judith and Jack married before either of them were even born."

"Well, I didn't have a daughter after Roslynn did just to spite him, I do assure you," George replied, then added with a conspiratorial smile, "Although, that's an interesting idea. I might try it next time, especially since I'm sure James would love it."

"Spiting my Tony?" Roslynn piped in. "Oh, I don't doubt James Malory would jump on any chance to do that."

"But aren't they brothers?" Kelsey asked, confused.

"Oh, yes, m'dear, and all four of those brothers just love to bicker and argue and get digs in on each other, especially Tony and James," Roslynn said. "The elder two are great arguers, but those younger two, they are forever cutting each other up — verbally, that is — and delighting in every bit of it. Och, you'd think they are the worst of enemies, but they're really quite close."

"And they band together against anyone else, especially my Nicholas," Reggie added with a sigh. "I do hope the blood isn't too difficult to clean up from the dining room, now that we've left them alone together."

Kelsey blinked, but both Georgina and Roslynn laughed. "I wouldn't worry about it, Reggie, not with Derek there," Roslynn said. "He tends to have a tempering influence on both James and Tony."

"I've noticed that as well," Georgina remarked. "Perhaps because they see a bit of Jason in him, and they do tend to be on their better behavior when Jason is around — that is, unless it's him they're arguing with."

"They seemed to get along fine earlier," Kelsey said, confused yet again. "Am I to understand they don't actually like your husband, Reggie?"

" 'Course they do," all three women said at almost the same moment.

Reggie chuckled, explaining, "Well, you see, Uncle James and Nicholas used to be enemies of a sort, at least they were out for each other's hides — quite seriously. But then I met Nicholas and ended up marrying him, and that put an end to their private feud. Uncle James couldn't very well continue to seek revenge against his nephew by marriage. We are a very close family, after all. As for Uncle Tony, well, he was rather upset with Nicholas for compromising me. He was all for shooting him rather than giving him to me for a husband. Didn't think he was good enough for me, either, rake that Nicholas was at the time."

"As if Anthony wasn't one himself," Roslynn said in amusement.

"And James the worst of the lot," Georgina added. "But that's so typical of men. What was good for them *wasn't* good enough for their favorite niece."

"So now, it's just a — well, a friendly feud, you could call it," Reggie said. "Only my uncles *always* best my poor Nicholas in their verbal skirmishes."

"Cheer up, Reggie," Roslynn remarked. "You're forgetting they now have Warren to rake over the coals. I'm sure he'll take some of the heat off Nick."

"Who's Warren?" Kelsey asked.

"My brother," Georgina replied. "He just married into the Malory clan last week. But there was a time when he tried to have James hanged, and James nearly killed him with his bare hands. But that's another story. Suffice it to say, they were serious enemies, too. Having Warren as a brother-in-law didn't stop James from wanting to clobber him. But now that Warren has joined the family yet again, this time as a nephew by marriage, they've called a truce, though it still doesn't exclude very pointed barbs."

"Amy has changed Warren, though," Reggie pointed out. "He used to have the most horrible temper, but now he's much too happy these days to take heed of their baiting. Or haven't you noticed that when they start in on him, he just smiles and ignores them now?"

Georgina laughed. "I noticed. It drives James crazy when Warren does that."

"I wouldn't doubt Warren knows it."

"Oh, he does." Georgina grinned.

Kelsey was beginning to figure it out —

somewhat. She'd asked earlier why James called his daughter Jack. The unanimous answer had been "Because he knew his brother-in-laws wouldn't like it." Which, she supposed, said a lot about James Malory right there.

"Which reminds me," Reggie said, turning to Kelsey, "if you haven't set your cap for Derek yet, one of George's brothers would be an excellent catch. She's got five, you know, and the other four aren't married."

"Watch out, Kelsey," Roslynn warned with a laugh. "Reggie's an irrepressible match-maker."

"So you're interested in our Derek?" Georgina asked Kelsey. "I rather thought so, with the way you two were looking at each other tonight."

Kelsey was blushing furiously by then. She knew she shouldn't have gone there, even though Derek had said there was no help for it, with the way Reggie had cornered them today at the races. These were such nice women, so friendly, but they would be horrified if they knew she was Derek's mistress. And how was she supposed to deal with a subject like this?

They actually thought she was looking for a husband, and why wouldn't they think so? She was, after all, at the age when most young women did look for husbands. Yet she had burned her bridges, would never be marrying. But Percy's cousin would be expected to. Percy's cousin was pure, and sweet, and still a virgin, or so they thought.

"Derek is very nice," Kelsey began uneasily, not sure how to get out of this. "But —"

"And very handsome," Roslynn cut in.

"And titled, if that matters," Georgina added, cringing.

Roslynn chuckled. "You'll have to excuse my American sister-in-law, Kelsey. She doesn't put much stock in titles, was appalled when she found out one came part and parcel with James when she married him."

"Titles are fine if you happen to like them. I just don't," Georgina clarified.

"Derek *is* a fine catch," Reggie continued. "But I don't think he's quite ready to settle down yet. And she hasn't even met your brothers yet, Aunt George. Drew is an absolute charmer, and —"

"And what makes you think my brothers are ready to settle down?" Georgina asked Reggie with a grin.

Reggie chuckled. "Actually, I don't think *any* man is quite ready, they just need a little nudge in the right direction. In my Nicholas's case, he had the entire Malory clan breathing down his neck, and Uncle Tony threatening to geld him, if he didn't agree to marry me."

"To be expected, after he compromised

you, m'dear," Roslynn said.

Reggie grinned. "But he didn't. Everyone only thought he did."

"Same thing, as you well know. The truth doesn't amount to much if a scandal is involved. The issue becomes what everyone else assumes, more's the pity."

"Well, I'm certainly not complaining," Reggie replied. "It *was* the only way I was going to get him, after all. And he's not complaining, either, for having been forced to the altar, any more than James ever did."

"Oh, James complained." Georgina laughed. "James wouldn't be James if he didn't disagree on *every* issue."

"But I'm not looking for a husband — yet," Kelsey said, hoping that would end the subject. "I only came to London for a new wardrobe, as Percy told you, not to get married," she added, hating having to further the lie, but there was no help for it. "I will be going home in a few days."

"Which is *such* a shame," Reggie replied. "I'll have to talk to Percy about extending your stay. Why, you haven't even been to a ball yet. I'll even stay in town longer myself and accompany you. It will be such fun, Kelsey, so do think about it."

Think about it? The only thing Kelsey was thinking just then was why couldn't the lie be the truth? What Reggie was suggesting did sound like fun. And Kelsey had never been to a formal ball, had always figured she would one day, but now . . . now she had to force herself to remember what she was and that such things were no longer possible.

29

Jason couldn't remember ever having to do anything as hard as telling his family that he and Frances were divorcing. The fact that he would be creating a scandal himself, deliberately, when he had so often lectured them on keeping the family name out of the gossip mills . . . well, he was sure he wouldn't be living this down any time soon, especially where James and Tony were concerned.

They might be, amazing as the thought was, settled down in marriage now and behaving themselves, but those two had always been scoundrels. And he had never stinted on letting them feel his displeasure. He didn't doubt for a minute that they would relish having the tables turned.

He hadn't asked the entire family to show up for this meeting. He had only requested his brothers to be present — and Derek. They could see to telling their wives and children later. Edward would possibly understand. James and Tony would likely be highly amused. It was Derek he was worried about, and how he would take the news. Frances was the only mother Derek had ever known, after all.

He should have told Derek first, and in

private. It was cowardly of him to choose to do it this way instead. But he was hoping for some little support, at least from Edward. And he was hoping that, with the others present, Derek wouldn't question him too deeply as to the whys.

Everyone had arrived except James. Anthony had questioned him already, twice, about why they were there, but he'd given no hint, had said as soon as all were present, he'd get to it.

He stood by the mantel, waiting. Edward and Anthony had settled into a friendly argument about some mining investment. Edward would win, of course. Where investing was concerned, he was a genius. Derek was looking a bit uncomfortable, almost guilty, but the lad hadn't been involved in anything untoward that Jason knew about. Though perhaps he ought to visit a few friends before he returned to Haverston, just to keep abreast of the current gossip.

James finally appeared in the doorway to the parlor where they were gathered. Anthony complained immediately, "You're late, brother."

"I am?"

"He wouldn't fess up to what this is about till you got here, so yes, you're bloody well late."

James snorted. "Put a lid on it, puppy, I

ain't late. You, obviously, arrived too early."

"Redundant, now that we're all here," Edward pointed out placidly.

"Have a seat, James," Jason suggested.

James's brow rose. "This calls for sitting down? That bad, is it?"

"Bloody hell, I'm on tenterhooks here, James, so sit!" Anthony said.

Jason sighed inwardly. There was no easy way to work up to a subject like this, so as soon as James joined Anthony on one of the couches, he said, "I've asked you here today because I wanted you to be the first to know, before it starts making the rounds, that Frances and I are divorcing."

He said no more, waited for the barrage of questions, but received only silence and blank stares. He shouldn't have been surprised. He'd had time to digest the thought, unpalatable as it was, but they hadn't.

Anthony finally asked, "You ain't pulling our leg here, Jason?"

"No."

"You're positive?"

"Have you ever known me to jest about something this serious?" Jason replied.

"Just making sure," Anthony said before he burst out laughing.

That brought out Edward's frown and the remark, "There's nothing funny about this, Tony."

"Oh, yes — there is," Anthony got out between guffaws.

"I fail to see —"

"You wouldn't, Eddie," James cut in dryly. "Perhaps because you've never been called on the carpet by our esteemed eldest."

"That has some significance, I suppose?" Edward asked stiffly.

" 'Course it does. What Tony would find amusing is that Jason will be making the scandal for a change. I find it rather refreshing myself — and long overdue."

"You would," Edward said in disgust.

"I was referring to the divorce, not the scandal. It was an absurd marriage to begin with and should have been ended long ago. That Jason finally came to his senses —"

Jason interrupted, explaining, "It's Frances who wants the divorce."

"*She* does?" Edward said. "Well, that puts a different face on it. Simply prevent it."

"I've already made the decision not to."

"Why ever not?" Edward demanded.

Jason sighed. Edward was the one he had expected support from, not opposition. And he had figured James would be falling off the couch laughing as Anthony was doing. Instead, James was in agreement with him. Incredible. And Derek had said nothing yet. He wore a slight frown, but one of concern rather than upset.

"She wishes to marry elsewhere, Eddie,"

Jason said. "It would be selfish of me to deny her that when we haven't had a normal marriage, as you well know."

Edward shook his head. "You knew you wouldn't have a normal marriage to begin with. Warned you at the time that you would be regretting it, that there would be no backing out of it. But no, you said it wouldn't matter, that you had no intention of ever marrying anyway."

"Yes, you did warn me," Jason agreed. "And it didn't matter at the time. But am I to be held accountable indefinitely for a decision made in my youth when I was worried about the welfare of two younguns?"

"This isn't *your* wish to divorce, it's hers, and she should bloody well know better," Edward insisted.

Anthony was sitting there grinning, delighting in watching the elders duke it out verbally. James had his arms crossed, looking his usual dispassionate self. Edward was red-faced, he'd gotten so worked up over the subject. And about the only thing that might change his tune was a bit more of the truth.

"She's got a lover, Eddie. She admitted it. That's who she wants to marry."

Anthony blinked. "Frances does? Gad, that's rich," and he went off into another peal of laughter.

"Do restrain yourself, dear boy," James said to Anthony. "This ain't *that* funny anymore."

"But Frances? *His* Frances? I bloody well can't imagine it," Anthony replied. "She's such a timid little mouse. Who'd have thought she'd ever have the guts to — well, with Jason's temper'n all, she was bloody well taking her life in her hands, and especially to admit it to him. Just can't credit it, indeed I can't."

Since it *was* rather hard to believe, James glanced at Jason again for confirmation and got a curt nod, as well as, "It's true. I was shocked myself, as you can imagine. But after digesting it, I could hardly blame her for being unfaithful when I've never — that is to say, she's never had a true marriage with me."

"Jason, that's hardly pertinent," Edward said, still frowning. "Marital ties have been known to be ignored by both spouses, but divorce has never been the answer, not in our circles."

"*Never* is incorrect," Jason replied. "There have been divorces in the *ton*, they are just rare."

"My father knows well enough the stigma that will follow a divorce," Derek said, finally speaking up. "I think it's rather decent of him to give the old girl what she wants."

Jason smiled at his son, his relief tremendous. Derek's opinion, after all, had been the only one he was truly concerned with.

"Come now, Eddie boy," James added at that point. "Even the lad can see that this dead horse has been beat enough." And then to Jason, "You should have made it clear that you weren't asking for a vote here, that your decision has been made. Your problem, brother, is you've always put too much weight on the opinion of your peers, when as long as *you* have no regrets over what you do, then it's bloody well no one else's business, is it?"

"That is a luxury not all of us can enjoy," Jason pointed out. "Not when we must deal with the peerage on a regular basis. But as you say, the decision has been made, and it will be acted upon today. And thank you, James, for siding with me on this."

"Good God, is that what I've done?" James exclaimed with feigned surprise. "Come along, Tony, let's adjourn to Knighton's, where you can beat some sense back into me. I seem to have misplaced mine this morning."

Anthony grinned. "That was probably as hard for him to say as it was for you to stomach, but I'm all for beating some sense into you, for whatever reason."

"I don't doubt," James snorted.

Jason smiled fondly after his two younger brothers as they left the room. And then he met Edward's disapproving gaze and sighed.

"You're making a mistake, Jason."

"It's been duly noted that you think so. I prefer to think of it as correcting a mistake I made long ago."

30

"Found out what m'father called a family meeting for," Derek said the moment he entered the parlor.

Kelsey had been sitting in an overstuffed chair by the window sewing on something. She quickly stuffed that something in the corner of the chair before she glanced up at him, looking rather flustered.

But her voice was as calm as usual. "I wasn't aware of any meeting that was called. Was I supposed to be?"

"That's right, you'd left the room last night with the women before that subject came up."

Her frown was abrupt. "Let's not bring that up again, if you don't mind."

He winced. She had been more than a little displeased the night before when he had taken her home. She had been bloody well furious that he had put her in a position where she'd had to lie and pretend.

One of the things she had said in particular had stuck in his mind. "If you are obviously so ashamed of me that you have to call me a widow or someone's cousin when you introduce me, then do *not* take me to places where it will be necessary to introduce me."

Ironically, he'd realized he wasn't the least bit ashamed of her, that he was actually proud to be seen with her. And it had occurred to him, after he'd thought about it, that the real reason he hadn't tried very hard to come up with an excuse not to take her to Reggie's the night before was possibly that he had *wanted* his family to meet her. And that was so bloody absurd, it didn't bear examining. No, he wasn't ashamed of her, not at all. It was her relationship to him that was shameful and needed to be concealed, and there was, unfortunately, no way of getting around that.

"Was it so difficult, dealing with my relatives?" he asked.

"Your family is very nice, at least the women are. Your uncles are rather strange in that they *like* to argue and bicker, but that is nothing to me. The point is, they were deceived and shouldn't have been. You know very well you should never have taken me there."

He knew it. But it was done, couldn't be undone.

And as long as they were on the subject, he told her, "My uncles know."

"Know what?"

"That you're my mistress."

"You *told* them?" she cried, appalled.

"No, they both figured it out for themselves. They've each had countless mistresses of their own, you see — before they were married, that is. It was still my fault, though, because it was apparently the way I was looking at you last night that gave it away."

"And how were you looking at me?"

"Rather . . . intimately."

"Why ever did you do that?"

"I didn't *know* I was doing it until they pointed it out," he insisted.

She was blushing by then. And he was reacting as he usually did, his body responding to her sweet innocence in a purely primitive way. He took a step toward her but caught himself and stopped, raking a hand through his golden mane, annoyed with himself.

He'd already broken one of his own rules by going to her before it was even noontime. He'd received startling news that morning, and although it was really none of her concern, he had wanted to share it with her. But making love to her now was out of the question. *She* wouldn't expect it.

A mistress was to be visited in the dark, secret hours of the night. He'd already made allowances to come earlier so he could dine with her each evening. If he kept making allowances like these, he might as well move in with her so he could spend all his time with her.

What an incredibly tempting thought. To

wake with her each morning. To breakfast with her. To tell her his thoughts as they occurred to him, rather than to keep them until he saw her again. To make love to her when he felt like it, not just at what was considered the appropriate time.

He mentally shoved the thought aside because it was *too* tempting by half. What the deuce was wrong with him? He hadn't even wanted a mistress in the first place. He might have changed his mind because of Kelsey, was very pleased that he had her, but still . . .

"You mentioned a meeting?" she said to end the long silence that had fallen.

"M'father's getting a divorce."

"I beg your pardon."

"That's what that meeting was about," he explained, blushing slightly for having blurted it out like that. "So he could announce it."

Sympathy filled her soft gray eyes, and she came out of the chair to put her arms around him. "Your mother must be devastated."

"Actually —"

"You must be as well."

She was trying to comfort him, and damned if he didn't like that very much, enough to savor it for a few moments before he confessed, "No, it's not like that a'tall. She's my stepmum, you see, and although

I'm quite fond of the old girl, she was never around often enough for me to form a strong attachment to her. Besides, she's the one who wants the divorce."

"Then your father must be —"

"No, no, dear girl, no one is devastated, really they aren't — well, except perhaps for my Uncle Edward," he added with a slight grimace. "He tried his damnedest to talk m'father out of divorcing, but there's no changing Jason Malory's mind once it's set."

"Why did your uncle object?"

"I would imagine because it's going to be a bit of a scandal."

"But I thought you said it was your father who abhorred scandals."

"He does, but he's making an exception to grant Frances her freedom. They never had a normal marriage, you see. He only married her to give Reggie and me a mother. But that didn't exactly work out as he had hoped. As I said, she was rarely home."

"Why not?"

"Well, she's rather sickly," he explained. "So she went to Bath for the water cures quite often, until she finally just bought a cottage there and simply lived in Bath most of each year."

Kelsey sighed, laying her head against his chest. "People shouldn't marry for other than love."

"Ideally no, yet many do."

"Well, I'm glad you aren't very upset about this."

"And if I was?"

"Then I would endeavor to help you get over it, of course," she replied.

"Why?" he asked softly.

She looked up at him, somewhat surprised. "Because that would be the mistressly thing to do, wouldn't it?"

He almost laughed. That would be the *wifely* thing to do, certainly, but mistressly? A mistress might worry if her protector was angry or not, but whether he was happy or sad wouldn't concern her very much, not unless it related directly to her.

"That would be very generous of you, m'dear," he said, cupping her cheek. That she had been leaning against him for the last five minutes had quite done him in. "Perhaps I could use some of that help after all."

Since he had picked her up as he finished, and was already heading toward the door, she asked, "You aren't going up to the bedroom, are you?"

"Oh, yes."

"But that wasn't the kind of help I was referring to," she pointed out reasonably.

"I know, but it's the kind I need just now, and I don't give a bloody damn what time of day it is."

He said that so belligerently, she blinked. "Neither do I, actually."

"You don't?"

"No, why should I?"

"No reason a'tall, m'dear," he said, grinning from ear to ear.

31

Derek had a few errands to attend to that afternoon, and he decided to take Kelsey with him. It had been an impulse to do so, one he should have ignored, but he didn't. His extremely mellow mood was likely to blame, and he could blame Kelsey for that.

She was turning out to be a splendid lover; at least, the pleasure he derived from making love to her was much more intense than he was used to, on a par with pure ecstasy. And after such an enjoyable hour as they had just spent, he was a bit more reluctant to leave her than usual.

The dress she donned for the outing was a surprise, though. Aside from that red dress she'd worn when he bought her, every time he'd seen her she had been dressed — well, more like a lady, and he supposed he had become used to that.

He was so surprised by the bright orange velvet with lime green trimmings that he remarked thoughtlessly, "I can barely see you in that, it's so glaring."

Which was true. Her other clothes had been tasteful and subtle in hue, so that her beauty was the first thing noticed, her gowns merely an enhancement to that beauty. But no one would be seeing anything but that atrocious orange when they looked at her this day, its brightness so hid her beneath it.

Belatedly, though, he realized he'd just insulted her. But she didn't look insulted when he glanced at her.

She looked merely thoughtful as she said, "I thought it was rather awful myself, but it's one of Mrs. Westerbury's selections that were made per your instructions."

He flushed with color immediately. He *had* told the dressmaker that Kelsey was his mistress and to dress her accordingly. But the woman must imagine all mistresses were culled from the theater district, where many of the actresses deliberately dressed flamboyantly to call attention to themselves.

"The neckline is quite risqué as well," she added, and when his eyes went immediately to her breasts, which she had already completely covered with her jacket, she shook her head. "No, I will *not* show you."

"Quite risqué?" He grinned.

"Yes, quite."

She sighed and scowled at him as his fingers came to her jacket to undo the buttons, but she didn't try to stop him. And spreading the jacket wide a moment later, he changed his mind completely about the dress's being the only thing noticeable. No one was going to miss *those* despite the eye-catching material just barely covering them.

With some throat clearing, he closed the jacket again and buttoned her back up. She had a brow raised, waiting for his comment. He merely grinned sheepishly at her and led her out to the waiting coach.

But he added one stop to his list of errands, and when he came out of the dressmaker's a while later, having left her in the coach, he told her, "Just arranged for a few changes on the rest of your order."

She didn't need to ask what. He hadn't liked the color selection any more than she had, but he had very obviously liked the low bodice. She supposed she could live with that. Lace fichus could be added when she wasn't with him, and she could easily sew those herself. She made a mental note to go out and buy some materials tomorrow.

They were halfway to his solicitor, where his signature was required on some document, when he suddenly pounded on the roof for the driver to stop. The coach had barely done so before he was jumping out of it. Kelsey stayed behind again, but was able to watch from the window, since Derek didn't go far. He had hailed a middle-aged couple he apparently wished to speak to.

Frances stopped at Derek's shout. Her companion stepped back, as if he didn't want to be associated with her, but Derek barely noticed him anyway, he was so non-descript.

"I didn't know you were in town," Derek said, giving her a hug.

"I had some — ah, business to attend to, so I stayed in London after Amy's wedding," Frances said.

That surprised a frown from him. "Where? I haven't seen you at the town house."

"Perhaps because you're rarely there?"

He grinned. "That's true. But surely Hanly would have mentioned it to me."

"Actually, Derek, I'm staying at a hotel this trip," she admitted.

"Why?"

"Because I didn't want to be in residence if Jason showed up."

He nodded in understanding. "M'father told us about the divorce this morning."

Her eyes lit up with excitement. "Then he's agreed to it?"

"You didn't know?"

"No, he never sees fit to tell me anything," she replied with a sigh. "Though to be truthful, I haven't been in contact with him since I told him I wanted it. I sent him word where I could be reached, but — well, I suppose he will get around to telling me."

She was fond of Derek, but she'd never felt motherly toward him. It wasn't in her nature to be motherly, she supposed. And had she known that was all Jason had wanted from her, she probably could have prevented their disastrous marriage before it began.

Actually, no, even she hadn't known at that young age that she had no motherly instincts, didn't even particularly care for children being underfoot. But regardless, she hadn't wanted the lad to be upset over the termination of her so-called marriage to his father.

"I hope you weren't too distressed?" she asked uneasily.

"It was — surprising, to say the least, but understandable, considering the circumstances. Only Uncle Edward had any complaints, because of the expected scandal."

"The scandal shouldn't affect your family very much, since I've given Jason grounds to divorce me, the kind that will have his acquaintances in sympathy with him. I fully expect to take the brunt of it, but then I've never been socially active, so it won't even affect me that much."

She was talking about her having admitted to having a lover, he knew, and the very mention of it brought his attention straight to her companion. He was a scrawny beanpole of a man who couldn't have weighed more than a hundred pounds or so. And he was no more than a few inches taller than Frances, which meant he barely reached Derek's shoulder. But Derek knew instantly, just by the fellow's wary expression, that he was the culprit.

Derek's protective instincts rose, as did his anger. This fellow had caused his family grief, was going to be responsible for his father's embarrassment during the divorce. Bloody hell, not without paying for it, he wasn't.

Derek's long-armed reach caught the man's lapels and lifted him clear off the ground. He squeaked, gripping Derek's forearm, his eyes bulging with fright that did nothing to ease Derek's fury.

"Did you know the Lady Frances was a married woman when you put your hands on her?" Derek demanded. "One blow and I could smash your face in, you little twit. Give me a single reason why I shouldn't do just that."

"Put him down, Derek, this instant!" Frances shouted, revealing some anger of her own. "Have you lost your reason? Would I have been unfaithful to your father if he had made me happy? Well, he never did! And furthermore, he has been unfaithful to me since the day we married, a marriage that was never even consummated, I might add."

Derek's head swung around to look at her incredulously. "Never?"

"Never," she said stiffly. "Yet *he* certainly

hasn't slept alone since."

"That is an absurd accusation, madam," Derek said just as stiffly. "When m'father rarely leaves Haverston."

"He doesn't have to leave Haverston when his mistress lives under his very roof!"

Derek was so surprised he dropped the fellow he was still holding to the ground and demanded, "Who?"

Frances had already flushed with heated embarrassment. She shook her head. She looked quite wary now, and quite upset, as she helped her companion back to his feet.

"Who?" Derek was shouting now.

"I don't know who," she lied.

"You're lying, madame."

"Well, it doesn't matter who," she insisted. "The point is, I certainly wasn't the first to be unfaithful. The amazing thing is that I wasn't unfaithful from the very beginning, when Jason Malory certainly gave me every reason to be. But enough is enough. And you have no call to harm Oscar. He has only helped along what should have been done years ago, the ending of an intolerable relationship."

Having said that, she huffed away, dragging her Oscar with her. Derek stared after them, trying to digest what had just been said.

After a moment, a hand slipped into his and he looked down, startled, to see Kelsey standing beside him. "Gad, I forgot you were waiting."

She smiled. "That's quite all right. What was that all about?"

He nodded toward the departing couple. "My stepmum — and her lover."

"Ah, so that's why it looked like you were going to kill the little fellow."

"I bloody well felt like it," he mumbled as he led her back to the coach.

"Amazing," she said, looking thoughtful.

"What is?"

"Well, if your father looks anything like you, I just can't imagine your stepmother preferring anyone else, and *certainly* not that little chap."

He smiled at that roundabout compliment and gave her a hug before he hefted her into the coach, then pulled her next to him on the seat. "What *is* amazing is that she claims my father never once touched her in all these years, that he's had a mistress instead who's been living right under his roof."

"Imagine that," she said. "Actually, that's rather — shocking."

"Well, it's a very big roof," he said, as if that made it a little more palatable.

"I take it you didn't know?" When he shook his head, she added, "And you still don't know who it is? No guesses?"

"Not a clue." He sighed.

"Well, with his marriage ending, it hardly matters now who she is, does it?"

"No — except it's going to drive me crazy until I find out."

"Should you?"

"What?"

"Find out?"

"Absolutely."

"But the fact that you didn't know, Derek, means your father has kept this woman a secret intentionally. That makes it a pretty safe guess that he'd like to keep it that way, don't you think?"

"Probably," he agreed.

"So you'll leave it alone?"

He grinned. "Not a chance."

32

For what should have been some simple errands that required no social discourse, Derek was running into too many people he knew. First Frances. Then, at his tailor's, his cousin Marshall showed up.

That wasn't so bad, though, with Kelsey out in the coach and Marshall being left behind in the tailor's shop — or so he'd thought. But Marshall was apparently full of gossip, and he hailed Derek once more just as he reached his coach to impart some additional tidbit. And there he spotted Kelsey, even though she was doing her best to squeeze into the corner so she wouldn't be noticed — impossible, of course, with that bloody orange dress.

Marshall was Edward's oldest boy, though still three years younger than Derek. And he wouldn't be put off from meeting Kelsey. But that went well enough. Marshall didn't ask who she was or what she was doing alone with him, and Derek didn't volunteer the information. But then two of Marshall's cronies came along, and Sir William, the more outspoken of the two, after ogling Kelsey for a good five minutes, brought up a subject that seemed to come up all too frequently.

"Related to Lord Langton, the earl whose wife shot him?" he asked baldly.

A simple "No" just didn't suffice.

"Who is she, then?" William persisted.

"I'm a witch, Sir William," Kelsey answered before Derek could. "Lord Malory has hired me to put a curse on someone. Is this the person, Derek?"

Derek blinked in surprise, but William paled and looked so comical in his horror that Derek couldn't help but burst out laughing. And Kelsey merely looked on innocently.

"Oh, I say, that ain't funny, Derek," Marshall declared.

"Well, obviously, it ain't William here that he wants to have cursed," William's companion pointed out logically, given Derek's present amusement. But then, "So who is the unlucky chap?"

Derek's cousin rolled his eyes, having caught on by then. But Derek went into yet another round of laughing over that question. And obviously, he wasn't going to be answering it any time soon.

So Kelsey said quite calmly, "Surely you realize I was jesting, gentlemen? I'm not a witch — at least, not that I'm aware of."

"Just bewitching," Derek finally got out with a tender smile for Kelsey, and in response he got the expected blush that compliments always caused her.

But he managed to extricate them soon after and he left before the question of Kelsey's identity came up again. He remarked on that on the way to their next stop.

"That was rather brilliantly done, damn me if it wasn't," he said, giving her a squeeze. "A jest instead of a lie. Glad you thought of it, m'dear."

"And which lie would you have used this time, widow or cousin?"

He winced. "That *really* was not supposed to happen, Kelsey. Marshall was in the tailor's, yes, hadn't expected that, but I'd bid farewell to him three times. He kept recalling something else he wanted to tell me, and caught up with me each time, until as you saw, he stopped me once again just as I reached the coach."

She smiled at him, allowing that it wasn't his fault. This time. And she had been enjoying keeping him company, even if she was spending half the time alone in the coach.

So her rebuke was a mere "We will endeavor to keep it from happening again, won't we?"

"Absolutely," he assured her.

And yet at their last stop, at the crystal shop, where he hoped to find a birthday present for his cousin Clare, he asked Kelsey to come in with him to help him choose.

And here they did run into yet another acquaintance. Only this time there was no need for introductions to be made. This time it was someone they *both* knew — and both wished they didn't know.

It was the worst luck that David Ashford would be in that particular store at that exact time of day, and that they would run into him, literally. He had turned about to leave without noticing that anyone had come up the narrow aisle behind him and plowed right into Derek, who had to release Kelsey's arm to shove the man back.

Ashford was startled by the collision, but then his blue eyes narrowed as he recognized who stood before him. "If it isn't the do-gooder," he sneered. "The rescuer of damsels in distress. Did it ever occur to you, Malory, that some damsels might enjoy distress?"

A bald remark like that made Derek's hackles rise. "Did it ever occur to you, Lord Ashford, that you are sick?"

"There is nothing wrong with my health."

"I was referring to your mind."

"Ha!" Ashford scoffed. "So you'd like to think, but I am quite sane. And I also have a long memory. You will regret stealing this pretty from me."

"Oh, I doubt that, indeed I do," Derek replied with seeming indifference. Then he pointed out coldly, "But nothing was stolen from you. It was an auction. You could have continued to bid."

"When everyone knows how rich the Malorys are? Don't be absurd. But the day will come when you will regret crossing me."

Derek shrugged with little concern. "If I have any regrets, Ashford, it's knowing you're alive, when scum like you should have been tossed in the rubbish at birth."

The man stiffened, his face suffusing with color. Derek wished he would have challenged the man, but he'd pegged him correctly: a coward who only felt powerful when dealing with the weak and helpless.

"That will be remembered as well," Ashford said impotently. But then his icy glare lit on Kelsey and he added, "When he tosses you aside, I'll be waiting, and you'll pay for making me wait, my pretty. Oh, indeed, you will pay. . . ."

He had shoved his pointed finger at Kelsey as he said that, would have stabbed her in the chest with it if Derek hadn't grabbed his hand. Ashford howled when the finger happened to snap in the process. But Derek wasn't done. Threats to himself he could easily shrug off. A threat to Kelsey had made him berserk.

"You broke — !" Ashford was shouting, but a swift punch to his mouth cut him off.

Derek caught the other man before he could fall and, still holding him, said furiously, "You think I won't smash you to bits in here, with all this crystal surrounding us? Think again, Ashford, because I don't give a bloody damn what breaks, as long as you break with it."

The man paled, but the owner of the shop intervened. "I would rather not go out of business," he said in a worried voice, "m'lord, due to your little altercation. Could you *please* take this argument elsewhere?"

And Kelsey whispered, "Don't let him provoke you into causing a scandal."

It was perhaps too late for that warning. Yet a glance around revealed no other customers in the shop, just the owner wringing his hands.

Derek nodded curtly and released Ashford, but he did some finger jabbing of his own. "You like to mention regrets? Let me mention one that you won't have to worry about, because you won't have any if you ever come near her again, nor any memory of it, nor any breath left to pollute this city with. You will quite cease to exist."

He then snatched up a vase on a stand beside them, without even looking at it, and shoved it at the owner. "I'll purchase this."

"Certainly, m'lord. Please come this way, if you will," the man said, and quickly hurried to his sales counter in the back of the shop.

Derek took Kelsey's arm and followed the

owner. Neither spared another glance for Ashford. And within moments, they heard the door to the shop open and close behind them as Ashford left.

Kelsey sighed in relief. The owner sighed in relief. Derek was still too agitated to feel anything other than anger. He should have beat the man senseless again and to hell with scandal. He had a feeling he was going to regret *not* doing so.

Annoyed with himself for not doing more while he had the chance *and* the provocation, he tossed the owner a large amount of money and told him, "Keep the change — and this unfortunate incident to yourself."

"What incident?" the owner replied with a smile, now that all his wares were safe and his pockets lined.

33

There was such a boyish quality about Derek Malory, with his thatch of unruly blond hair and his charming smiles, that made him seem quite harmless. But on this day Kelsey had found out that the surface wasn't exactly the whole story. She had been frozen in fear upon meeting Lord Ashford again and having the horror of the auction recalled so vividly. But Derek had turned into another man entirely. And she was immensely glad that he wasn't as harmless as he usually seemed to be.

Far from it. He'd actually broken the man's finger. Deliberately. And she had little doubt that he would have broken much more if it hadn't been pointed out that he would be making a scandal if he did so.

She had said that because she knew how he felt about scandals, and knew it would likely put an end to the altercation, which it did. Why she had done so she wasn't sure. Perhaps because she didn't want to witness him being so violent. Or because the poor owner of the store was so worried for his goods. Or maybe just because she was feeling some protective instincts suddenly where Derek was concerned and didn't want him doing something that he would later regret. The latter was definitely worth worrying over.

She had previously determined that this business of being a mistress needed to be kept as impersonal as possible. But trying to keep it that way was becoming more and more impossible. She *liked* Derek, liked being with him, liked making love to him, liked everything about him. And unless he did something drastic to alter that, she was afraid those feelings were going to get much stronger.

That was a horrible thought. She didn't *want* to love Derek. She didn't want to agonize over the day he would tell her he had no further use for her. And that day would eventually come. When it did, she wanted to sigh in relief, not cry her heart out.

He'd had a mistress before, she knew, so she had reason to worry. In one of the conversations with Percy and Jeremy, it had been mentioned that Derek had ended the relationship in a matter of months, not years.

The exorbitant extra cost he had spent to acquire Kelsey didn't matter very much to him, as wealthy as his family was. So she couldn't count on that coming into the equation. No, when he was ready for someone new, she would definitely be sent on her way, regardless of her own feelings. It was that simple. And she didn't know how to make it any easier to bear when that day came around, not if she was going to do a stupid thing such as fall in love with him.

Derek was silently brooding now over the incident with Ashford, though he sat with his arm protectively around her, his hand absently rubbing her arm. Since Kelsey was doing her own brooding, it was a quiet ride.

When they arrived at the next stop, Kelsey wasn't going to budge from the coach. Derek didn't ask her to. But he wasn't gone long. And when he returned, he handed her a package.

"It's for you," he said simply. "Open it."

She looked at the small box in her hand warily, afraid she knew why he was giving her a gift, especially since he was looking rather guilt-ridden. Opening it, she found a heart-shaped pendant made entirely of tiny diamonds and rubies, on a short, thin golden chain that would hang just below her neck. Very simple, very elegant, very expensive.

"You didn't have to do this," she said softly, still staring at the pendant.

"Yes, I did," he replied. "I'm feeling so guilty right now that if you don't say you forgive me, I'll probably burst into tears."

Her eyes shot up, wide with the thought that he was serious, but his expression told her otherwise. She chuckled, but only briefly. He wasn't serious about crying, but he did feel guilty.

He smiled ruefully. "Today has been somewhat of a disaster all the way around, hasn't it?"

"Not completely," she said, and her blush gave her away.

"Well, not that," he agreed with a grin. "But the rest — I am *truly* sorry you had to even be in the same room with that bastard Ashford, let alone be subjected to that distasteful encounter."

She shuddered inwardly. "He's a cruel man, isn't he? I saw it in his eyes that night he was bidding on me, and again today."

"Worse than you can imagine," Derek said. He went on to explain just how sick the man really was, telling her everything, or at least alluding to it, so she would understand his warning.

"If you ever see him again, Kelsey, when I'm not with you, leave wherever you happen to be immediately — that is, if it's safe to do so."

She had lost nearly all of her color and actually felt sick to her stomach. "Safe?"

"As long as there is no likelihood that he will follow you. You *never* want to find yourself alone with him, Kelsey. Intrude on strangers if you must, scream for assistance, but whatever you do, don't let that man anywhere near you."

"No, I wouldn't," she assured him. "Ideally, I hope I never see him again. But if I do, and I see him first, he'll never see me, I promise you."

"Good, now say you forgive me."

She smiled at him. "I do, even though you have nothing to be forgiven for. Now, take this back and get your money returned. You don't have to buy me jewels."

He chuckled at that. "Kelsey, m'dear, that is a very *un*mistressly thing to say. And I'm not taking it back. I want you to have it. It will go very nicely with your lavender gown."

And a half dozen more that were yet to be delivered, she could have added but didn't. She sighed. "Then I suppose it would be churlish of me not to thank you."

"Yes, very churlish."

She grinned. "Thank you."

"You are very, very welcome, m'dear."

That had been their last stop. After that he took her home and stayed for dinner — and stayed the night, too.

He had not planned to do this. Whenever Jason was in town, and staying over, it was Derek's habit to at least join him at the town house for dinner. And he didn't know when Jason would be returning to Haverston, so he didn't know if he'd have the opportunity to catch him the next day.

But as much as he wanted to talk to his

father about the divorce — and the woman he'd managed to keep a secret for so long — he wanted to stay near Kelsey much more.

She had been shaken by the encounter, he knew. But Derek was more concerned, worrying about her.

Unbelievably, Ashford had treated her as if she belonged to him and had just been temporarily stolen from him. His remarks had also indicated that he was going to make her pay for being stolen when he got her back, and he had also seemed confident that he *would* get her back. And who was to say what plans his crazy mind could conjure.

Derek couldn't be with her all the time. She did go out on her own, to the dressmaker for her fittings, shopping, and whatnot. Nor could he ask her not to, when his fears so far were based on simple threats.

He would pay his Uncle James a visit again the next day, to get his advice. He was likely worrying over nothing, but tonight he still wasn't letting Kelsey out of his sight.

34

Derek did indeed visit his Uncle James the next morning, before he even returned home for a change of clothing. And after a short chat with James, he was much relieved. Kelsey could not be in any immediate danger, because his uncle had already set his two butlers to following Ashford.

Artie and Henry were in no way typical butlers, though, which was why Derek was so relieved. They had been members of James's pirate crew and had served under him for most of his ten years at sea.

They had both elected to stay with James after he sold the *Maiden Anne*, and they now shared the job of butlering at his London residence, a job they thoroughly enjoyed because they weren't what one might expect. And they got a hoot out of shocking visitors.

That they continually bruised a few feathers with their unorthodox ways didn't bother James in the least, and Aunt George had long before given up trying to teach them better manners. To knock on their door these days — if you weren't a relative — could get a barked "They ain't home!" and the door slammed in your face, or a "What in the bleedin' hell d'you want?" Unless it was a comely lady knocking, of course. Ladies invariably got dragged right in and the door shut behind them before they could get two words out.

But both ex-pirates were quite suitable for the job James had set them to. And so far, James informed Derek, they had followed Ashford to two separate residences, his main house in the city and one just outside the city that looked all but deserted, and where he didn't actually spend the night, just a few hours of an evening.

They had also followed him to a tavern in one of the poorer sections of town. Derek had stiffened, hearing that, until James related that Artie had caused such a commotion there, in the guise of being utterly foxed, and accosted Ashford in the process, that the man had quickly canceled whatever plans he'd had and left.

Derek had immediately sent off a note to Kelsey so she could stop worrying, if she still was, and could relax her guard somewhat. He'd then returned home and found his father still there. Whether he could consider that fortunate or not was in doubt, since Jason looked none too pleased as he called Derek into his study.

Derek immediately assumed that Frances had gotten in touch with Jason and had informed him about their little encounter the day before. Not so. Actually, Derek later wished that had been the case.

"You actually bought a mistress in a *public* whorehouse in a room full of your *peers?*"

Derek practically fell into the chair he'd been about to sit in, feeling more than a little poleaxed. Any time his father stressed words, you knew he was just barely in control of his temper.

"How did you hear of it?"

"How did you think I *wouldn't,* when the thing was done so damned *publicly?*" Jason demanded.

Derek cringed inwardly. "It was to be hoped, considering the gentlemen there don't usually admit to being in such places."

Jason snorted. "As it happens, I stopped by my club last evening. A friend of mine was there who felt I should be apprised of it. He happened to have another friend, who was a friend of someone who was there that night. It's bloody well made the rounds of all the clubs already. And Lord knows how many wives it's been shared with by now, who are passing it around in *their* groups."

Derek was flushing furiously already, but in his defense, he said, "You know very well it isn't likely to be shared with *any* wives."

"Beside the bloody point," Jason replied, his frown just as dark. "What the devil were you thinking, to participate in an auction like that?"

"I was thinking I would be saving that innocent young girl from —"

"Innocent?" Jason cut in. "Who is she anyway?"

"Kelsey Langton, and no, she's no one of importance, so you needn't worry about that. But as I was saying, I bid on her to keep her from being scarred for life."

"I beg your pardon?"

Derek sighed. "I'd had no intention of getting involved, Father. We'd only stopped by that place for a few hands of cards while Jeremy visited with one of his ladyloves who worked there. But then —"

"You took *Jeremy* to such a place? He's only eighteen years old!"

"Jeremy has been going to such places probably longer than I have, or have you forgotten that he was raised in a tavern before Uncle James found him?"

To that Jason merely glowered, so Derek continued, "As I was saying, I'd had no intention of getting involved, but then I noticed who was bidding on the girl."

"Who?"

"He's a man I've run into before, a lord, and I've witnessed firsthand what he does to the prostitutes he uses. He whips them bloody, so severely that they are permanently disfigured. It's rumored it's the only way he can get any pleasure out of sex."

"Disgusting."

"I couldn't agree more. In fact, as a favor to me, Uncle James is looking into a means of putting a stop to the man's perverted practices."

"James is? How?"

"I — ah — didn't bother to ask."

Jason cleared his throat. "Quite right. Where that particular brother of mine is concerned, it's better not to know. But, Derek —"

"Father, it really couldn't have been helped," Derek cut in. "I couldn't think of any other way to keep the girl safe, except to buy her myself. And she did turn out to be an innocent, so I'm bloody well glad I kept her out of Ashford's hands."

"David Ashford? Good God, I would have thought some woman would have gelded him years ago."

"You knew about him?"

"I'd heard rumors, back before he'd reached his majority, that he used to torture his female servants. Nothing that was ever proven, of course. Then there was another rumor that someone had brought him up on charges, but it never reached a trial, since the woman in question refused to bear witness against him. They say it cost him most of his family fortune to pay the woman off. As I recall, a cheer went up in my club the night we heard that. At least it was some punishment — if the rumors were true."

Derek nodded. "I imagine they were true, and he has progressed to worse tortures."

"And there's nothing the courts can do without a victim to accuse him." Jason sighed.

"Oh, he covers himself very well these days," Derek said. "I found one of his victims, the same one I had come upon him beating. I'd hoped she would help to bring him to trial. But he not only pays them handsomely, he warns them of what he means to do and gets their agreement first."

"Smart as well as dreadfully demented. A dangerous combination, that. But you have involved James. Leave it to him. I can almost guarantee he will find a way to keep that man from hurting anyone else."

"Which was my hope, especially since I just had yet another run-in with the fellow, and he indicated that he feels Kelsey was stolen from him when I outbid him and that he'll have her back eventually."

Jason raised a brow. "Are you saying you still have the girl?"

"Well, she was sold as a mistress, and I did pay a great deal of money for her."

"How *much* money?"

"I'd rather not sa—"

"How much?"

Derek hated that better-fess-up-or-else tone, he really did. "Twenty-five," he mumbled.

"Twenty-five *hundred!*"

Derek sank a bit lower in his chair before he admitted, "Thousand — pounds."

Jason choked, sputtered, opened his mouth to say something but snapped it closed again. He dropped into the chair behind his desk. He raked both hands through his golden mane. He finally sighed, then pinned Derek with one of his darkest frowns.

"I must not have heard you correctly. You didn't say you paid twenty-five *thousand* pounds for a mistress. No —" He held up a hand when Derek started to speak. "I don't want to hear it. Forget I asked."

"Father, there was no other way to keep Ashford from buying the girl," Derek reminded him.

"I can think of a half dozen at least, including simply taking her out of there. Who, after all, would have stopped you, when that auction was hardly legal?"

Derek smiled at what was a typical Malory response. "Well, the proprietor, Lonny, might have had a thing or two to say about that, considering the profit I would have been snatching out of his hand."

"Lonny?" Jason frowned a moment, opened the *London Times* on his desk to the second page, and pointed. "That Lonny, by any chance?"

Derek leaned forward to briefly scan the article, but was so surprised that he went back to read it more thoroughly. It was a report on Lonny Kilpatrick, who had been murdered in a house of ill repute that he had run for a little more than a year and a half. The address was given, and the details of his death. He had apparently been stabbed in the chest repeatedly. There was mention of a great deal of blood. And no clue as to his murderer.

"I'll be damned," Derek said, leaning back.

"I take it that's the same Lonny you dealt with?" Jason asked.

"Indeed."

"Interesting, though I doubt there is any connection between the murder and the auction. All that blood on the body, all around it, does, however, remind me of what you said about Ashford and his predilection for blood."

"He's a sniveling coward," Derek scoffed. "He wouldn't have the guts to kill a man."

Jason shrugged. "From what you've said about him, and from the previous rumors I'd heard myself, that man is deficient up here." And he pointed at his head. "There is no telling what someone like that is capable of. But I tend to agree. He does sound like a coward who prefers to torment the weak. Besides, for what reason would he kill this Lonny person, when it's apparently only women he enjoys hurting. It's likely no more than a coincidence."

Derek would have agreed, wanted to agree, but blister it, that small bit of doubt had been raised. He was back to worrying again. And he went straight back to James's house as soon as he left his father, to apprise his uncle of this newest development.

Unfortunately, he forgot all about wanting to ask his father about the mistress he had been keeping all these years. And by the time he returned home again, it was to find a note from Jason reminding him that he was expected at Haverston for the Christmas holidays. His father was already on his way back there himself.

35

Despite Derek's assurances that she had little to fear from Lord Ashford now that he was being watched, Kelsey still wouldn't leave the town house for nearly a week. She sent her footman around to the dressmaker to cancel two fittings — she had fortunately just hired a footman, as well as the rest of the servants she needed, that week.

She also held off returning to that nice little yardage shop that she'd found, where she had purchased the material to sew Derek a few things for Christmas. A monogrammed cravat and handkerchiefs, some silk shirts, several of which she had already finished.

Ironically, she hadn't been quite as fearful the day they encountered Lord Ashford as she was the next day, after spending the evening with Derek. She had sensed his fear, though he hadn't said anything more after his warning.

Staying holed up in the house did have its advantages. After three days of agonizing over it, she was able to finally get off a letter to her Aunt Elizabeth. In it she had explained that her friend had had a new medical opinion that actually offered some hope, and that they had moved to London to be close to the new doctor.

Continuing the lie to her aunt was what was so difficult, that and supplying a return address, which Elizabeth would naturally expect. In the end, Kelsey used her own, since she knew of no others aside from Derek's, and using his was out of the question.

She had also included a letter to her sister filled with gossip about their hometown, all of it fabrications, of course. Both letters, once finished, made her feel so despicable that she certainly hadn't been very good company for Derek. He'd noticed, and remarked on it, but she'd put him off with more lies about feeling under the weather and such — and got lots of flowers the next day that made her want to cry.

She finally convinced herself that she was being silly, hiding indoors. The fact that it was a lovely winter day when she did might have helped. At any rate, she took herself straight to the dressmaker for those final fittings, and those were seen to in quick order. And she was only a little bit hesitant in leaving the back of the shop, worrying that she might run into Lady Eden again on the way out.

But the showroom was quite empty that early in the morning, most of the ladies of the *ton* being late risers due to late-night entertainments. There was one exception, however.

Just as she reached for the door to the street, it opened, and in walked her Aunt Elizabeth with her sister, Jean, just a step behind. Jean, of course, shrieked in delight upon seeing Kelsey and threw herself into Kelsey's arms. Elizabeth was as surprised as Kelsey was, though not unpleasantly, as Kelsey most surely was.

"What are you doing in London?" they both asked at the same instant.

"Didn't you receive my letter?" Kelsey added.

"No . . . I . . . did . . . not."

The pauses between those words added a sting to Elizabeth's reproach, if Kelsey didn't feel it enough from her expression. She should have written sooner. She knew it. Elizabeth had been expecting a letter. But it was just so *hard* lying to her own family that she'd put it off as long as possible. Now she was going to have to explain again.

"I did write, Aunt Elizabeth, to let you know that I was moving to London with Anne. She's found a new doctor here, you see, who's actually given her some hope, so she wanted to be near him."

"But that's wonderful news!"

"Yes, it is."

"Does that mean you will be coming home

soon, Kel?" Jean asked hopefully.

"No, sweetheart, Anne is still very sick," Kelsey said, hugging Jean close.

"Your sister is needed here, Jean," Elizabeth added gruffly. "Her friend needs her spirits kept up, and Kelsey is good at that, kindhearted as she is."

"But what are you doing in London, Aunt?" Kelsey asked again.

Elizabeth humphed. "Our seamstress at home moved away, and without a by-your-leave. Can you imagine that? And I won't use that French hussy who competed with her. So I decided that as long as Jean and I were going to get a few new dresses for the holidays, we might as well come to the best, and Mrs. Westerbury has been well-recommended by several of my friends."

"Yes, she is excellent," Kelsey agreed. "I've ordered a few dresses for myself as well, since I didn't bring too many along with me."

"Well, if you *are* going to be needed here for much longer, do let me know and I'll send your trunks to you. You shouldn't be deprived on this errand of mercy. But, goodness, as long as you are in London, do you realize this is the height of the season? And I have numerous friends here who I'm sure would be delighted to take you in hand and launch you. And I'm sure your friend wouldn't begrudge you a few hours here and there to keep your own spirits up."

Aunt Elizabeth was well-meaning, of course, but Kelsey had passed beyond taking advantage of a London social season for marriage prospects. Since she couldn't mention that, she said simply, "That will have to wait, Aunt Elizabeth. I'd feel so terrible, going off to enjoy myself while Anne couldn't, that I wouldn't enjoy myself a'tall."

Elizabeth sighed. "I suppose. But you do realize that you *are* at an age to marry? And as soon as you return home, we *will* plan a proper season for you. I will begin working on the arrangements immediately. I owe it to my sister to see you well sponsored."

Kelsey cringed inwardly. She hated thinking of her aunt's wasting her time making plans for something that would never come about. But she couldn't tell her not to bother, not without telling her the truth. And what was she going to tell her six months from then? A year from then? That Anne was *still* lingering? That excuse was going to wear thin as the months passed.

The best she could do was warn, "Don't make any specific plans yet, Aunt. I really can't say at this point how long I will be needed here."

"No, of course not," Elizabeth concurred.

"Speaking of which, I'd like to pay my respects to your friend as long as we are here in London."

That simple statement threw Kelsey into a complete panic. Her mind went blank. Not a single excuse occurred to her. And worse, she realized that Elizabeth would want to visit her as well while she was in town, and if she did, Anne wouldn't be there, of course, because *there was no Anne.*

Elizabeth didn't have the address now, wouldn't have it until she returned home and got Kelsey's letter. *Why* had she put her real address on it? Because she had assumed her aunt wouldn't be traveling to London. Elizabeth *never* came to London. She hated the congestion. But here she was . . . and Kelsey didn't dare give her the address when there was no telling what time of day she might drop by.

With that realization coming to her, thankfully, so did an excuse. "Anne isn't well enough to receive callers right now. The trip to London took a severe toll on her, and now she has to conserve all her strength just to visit her doctor."

"Poor girl. She's still that bad?"

"Well — yes, she *was* at death's door before she started these new treatments. The doctor said it will take several months before we will even know if it's going to help her. But I do want to see you both again while you are here. What hotel are you staying in?"

"We're staying at the Albany. Here, I have the address written down." She searched in her reticule until she found it and passed it to Kelsey.

"I will be sure to call, then," Kelsey promised. "I've missed you both. But just now, I really must run. I don't like to leave Anne alone too long."

"Tomorrow morning, Kelsey," Elizabeth said, and it might as well have been an order in that tone. "We will be expecting you."

36

"Well, it's about bleedin' time 'e's left that coach behind," Artie said to his French friend as he reined in the horses on the carriage in which they had been following David Ashford. "I was beginnin' to think we was never goin' to find 'im off alone."

"You call that alone, *mon ami?*" Henry asked casually as he kept his eyes on their prey. "He has already picked up some wench."

Artie sighed. "Well, 'ell, it were easier nabbin' the cap'n's niece outta 'er backyard than it is this nabob."

"I would agree, but since she turned out to be his niece, rather than just his enemy's wife, I would rather not repeat the disaster that turned out to be."

Artie snorted. "As if we knew. The cap'n didn't even know, not till she tol' 'im. Besides, wot's to mistake this time? That's our target. We just need to get 'im away from 'is servants long enough to grab 'im."

"We have been waiting a week now to do that," Henry reminded his friend. "But he does not seem inclined to stray far from his coach or house."

"I still say we shoulda took 'im from that tavern. We coulda whisked 'im out the back

313

way, an' 'is driver out front would still be sittin' there waitin' on 'im."

Henry shook his head. "The cap'n said to avoid notice. That tavern was much too crowded."

"And this street ain't?"

Henry looked up and down it first before he confirmed, "Not nearly as crowded. And besides, people tend to mind their own business on the street. Who will notice if we quickly escort him to our carriage instead of his?"

"I still say we oughta just take 'im from that 'ouse 'e visits outside o' the city. It's so isolated, can't be no one else in it."

"There was a light from within the last time we followed him there. You were sleepin'."

"You still bitchin' 'bout me fallin' asleep that *one* bleedin' time?" Artie complained.

"Two times, but who is count— ?" Henry paused, frowning, as he continued to keep his eyes on Ashford and the woman who had just joined him. "She looks scared."

Artie squinted at the couple. "Maybe she knows 'im. If I was a wench and I knew what 'e was like, I'd bleedin' well be scared, too."

"Artie, I really do not think she is going along with him willingly."

"Wot the 'ell? You mean 'e's kidnappin' 'er when we're supposed to be kidnappin' 'im?"

Kelsey's driver had had to move her coach to accommodate a delivery wagon, so he wasn't where she'd left him. He was quite far down the block, waving at her to get her attention. She started walking that way, but as for her attention, it was still on that unexpected meeting with her aunt and sister.

So she didn't see Lord Ashford approaching her. She didn't notice him until he grabbed her arm in a painful grip and began walking with her.

"Make a sound, my pretty, and I will break your arm," he warned her with a smile.

Had he realized that she was about to scream her head off? She had already blanched completely just at the sight of him. And he was pulling her along, but moving toward her own coach, thank God. Would her driver realize that she needed his assistance? Or did it merely appear that she had met up with an acquaintance?

"Let go of me," she ordered, but it came out as a timid squeak.

And he laughed. He actually laughed. The sound turned her blood cold.

She was going to have to scream despite his warning, she knew that now. What was a broken arm, after all, compared with what she now knew him to be capable of?

But he must have sensed that she was about to cause him difficulty, because he shocked her into utter silence by telling her, "I killed that bastard, Lonny, you know, for getting my hopes up with the promise of a virgin. He should've just sold you to me, instead of auctioning you. But I'm sorry I did so now, because his brother has taken over the place. He's a much straighter arrow and probably won't permit whipping the whores. Ah, well, that place only ever offered me appetizers. I still had to go elsewhere to have my full pleasure, as I intend to have with you."

He said it all so casually, as if he were speaking of the weather. Even the mild regret he was showing was not for killing a man but because it had caused *him* to lose something he was used to.

She was so horrified that she didn't even realize that he had steered her off the walkway and into the street, where his coach waited, until he was thrusting her into that coach. She did scream then, but the sound was cut off abruptly as he shoved her face into the cushioned seat.

He held her like that until she discovered that she couldn't breathe and complete panic set in. Was he going to kill her right then? When he did release her head, all she did was gasp for breath. That was all she could do, really. But it allowed him to gag her before she even thought to try to scream again.

Had her driver seen what happened? Had he even tried to help? But it was too late now. Ashford's coach had taken off as soon as they were inside it, and at no slow pace.

The gag wasn't all that restrained her. The moment she was able to sit up, she turned to attack him, but she barely got in one swipe toward his face with her nails before her hand was caught and twisted behind her back, where it was then tied to the other.

The cords there were so tight that her fingers quickly numbed. The gag, tied behind her head, was just as tight, cutting into the sides of her mouth.

But those were minor discomforts. She knew that now. She wished she didn't. She wished Derek had not told her exactly the kind of cruelties this man enjoyed inflicting.

She had to escape before they got to where he was taking her. She could still use her feet. He hadn't tied those. Would the door open if she kicked it? Could she manage to dive out of it before he pulled her back? She was desperate enough to try. She just had to turn sideways so she could manage the kick . . .

"I would have waited until he got tired of you and tossed you out, but with the way he protected you, I knew he wasn't going to give you up within a reasonable time period. My patience doesn't last long. And unfortunately for you, my pretty, because of him, I won't ever be able to release you now."

"He," of course, was Derek. But Ashford had caught her attention completely with that "won't ever be able to release you now." Did he fear Derek that much? If she escaped, she would naturally tell Derek what he'd done, and then Derek would go after him . . . yes, he had reason to fear Derek. And maybe she could make use of that — if he removed her gag long enough so she could speak.

"Unless I kill him, too, of course."

Her blood went cold again when he added that. And he wasn't even looking at her as he said it, but was staring out the window. It was almost as if he were talking to himself. Did insane people do that?

"He deserves it, for the inconvenience he's caused me. But I haven't quite made up my mind yet." His eyes went to her then, so chillingly cold they could have been shards of ice. "Perhaps you can persuade me to let him live, eh?"

She tried to speak through the gag, to tell him what he could do with bargains like that. Only muddled sounds came out. But her eyes told him, showing the rage and fear and hate she felt. He only laughed.

She wasn't stupid. If he was going to try to kill Derek, nothing she could do would change his mind. But Derek wouldn't be unsuspecting of him, like Lonny must have been. Derek wouldn't be easy to kill, either, which he'd already realized, or he wouldn't fear him so much. If only she could work on that fear . . .

37

The large, musty old house showed very few signs of habitation. Sheets covered what little furniture could be seen through open doorways. Drapes were closed against any light, making a lamp necessary to light the way. Cobwebs had gathered in corners.

But an old man had let them in, so someone did reside there. Only on closer inspection, he wasn't very old, just very misshapen and very, very ugly. One arm was longer than the other, or perhaps it just seemed to be so because of the way his body was twisted. And his face was grotesquely disfigured; his nose had actually been cut off, and with cheeks that puffed out, he now bore close resemblance to a pig. The gray hair was what made him appear old when he really wasn't.

Kelsey's first horrified thought when she had that closer look at him was that Ashford had caused his deformities. Then she started paying attention to what they were saying as she was dragged down the hall.

The caretaker, John was his name, seemed to worship Ashford for giving him a job when apparently no one else would. And she had to wonder what that job was. John didn't seem the least bit surprised that Ashford had brought in a gagged and bound woman.

But then he asked, "A new pretty for yer collection, m'lord?"

"Indeed, John, and very troublesome to obtain, this one was."

They came to some stairs that led down into abject darkness. John went ahead of them to light the way. Kelsey had to be yanked down those stairs, because she would *not* go down them willingly.

Collection? Dear God, she hoped that didn't mean what it had sounded like, but she was afraid it did. They went through a long cellar, then came to yet another set of stairs that led still deeper under the house . . . and she could hear the moans.

It was like a prison. It *was* a prison, she realized when they passed one door after another with barred openings in them and heavy padlocks — and there was a stench that emanated from each room they passed that was foul enough to gag. The only light was a torch on the wall at the end of the corridor by the stairs. No light showed through the bars.

There were signs of construction at the end of that long corridor, where even more cells were being built. She had counted four locked doors. Four occupied rooms? She was pushed through the fifth door.

John was there. He had set his lamp aside

on the floor. There was a bed in the center of the small room with just a sheet on it. The room was new and clean. It smelled of fresh wood. Four buckets of water were set against one wall — to wash away the blood on her afterward?

"Very nice, John," Ashford remarked, looking about the room. "And you've finished it just in time."

"Thank ya, m'lord. I would've had it done a bits sooner if I'd had some help with it, but I understand why no one buts me can be allowed down here."

"You do very well on your own here, John. Help would mean you would have to share."

"No, I don't wants to share. I'll get the next room done by the end of the month."

"Excellent."

Kelsey wasn't listening to them. She was staring in mesmerized horror at that narrow bed out in the middle of the room; the bed had leather straps with thick buckles attached to its four corners. Her fear got the better of her, seeing those straps. She'd have no hope left if they were put on her, and she didn't doubt by then that that was exactly what Ashford intended.

She had tried kicking that coach door open. She'd only hurt her feet and amused Ashford in the process. He'd had a good chuckle over her effort. And his grip on her arm now was no looser than it had been when he'd first grabbed her, which was too tight to jerk free of. Yet she had to do something. And while they were talking and not paying attention to her was the perfect time . . .

She fell into Ashford as if she'd stumbled against him by accident. It was the only thing she could think of that might make him loosen his hold. Pretending to faint might have done the same thing, except she wouldn't have been able to get back up easily with her hands still tied behind her back.

And he did let go of her arm, so that he could push her back away from him. He did it so quickly that it was rather obvious that he didn't like the contact with her, which she would have found quite strange if she'd had the time to think about it.

She didn't. She took those few precious moments when she wasn't restrained at all, and dashed out of the room. Behind her, she heard Ashford make a sound like a chuckle and say something that she didn't catch.

She couldn't credit the amusement, must have been mistaken, because it made no sense. But he didn't give immediate chase, nor did his caretaker. And she found out why as soon as she reached the stairs and tripped on the first step, falling hard on those above it.

Her stupid skirt! She couldn't lift it out of the way to climb the stairs, not with her hands still tied behind her back. That's why the bastard was amused. He knew her long hems would hamper her.

Damned if she would let it. She *would* climb the stairs, just not as quickly as she would have liked. And lifting her legs as high as she could to make each step, she reached the cellar above, and then the top of the other stairs to the first floor.

She made it so far that she actually thought she'd make it all the way out of the house. But she found the front door bolted closed. She was able to twist around to reach the handle and turn it, even though her fingers could barely move, they were so numb, but she couldn't quite reach the bolt. It was too high up on the door.

Her disappointment was so overwhelming that she almost collapsed in defeat. But there had to be other doors leading outside. They couldn't all be locked. Only she was running out of time to find one. And the pain in her hands, now that the blood was circulating in them again, almost immobilized her.

She should have looked for the kitchen instead, where she could find a knife to work on the cords binding her while she hid . . . she had to hide. And it was too late to find the kitchen, which was undoubtedly at the back of the house, where the entrance to that cellar had been — and where Ashford would be appearing soon.

The darkness in the house was a blessing. At least Kelsey prayed it would be. But the rooms on the first floor, they had so little furniture in them, would they offer her any hiding spot at all? She didn't have time to look.

She could just barely make out the stairs leading to the upper reaches of the house, and she ran toward them. Stairs again, but what choice did she have? The avenues to the back of the house and another door leading outside were going to be cut off at any second.

She made the right choice. She could hear Ashford before she even reached the top of the stairs. But even if he looked up, he probably wouldn't see her. The lamp he carried didn't cast a far-reaching light, held close to him as it was, and it created as many new shadows as those it dispersed.

"The time has come for your punishment, my pretty. You can't escape. You must pay for her sins, just as the others do."

Her sins? Was there actually a reason for his madness? Who the devil was "her"?

The doors upstairs were all closed. She tried to open the first one and found that her hands had fallen asleep again, and she cringed as that horrible tingling started all over. And the damned room, when she got the door opened, didn't have a speck of furniture in it that she could see.

The second room she came to and opened was so cluttered, it was obviously used. By that odious caretaker? But too much light filtered through the worn drapes there, making it too easy to find her if she only hid behind something. And under the bed was out of the question, a sure trap, and the first place Ashford would likely look.

The third room was so dark that she wondered if it lacked windows. She quickly worked her way along the wall until she found some drapes and shouldered them aside. Nothing. This room was as empty as the first.

Time was wasting. He would search downstairs first, thinking she wouldn't hazard more stairs. But he would be up there as soon as he'd looked everywhere below. She had gained a little time, but not much.

"You will be punished even more for this foolishness, I promise you. It will be better for you if you reveal yourself now."

His voice grew indistinct there at the end, indicating he'd entered one of the rooms downstairs. She still had a bit more time.

Kelsey hurried to the next door. An empty closet. The next . . . more stairs! To an attic this time? An attic would be good. An attic usually had a wealth of clutter and discarded things.

But she had hoped, prayed, that she would find another staircase up there that would lead down to the back of the house. She couldn't see the end of the hall, didn't know how many more doors she had yet to fight open. A good hiding place, or stairs that might lead to an outside door that wasn't locked? God, she couldn't decide!

Outside was the only real choice, to get away from this house completely. And the house was surrounded by woods. He'd never find her in the woods.

She continued on. Another door — and no drapery in that room at all. The bright daylight, even coming in through filthy windows, nearly blinded her. It took her a moment to see the broken bed, the large trunk with the lid open, the standing wardrobe missing one of its doors. The trunk? No, too easy, almost like a trap.

But the light from that room did show her that there was only one more door at the end of the hall.

When she reached it, she found that it was locked. But she wasted too much time thinking it might only be stuck and trying to turn the handle just a bit more. She could hear footsteps on the stairs . . .

She raced back to the lighted room next to her and nudged the door closed just enough so the light wouldn't be noticed in the hall, but so she could still get it opened quickly. Leaving it open could possibly lead Ashford right to her — if he knew that that door was usually closed. And she held her breath, straining to hear where he was, hoping he'd speak again so she could tell more easily, but he didn't. She heard only the footsteps, pausing, walking again, pausing . . .

Was he trying to listen for signs of her progress as well? Possibly. And then there was a marked difference when he reached the top of the stairs, his footsteps becoming much louder. He walked heavily. Deliberate? So she *would* hear him, would know when he was getting closer?

She could tell when he stopped to glance in that first empty room, letting his light fill it. And she realized she'd left all the doors open except these last two. All he would need to do was glance inside. His steps again, coming still closer, confirmed that.

He still had to enter the used room, though. There was the bed to look under, the wardrobe to open. She had a few seconds only, while he searched there, to get past that room and back downstairs. She might run into the caretaker down there, but up here, she was at a dead end.

She lost what little time she had when the door clicked shut when she tried to get it back open. And having to twist around to open it again . . . she wasn't even halfway to the room where Ashford was searching when she heard him walking toward the door.

She turned toward the attic instead, and prayed the panic that was gaining on her wouldn't trip her up on those damn stairs. There was still the hope that the attic would be big enough, and so filled with junk, that it would take him a very long time to search it completely.

And she still might have a chance to slip past him and head back downstairs.

Tears filled her eyes when she got the door at the top of the stairs open and closed it behind her. The attic was a very large, very long room that ran the length of the top of the house. And it was utterly empty.

She should have known it would be empty just from the sparsity of furniture down-stairs. Whoever had owned the house before had taken everything. Whoever owned it now, she assumed it was Ashford, had brought barely anything into it — because he had no intention of living in it. He used it, as isolated as it was, as a place to practice his cruelties where the screams of those he tortured wouldn't be heard. It was a prison. . . .

And she had finally run out of options. He was heading up the stairs behind her.

The door would open any second. And there was no place to hide in that attic. She was cornered, trapped, and still bound. If only she wasn't bound, she could fight . . .

The door opened. She stared at him, wide-eyed, only a few feet away. He smiled and set his lamp down, probably in anticipation. There was enough light in the attic from several small windows that he didn't need the lamp there.

The smile had chilled her. He ought to be angry that she'd made him search the house for her. He ought to be raving. But he didn't seem angry at all, he seemed very well pleased, actually amused.

She realized suddenly that this had all been part of his entertainment, to allow her some brief hope of escaping him, then dash it to bits. That's why he hadn't chased after her immediately. The bastard had *wanted* her to run, had wanted her to think she had a chance, when she didn't. All she had done was delay the inevitable.

"Come along, my pretty." He motioned her forward, as if he actually expected her to come to him. "You've had your little chance."

Those words just confirmed what she was thinking, and Kelsey saw red. She couldn't fight? The hell she couldn't.

Without thinking it through, she charged straight at him, throwing her full weight against his chest, uncaring if she fell down those stairs with him as long as he fell down them, too. And he did. But she didn't. She'd managed to catch him completely by surprise, and she caught her own balance before she tumbled after him.

In amazement, she stared at him sprawled at the bottom of the stairs, not dead, but definitely dazed. She practically flew down the stairs herself and leaped over his feet, running for the other stairs.

She finally had some real hope. The caretaker could still be on the ground floor, but then again, he might still be far below the house waiting for his lord to fetch her back. After all, Ashford hadn't really wanted her to be found quickly. That would have spoiled half his fun.

But she was wrong, and she found out in the worst way, running right into the caretaker as she rounded the corner to reach the other stairs. And the impact didn't send him flying down those stairs as Ashford had gone down the attic stairs. It knocked the breath completely out of her. But he was built like an ox and didn't even budge.

38

"Be very quiet, English. I do not wish to have to cut your throat."

The blade at the man's throat was the only warning that had been necessary. It had stopped his forward crawl through the brush instantly.

"What — what do you want?"

"I wish to know what you are doing sneaking about in these woods."

"I wasn't sneaking — that is — well, I was just trying to figure out what to do," the man tried to explain, though the words wouldn't come easily around that knife.

"Do about what?"

"I was following a coach, you see, but I lost it. Stupid wagon got in my way, delaying me. But it was heading this way, and with that house over there being the only one in the area, I was looking to see if I could spot the coach there. Wasn't sure if I should pound on the door and just ask, since something about this whole thing just ain't right."

The blade, which had relaxed against the man's neck, moved a little closer. "You have about five seconds to make sense out of what you just said, English."

"Wait! It's my employer, you see, Miss

Langton. I'm her coachman. I dropped her off at her dressmaker, but when she come out, this gentleman joined her and took her to his coach and took off with her. But she knew I was there waiting for her. She seen me. So she would have told me what was what, you see, before going off with that man — unless she didn't want to go off with him. And that's why I followed them. I think she's in trouble."

The knife was removed and the coachman was helped to his feet. "I think we are here for the same thing, *mon ami*," Henry said, offering the man an apologetic smile.

"We are?"

"Your Miss Langton, yes, she was taken into that house. And no, I am sure she does not wish to be there. The coach that brought her here returned to the city, but I have not been able to determine how many servants are in the house that must be dealt with before your lady can be rescued. My friend has gone for help, but unfortunately, he will lead it to the wrong address."

"Rescued? How do I know you don't come from that house yourself?" the coachman asked suspiciously.

"If I did, I have little doubt you would be lying there on the ground with your throat cut."

"She is in that kind of danger?"

"Did I fail to mention that?"

Derek arrived at his uncle's house just as James was leaving. Derek was already anxious, after that cryptic message he had received that didn't really tell him anything. And James's expression only increased his anxiety.

"Your man said it was urgent," Derek called out as he moved to leave his carriage.

James motioned him to get back into the vehicle. "I'll ride with you and explain on the way. Didn't think you were going to arrive before I left."

Derek had brought his carriage because he'd just come home in it when James's footman found him. James already had had his horse brought around, and directed that it be tied to the back of Derek's carriage.

Artie was still in the hack he'd hired when he and Henry had followed Ashford far enough to determine that he was heading toward his house in the city. He'd left Henry and headed back to Berkeley Square to let James know what had happened, and James had immediately sent for Derek, as well as for Anthony.

James ordered Derek's driver to follow the hack before he joined Derek in his coach. He said, "Looks like Tony won't make it in time to join us."

"For what? What's happened?"

"What we were rather certain wouldn't happen. Ashford has taken Kelsey — at least, the girl he forced into his coach fits her description. Artie hasn't actually seen her before, so he doesn't know for sure. The stupid man snatched her right off of Bond Street this morning."

Derek blanched. "She was going to Bond Street today to her dressmaker."

"It still might not be her, Derek. I would stop by her residence to be sure, but I really don't think we have that kind of time to spare —"

"Oh, God," Derek interrupted. "I'm going to have to kill him."

"I have other plans for him that are much more appropriate for —"

"If he's put even one mark on her, he's dead," Derek cut in again in a furious undertone.

James sighed. "As you wish."

It didn't take long to reach Ashford's residence, not with Derek repeatedly shouting up at his driver to hurry. But searching it took too long. Ashford's servants swore that he wasn't there, but James wasn't about to take any of them at their word.

But then Anthony showed up, having found out where they were headed from Georgina. And Anthony was quick to point out that with that many servants on hand,

and Ashford was well staffed, he wouldn't dare bring a woman he intended to abuse into his own home, especially since she would more than likely be screaming and kicking and generally hollering for help, unless he had restrained her, but then that would draw even more notice from his staff.

In fact, it would be a good guess that Lord Ashford's servants didn't even know of his despicable habits, or they wouldn't be likely to work for him — unless they practiced the same habits. He might have a few of them in his confidence, but hardly all of them.

Derek was frantic by then. Every minute that delayed them, Ashford could be hurting Kelsey. And they'd already wasted thirty minutes in searching his house.

39

"What kept you so bloody long?" Ashford growled at his caretaker as he rose slowly to his feet, rubbing the back of his head.

"Trespassers, m'lord," John replied as he ambled down the hall with Kelsey gripped at his side so tightly the wince wouldn't leave her brow. "Spotted 'em from the kitchen when I was searching it for the wench. They was moving around on the edge of the woods near the back of the house. That was too close for my liking."

"Trespassers? So far from the main road?" Ashford frowned thoughtfully. "Not just hunters?"

"Didn't have the weapons with 'em for hunters. And there was two of 'em. Figured I better round 'em up for ya to deal with."

"What a damned nuisance," Ashford complained. "Where are they?"

"Tied up in the stable. One I hits a might hard, though. Not sure if he's still alive. The other won't be coming 'round for a while."

Ashford nodded indifferently, as if this were a typical occurrence he'd dealt with many times before. "They can wait, then — but *she* can't. Excellent. I've waited too long for her as it is. You did well as usual, John."

He finally glanced down at Kelsey and

revealed to her for a brief moment just how furious he was over what she'd done. She'd managed to hurt him in that fall down the stairs. He probably wasn't used to his victims fighting back, or at least, not being hurt by them.

But then he smiled at her, that bone-chilling smile. She didn't need to hear him say that he'd be getting even, and very soon. It was there in his expression and his eyes, and he was savoring the thought.

He motioned for John to precede him. Kelsey was dragged down one set of stairs, then another, then the last, where that horrible stench assailed her again. Behind one of the doors, someone started crying pitifully. It sent shivers down her spine.

"Shut up in there!" John barked.

Silence was immediate. John ruled the cellars, and those who lived there obeyed or else — or else what? Kelsey supposed she would find out.

There was no stopping to chat this time before she was seen to. John didn't wait for Ashford's orders; he tossed her down onto that bed as soon as they entered the newly built room. She winced, landing on her bound arms. Enough time had passed that her hands had fallen asleep yet again, and yet again the pain shot through them as contact with the bed momentarily brought them to life one more time.

So it took her a moment to realize that he had immediately grasped one of her legs and was now wrapping leather around it. She tried to stop him, kicking him with her other foot, hard, again, again. He didn't seem to notice. The strap still went on — and was fastened.

She paled. She felt sick to her stomach. That strap put an end to whatever hope she had clung to. But she still tried to roll off the bed, panic making her desperate. Her other foot was caught, the grip on it so hard she moaned. She guessed he had felt her kicks after all. And within seconds, the other strap was in place.

She noticed Ashford then, standing there beside the bed. He was smiling down at her, and she could almost read his mind. He was relishing her helplessness and her fear, anticipating what was to come. Now? Would it happen now?

"The same rules, m'lord?"

The caretaker's question drew Ashford's eyes away from her, and his expression turned almost indifferent again. "Yes, you aren't to touch her until I've sufficiently broken her in, but then she'll be yours to do with as you please, just like the others."

"And the blonde who's had yer attention lately?" John asked hopefully.

"Yes, yes, you can have her back now," Ashford said impatiently. "It will no doubt be quite a while before I'll want her again, now that I have this one to amuse me."

"Thank you, m'lord. I have to admit, the blonde was my favorite, though I'm sure this one will be — soon as yer done with her. I like the new ones best and trainin' 'em. Withhold their food for a few days and they're happy to make old John happy, however I wants."

Ashford chuckled. "And I'm sure there are many ways to make you happy."

"Oh, aye, m'lord. I thanks the day ya offered me this job, indeed I do. All these pretty wenches that would never have let old John even gets near 'em, they change their tune once they're down here. And this pretty, ya wants me to prepare her for ya now?"

"Actually, I'm rather famished," Ashford said. "I believe I'll have a bite to eat before I initiate her. I've been looking forward to this one. I don't want anything to distract me from my pleasure once I begin. I trust the kitchen is still well stocked?"

"Aye, ya'll find all yer favorites there, just as ya ordered."

"Good, good. But you can finish the restraints. I don't want there to be any possibility that she won't be here when I return shortly."

"She'll be here. You've my word on it."

Ashford nodded, smiling at his caretaker.

"I do depend on you, John, indeed I do. I will see to the rest, though. I'm looking forward to that as well. Oh, and fetch my tools for me," he said as an afterthought. "I don't want to be bothered unlocking the blonde's cell to get them."

40

Tools? What tools? That sounded too much like instruments of torture, in relation to what went on down here. Or did he just call his whips tools?

Derek's words came back to haunt Kelsey. *He whips them until they are covered with blood. Apparently, he can't have sex with them without the sight of that blood.*

God, why did he have to tell her? She would have preferred not to know what was going to happen to her until it happened. Not knowing would have been frightening, but this? Ignorance is bliss. Knowledge, in this case, was absolutely terrifying.

Ashford had left to go eat his meal. Something so normal as that in the midst of her nightmare. Was he a fast eater? Slow? How much time exactly would she have until he returned to *initiate* her?

She'd delayed him only a little while when she had run from him. But he'd wanted her to do that. It was part of his overall entertainment. Since this delay was only for his own comfort, he could actually be back in a matter of minutes.

John was still there. He'd been told to finish putting on her restraints and he did just that, rolling her to the side so he could untie her hands, twisting her actually, farther than her muscles wanted to allow. And he kept her in that position while he strapped the leather about one wrist, because it kept her other arm from interfering, still trapped under and behind her as it was.

Not that she could have done anything to prevent those last straps from going on. One more time, her hands had gone numb from the tight cords, and her arms as well were sore from being twisted behind her for so long.

He left the room when he was finished, but he didn't go far. She could hear him working the lock on one of the other rooms, and the crying that started up just in anticipation of being visited, great wails that didn't stop until that door was locked again.

Kelsey shivered. Dear God, the terror she had just heard just because one of those women thought that Ashford or his caretaker was going to visit. Kelsey wouldn't last there, she knew she wouldn't. She would go quite mad if all she had to look forward to each day was pain and more pain.

John came back into her room. Across her stomach he laid three whips of different designs and lengths — and a knife. Ashford's tools. The ones he was going to use on her. She'd lifted her head to stare at them, couldn't take her eyes off them. She was going to be sick.

He chuckled at the look in her eyes. "There will be enough left of ya when he tires of ya, girlie, to suit me," he assured her. "I ain'ts particular."

Her eyes went to his. She saw that they were blue, actually a pretty shade of blue. It wasn't easy to notice with his misshapen face.

She had forgotten about hearing Ashford say that she would be John's later to do with as he pleased. Would she even care by then?

The caretaker didn't stay to gloat. And he closed the door behind him as he left, though he didn't lock it. The lamp was left behind. So she could continue to stare at what he'd brought her?

Kelsey heaved her back off the bed the second that door closed, to knock the whips and the knife onto the floor. But getting them off her body didn't get rid of them. She shivered again, feeling even sicker. And she wondered whether, if she didn't still have the gag in place, she wouldn't start screaming herself the next time that door opened. She might anyway.

The straps wouldn't give. She twisted and yanked and strained, but there wasn't the slightest bit of slack. She couldn't possibly work loose from them, or pull them free from however they were attached to the bed.

The door opened again, too soon, in what seemed like only a few minutes. It was Ashford. He'd rushed through his meal after all.

Kelsey's muscles went rigid with fear. He glanced at his "tools" on the floor and tsked. He sauntered forward to pick one up. It was the knife. Kelsey blanched. It came to her cheek. A tug, and she was able to spit out the sliced-open gag. She didn't thank him. She knew damn well he wanted it off so he could hear her screams.

But she wasn't going to scream. She was going to use her wits and talk herself out of this. It was the only chance she had left. He wasn't sane — not completely. If she could push him enough to snap the rest of his mind, perhaps he would leave her alone, maybe even let her go. It was a wild hope, but the only one she had.

"Release me now, Lord Ashford, before it's too late. You shouldn't have taken me, but I won't say anything about what you've done if you —"

"I didn't take you to release you, my pretty," he said as he walked to the end of the bed.

"But why take me at all? You already have other girls here. I heard them . . ." She managed to refrain from saying "crying."

"Yes, homeless urchins for the most part, that are never missed and don't have any friends who care what happens to them. Though I do have one other here that I bought at auction, just like you."

"Why do you keep them here?"

He shrugged. "Why not?"

"Do you ever let them go?"

"Oh, no, I can't do that. Once they come here, they can never leave."

"But they don't come willingly!" she cried. "At least I didn't!"

"So?"

"Why do you need so many?"

He shrugged again. "Scars tend to inhibit bleeding."

He said that so dispassionately, yet he was the one who caused the scars. It really didn't bother him, what he did here. He felt no guilt whatsoever. What she had heard only confirmed what she had already guessed.

He stuck the knife he still held under her skirt then and drew it toward him, opening the material. She gasped. He smiled.

"Don't worry, my pretty. You won't need these clothes anymore," he said, and ripped the rest of the skirt up to her waist, then moved up beside the bed again to examine the sleeve of her spencer. "You whores are always taking them off, count- less times a day, so down here, we are kind enough to save you the trouble."

He laughed at that, finding it quite amusing.

"I'm not a whore."

"Of course you are, just like *she* was."

There was that mention of another woman again, in a tone that implied that particular woman was the worst sinner in the world. "Who is she?"

A cold flame leapt into his eyes just before he slapped her. "Don't *ever* mention her."

Her face had been turned away from him with that slap. The knife slipped under her sleeve and began cutting before she turned back to glare at him.

"Or what? You'll beat me? Isn't that what you already intend to do?"

"You think there aren't ways to make you suffer even more, just like she did? I assure you, only these other whores down here will hear your screams."

God, they each could hear the other's pain. But she knew that, had already heard the sounds of their suffering. Only now they would hear hers, too.

Was that intentional, one more thing to add to the terror of every woman who was brought down there? He did seem to do things intentionally, as if he had played the same scene on this stage many times before. There was only one servant on the premises — and he was wholly devoted to

Ashford. There was no one, nor ever would be anyone, to carry tales of the atrocities that went on there.

How many years had Ashford gotten away with this? How long had some of these women been down there already? He whipped tavern women so badly that they were scarred for life. That was what Derek had witnessed. But those women still had their freedom after he was done with them. What about the women in the cellar, though, who were never let go to be able to tell? Were even worse things done to them?

She had to keep him talking. He stopped cutting on her clothes each time he said something. But she hesitated to mention "her" again.

"You have stolen me from Lord Malory. You think he won't know that and come after you?"

He paused. Just a trace of worry entered his expression, but he quickly shrugged it off.

"Don't be absurd," he admonished. "Whores run off all the time."

"Not when they don't want to, and he *knows* I wouldn't. And he's not stupid. He'll know exactly where to look for me. Your only hope is to let me go."

"If he comes, I will kill him."

"*When* he comes, he will kill *you*," she stressed. "But you already know that, Lord

Ashford. It's quite brave of you to court death like that."

He paled, but not nearly enough. "He won't do anything without proof. And he'll never find you here. No one knows of this place, no one ever will."

He had answers for everything. Mentioning Derek wasn't working. He feared him, yes, but he considered himself safe from Derek's retribution.

He moved to her other sleeve and began cutting it up to her shoulder. She was fast running out of time. She had to risk mentioning that other woman again. It was the only thing that really disturbed him.

"Did you bring *her* here?"

"Shut up."

She had jarred him, enough that the knife slipped, cutting her arm. She flinched, but she couldn't let that deter her. At least he hadn't slapped her again.

"Why do you hate her so?"

"Shut up! I don't hate you. I never hated you. But you shouldn't have run off with your lover when Father found out you were a whore. He beat me instead, because you weren't there. You should have just let him kill you as he wanted to. You deserved it. I didn't want to do it for him when I found you, but what choice did I have? You had to be punished. You still have to be."

Oh, God, he thought *she* was that other

woman now — his mother. He'd killed her, and he was going to kill her again when he was done "punishing" her for her sins, just as he had been punished for her sins. She had just condemned herself to much more pain than she would have been given — if she hadn't pushed him to the other side of his insanity.

41

The rented hack had stopped in front of them. Derek's carriage drew alongside it. "What have we stopped for?" James called out.

After a moment, Artie came to the carriage window to speak with them. "That's the 'ouse up yonder, Cap'n, the one I told ye about, that Ashford visited a couple times. This is the only other place I know of that 'e might've come to with the girl, but I guess not."

"Why not?"

" 'Cause there ain't no sign of 'Enry 'ere. 'Enry would be 'ere if this is where Ashford brung the girl. Besides, that place looks as deserted as ever. I'd say there ain't no one around here for miles."

James stepped outside to view the house and grounds. Derek and Anthony followed him.

"Bloody place looks haunted," Anthony said. "Someone actually lives here?"

Artie shrugged. "We never saw no one when we was 'ere before."

"We still have to search the house," Derek said. "If this is our last hope, I'm not leaving until every corner has been turned."

"Agreed," James replied, and began giving

orders. "Artie, cover the grounds and stable if there is one. Tony, to save time, try to find a back entrance that's open, or open one if it's not. Derek and I will take the normal approach and try the front door."

"Why do you get normal, while I get sneaky?" Anthony wanted to know.

"Put a lid on it, dear boy," James said. "No time for arguing just now."

Anthony took one look at Derek and coughed, saying, "Quite right."

"And let's be very quick about this," James added. "It's doubtful the bastard is here, since Henry's not. But this isn't our last hope. Henry will send word eventually where he's gone, just as soon as he can manage it. We will want to be there when he does."

He had said the last for Derek's benefit, but it didn't help. "Eventually," they all knew, would be too late where the girl was concerned.

"Well, looks like *someone* is here," Anthony said, staring at the house. "Or am I mistaken in seeing a light flickering in the attic?"

Indeed. It was very vague, barely noticeable, but there was a light up there. And that assured them that the place wasn't completely deserted.

They split up to approach the house separately. Derek sent his driver straight to the front door and bounded out of the carriage to try it. Finding it locked, he had to resort to pounding on it.

James followed a bit more slowly. He was worried about his nephew. He'd never quite seen him so bristling with fury and restless energy. Derek couldn't stand still. He rocked on his heels. He raked his hands through his hair. He pounded on the door again.

"Henry is a good man, Derek," James offered as they waited for the door to open — or not. "If he can safely get Kelsey away from Ashford, he will. He may already have her, for all we know."

"Do you really think so?"

The hope that came into Derek's eyes was difficult to look at. Bloody hell. A man did *not* invest that much emotion in his mistress. That James had planned to make his wife, Georgina, his mistress was a moot point. He hadn't, he'd married her instead. But this Langton girl wasn't the marrying sort. Not that it made any difference to James. It didn't. He'd always done what he bloody well pleased and always would. But the future heir of the Marquis of Haverston didn't have that luxury.

He was going to have to have a serious talk with the lad when this was over. Or better yet, with Derek's father. Yes, let Jason do his duty and pound the unpleasant facts into his son.

James wasn't given a chance to answer. The door opened and they were confronted with a very irate — what?

James had seen a lot of things in his well-traveled life, but even he was taken aback at the deformities on the creature standing in the doorway. But it did speak. It *was* a man, rather than a freak of nature.

"What's all the racket for, eh? You ain't got no business here —"

"I beg to differ," James interrupted. "So be a good chap and step aside. We need to speak with Lord David Ashford — immediately."

The name elicited some surprise in the fellow.

"He ain't here" was all he said.

"I happen to know otherwise," James replied, a bluff to be sure, but useful under the circumstances. "So take us to him or we will be forced to find him ourselves."

"Now, I can't let you do that, gents. I gots orders that no one comes in here — ever."

"You will have to make an exception —"

"I don't think so," the man said confidently, and the hand that he'd held behind him came around to show that it gripped a pistol.

He had come to the door prepared to back up his "no admittance" orders. And at such close range, they were indeed at a standoff

354

— at least until James could reach inside his coat for the pistol he'd brought along. But he hesitated to attempt that with Derek there and the man's weapon wavering between them. He took risks with his own life, but not with the lives of other members of his family.

"There was no call for weapons," James pointed out reasonably.

"Wasn't there?" The man smirked and then threw James's words back at him. "I begs to differ. And since ya ignored all them signs posted at the front drive to the property, that clearly warned ya to keep out, maybe I oughts to shoot ya both for trespassing."

But Anthony's voice suddenly came from behind the man at the door in a deadly calm tone. "This chap isn't actually threatening to shoot you, old boy, is he?" Anthony said.

The man turned, of course, to face the new threat at his back. Anthony had found another way into the house and had snuck up behind him down the hall.

"Excellent timing, old chap," James said as he knocked the pistol out of the man's hand and grabbed a fistful of his shirt to keep him there.

"You can thank me later," Anthony replied, grinning now that the fellow had been disarmed.

"Must I?" James shot back. But then, glancing at the fellow he held, and just before he landed his meaty fist in the center of the man's face, he added, "Bloody hell, how d'you break a man's nose when he ain't got one?"

James let the fellow go then. He was quite unconscious, slumped into a pile on the floor.

"Was that necessary?" Anthony asked, coming forward. "He *could* have told us where Ashford is."

"He wouldn't have," James replied. "At least, not unless we beat it out of him, and we've no time for such pleasantries. Derek, you search this floor. I'll take upstairs. Tony, find out if there's a cellar."

Anthony knew as well as James that Ashford wasn't likely to be on the main floor of the house that he'd assigned Derek to search. He'd either be in an upstairs bedroom, which was the most logical place for his purpose, or tucked into a room down in the cellar, where screams wouldn't carry very far. Obviously, James didn't want Derek finding him or the girl first if they were there.

"I get the dirty job again?" he grumbled as he turned back the way he'd come, but called over his shoulder, "Just make sure you save a piece of him for me, brother."

James was already halfway up the stairs, so he didn't bother to answer. And since most of the rooms were empty, it didn't take long at all to search the entire house. James arrived back downstairs just as Anthony came down the hall again.

"Anything?" James asked.

"There's a long cellar beneath us, but nothing but empty shelves and crates in it, and a few kegs of ale. What about you?"

"The attic was completely empty, just a lamp set on the floor up there, which don't make too much sense."

"Nothing else?" Derek asked as he came down the hall to join them.

"There was one locked door up there. Bloody hell, really thought I had him when I found it."

"You managed to get in?" Anthony asked.

"Certainly." James snorted. "No one was there, though. It was fully furnished, unlike the others, but doesn't look like anyone's lived in that room for years, more'n ten or twenty years by the look of the old-fashioned dresses in the wardrobe. The walls were covered with portraits of the same woman, some with her and a child. Looks like a bloody shrine, if you ask me."

"Told you this place was haunted," Anthony said.

"Well, it ain't haunted by Ashford. Not even another servant —"

James was cut off as the front door flew open and Artie rushed in. "I found 'Enry! 'E was tied up in the stable, 'im and another bloke, and they been 'urt bad. Someone nigh bashed their 'eads in."

"But they're alive?"

"Aye, 'Enry come around a bit, said some pig attacked 'em. The other man don't look too good, might not make it. They both need a doctor real quick."

"Take them back to town, Artie, and fetch a doctor," James ordered. "We will follow shortly."

"Thought he looked a bit like a pig myself," Anthony remarked as Artie left. He was looking down at the unconscious man, still sprawled on the floor.

"Whatever he is, it looks like he's in the bloody habit of killing anyone who wanders onto the property," James said in disgust. "I've a feeling that's what he had in mind for me and Derek as well."

"Ah, but at whose orders?"

"Ashford was here, damnit, or Henry wouldn't be," Derek put in.

"Yes, but he ain't here now. He must have taken the girl somewhere else after Henry showed up."

Anthony nudged the caretaker with his boot. "I'd wager he knows where."

"I'm inclined to agree," James said. "If any of Ashford's servants would be in his confidence, it'd be this one. Shall we wake him?"

"I'll fetch some water," Anthony replied, and took off down the hall again.

Derek was too impatient to wait. He hauled the man halfway off the floor and started shaking him and slapping his face.

"Easy, lad," James cautioned. "We'll have him talking in a few minutes."

Derek let the man drop back to the floor, but looked at James bleakly. "It's killing me, Uncle James, that he's had Kelsey long enough now to — to —"

"Don't think about it. We won't know till we find her, and I promise you, we *will* find her."

Anthony returned and dumped a bucket of water on the caretaker. The man came up sputtering and coughing, and quite cognizant, because he paused very warily when he noticed James standing by his feet.

James gave him a particularly nasty smile. "Ah, we meet again. Now, pay attention, dear boy, because I am only going to explain this once. I am going to ask you where Lord Ashford is, and if I don't like your answer, I'm going to put a bullet in your ankle. The bones will quite shatter there, of course, delicate as they are, but what matters a limp to someone used to deformity, as you most certainly are? Ah, but then, you see, I shall ask the question again. And if I again don't like your answer, I will put a bullet in your kneecap. The limp you will get from that will be much more pronounced. And then we will move on to your hands and other parts of your anatomy that I am sure you won't miss. Have I made myself quite clear? Nothing that you need explained further?"

The man nodded and shook his head at nearly the same time. James squatted down by his feet and put the nozzle of the pistol he held right against the man's ankle.

"Now, where is Lord Ashford?"

"He's downstairs."

"Here?"

Anthony tsked. "Damn me, didn't think he'd lie, really didn't."

"I ain't!" the man burst out.

"I've been downstairs. The only thing there is a cellar," Anthony said. "And there's only one exit from it, the same stairs used to get into it."

"No, there's another stairs, I tells ya. When the door's open, it looks like any stairs. When it's closed, ya only see shelves on the cellar side. The door's closed. It's always closed when he's down there."

"Show us," James said abruptly, and yanked the man to his feet to shove him down the hall.

What happened then occurred too quickly to prevent. The caretaker tried to dash ahead of them down the cellar stairs, perhaps to get behind that other door and lock it. But he had been sitting in a wide puddle of water in the entryway, from the bucket of water thrown on him. His boots were still too wet to take those stairs that quickly. He slipped and tumbled down them.

Anthony raced to the bottom of the stairs and checked the man's pulse, then glanced up at his brother. " 'Pears to have broken his neck."

"Bloody hell," James said. "We'll have to find the door ourselves now. Spread out. Check for hidden catches, obvious cracks, or strips of wood that could be used to hide the door seams. If we can't find it quickly — hell, start breaking down the walls."

42

Kelsey had tried everything she could think of, keeping in mind that Ashford had slipped far beyond reality. She took on the role of his mother, admonishing, apologizing, making up plausible explanations for what he was accusing her of, but it was set so deeply in his mind that his mother was evil that nothing worked. He wouldn't agree that his father was the one who had wronged him.

From some of the things he said, though, she gathered that the mother had deserted her husband and son, but it was possible that she had merely been trying to save her own life, running from a vengeful husband — at least until her demented son found her, years later.

He'd killed his own mother. He'd condemned her because his father had condemned her. He'd killed her because that was what his father had wanted to do. And at one point, he became his father. He spoke of his mother as his wife. His thoughts were his father's thoughts. And Kelsey had to wonder if he hadn't been in his father's mind when he'd killed her. The punishment, then the sex. Something his father would have done. And Ashford was reliving it again and again with each woman down there, with each tavern prostitute he'd paid to use.

He was a truly sick man. But she couldn't find any pity for him. He had killed people. Two deaths at his hands were all he had mentioned, but she was certain there were more. He had made too many people suffer with his sickness, and she was going to be one of them.

In speaking to him as his mother, she had merely delayed her punishment. She was frantic to continue putting it off. Not that she expected some miracle to occur to stop it altogether.

It was the terror of that beating that she couldn't face, had tried to postpone. She'd never been beaten before, in any way. She had no idea what she could withstand. And what came after? Death, if he still thought she was his mother? Or if he was partly rational by then, rape while she was still screaming from the pain already inflicted? Or both? She honestly couldn't say which she would prefer.

At the moment, he was himself again, not his father. But he still saw his mother when he looked at her. And she was still desperately trying to trigger some remorse or fear in him that would make him let her go.

"Your father won't be pleased if you kill

me," she told him. "He wants to do it himself. He will probably beat you again if — *when* he finds out."

That actually put a degree of terror in his own expression. Kelsey's whole body leapt with renewed hope.

"Do you think so?" he asked, confused.

"I know he will. You will be robbing him of his vengeance. He will be furious with you."

A noise upstairs distracted him. He glanced back at the last bit of material that still clung to Kelsey and slipped the knife under it. Her shredded clothing draped each side of the bed to the floor. None remained to cover her.

"Did you hear me?" she asked frantically, her panic soaring.

He didn't even look at her. He dropped the knife to the floor, done with it — for the moment. He then looked down for his whips and tsked when he couldn't find them right off. He had to bend down to lift the material of her dress to find one of them, but he stood back up with it in his hand. It was short-handled, with many long, thin strips of leather dangling from it. He rubbed the handle against his cheek fondly.

"Answer me, damnit!"

He scowled at her tone. "Answer you?"

"Your father is going to be furious with you. Don't you realize that?"

He chuckled. "I hardly think so, my pretty. The old man died quite a few years ago. His heart stopped while he was — amusing himself. Not an unpleasant way to die."

Oh, God, he was back to his *normal* self again, which meant she was out of time. Would begging help? She doubted it.

He laid the whip across her bare legs so he could remove his coat. Her legs wouldn't bend enough to dislodge it. And just the feel of that leather on her bare skin started her trembling.

He laid the coat over her legs as well while he started unfastening his shirt. It didn't cover but a small portion of her shins. But she hadn't expected this. Was he going to rape her first after all?

"What are you doing?"

"You don't think I'm going to ruin a perfectly good set of clothes, do you?" he asked. "It's too tedious, getting blood out of good broadcloth."

Kelsey blanched. He expected enough blood that he was going to be splattered by it? Then the buckets of water were probably there to wash the blood from *him* afterward, not her. The fastidious bastard thought of everything, didn't he? But, then, he'd done this so often he'd learned how to keep things simple.

She couldn't stop him. There was nothing

else she could do — but let him know her rage.

"I hope when Derek finds you he cuts your heart out — slowly. You're a pathetic excuse for a man, Ashford, as crippled as your caretaker is. You can't even —"

She sucked in her breath sharply. He'd picked up the whip and slashed it across her thighs. Welts rose up in several places, but the skin hadn't broken. And he laid the whip back on her to finish undressing himself.

He'd done it to shut her up, and it absolutely enraged her, that she wasn't even going to be allowed that outlet for her emotions. Like hell she wasn't.

"Coward!" she spat. "You're even afraid to face the truth."

"Shut up! You know *nothing* about me."

"Don't I? I know that you wouldn't know what to do with a woman if she wasn't tied down for you. You're a sick little boy who never grew up."

He picked up the whip again. She stiffened, waiting for the blow. It didn't come. He glanced at the door instead, frowning. She followed his gaze but didn't know what had drawn it. She hadn't heard anything. But he had.

"John, stop making that noise!" he shouted. "You know better than to disturb me when I — how did *you* get down here?

You can't come down here!"

Kelsey burst into tears at seeing James Malory suddenly filling the doorway. Her relief was so incredible it controlled her utterly. All she could do was sob. Perhaps because she couldn't really believe it. And if her mind was playing tricks on her . . .

But then Derek was there behind James as well, and pushing his way past him. Ashford, well, he was merely indignant that James was there. But Derek, Derek he was terrified of, because Derek he had already tangled with twice, and both times had lost.

Derek took one look at Kelsey, then at Ashford behind her with the whip in his hand, and he tore across that room. He didn't even go around the bed to get at his target, but dove over it, taking both him and Ashford to the floor, where Kelsey couldn't see them very well, could only hear . . .

James came over to the bed, removing his jacket as he did so to cover her with when he reached her. "Shh, m'dear, it's over now," he said gently.

"I — I — I know! I — I can't help — it!" she cried.

He smiled at her, keeping his eyes tactfully away from any of her still-exposed limbs. And he made haste to unbuckle her straps. Anthony Malory was there, too, she finally noticed, standing by the end of the bed and watching his nephew pound away at Ashford.

"Bloody hell, he's not going to leave any for us, is he?" Anthony complained to his brother.

James chuckled. "You might as well break that up, Tony. I don't believe the bastard is feeling any of those blows just now, and I hate to see good retribution going to waste, especially when he deserves so much. Besides, the lad needs to take Kelsey out of here."

Kelsey was sitting up by then, and quickly slipped into James's jacket. She could see for herself that Ashford was unconscious. But that wasn't stopping Derek from hitting him.

Anthony had to literally pull Derek away. It took a moment for the fury to fade from the younger man's eyes. But the moment they met Kelsey's, he came to her and held her close, very, very close . . . and she burst into tears again.

James rolled his eyes. "Women. She was giving him hell as we walked up the hall, now she's safe, she cries. I will never figure that out, damn me, but I won't."

Anthony chuckled. "It's a womanly thing, old man. We ain't supposed to understand it."

James snorted, but he glanced at his

nephew again and nodded toward Kelsey. "Derek, take her out of here — back to town, if you like. Tony and I will see to this scum."

Derek hesitated, glaring down at Ashford again. "He hasn't suffered enough yet."

"Enough? Believe me, youngun, he hasn't even begun to suffer."

Derek stared at his uncle for a long moment, then nodded in satisfaction. Whatever James had planned for the man, it wouldn't be the least bit pleasant.

Derek gently lifted Kelsey and carried her out of the room and down the hall. Her arms had wrapped tightly about his neck, almost in a death's grip.

"I can't believe you came — that you found me," she whispered. "How?"

"My uncle had men following him."

"There was mention of trespassers," she said as they mounted the stairs. "The caretaker put them in the stable. One might be dead. Your uncle's men?"

"One of them was, yes. The other was your coachman. But they're both alive. The other of James's men came to tell him that you'd been taken. And they had followed Ashford here before, so we knew this was one place to look for him."

He didn't mention that he had feared they would be too late. She didn't mention the hell she'd gone through to postpone her "punishment."

She gripped his neck harder. "There are other women locked down there. This place has been their prison. We have to release them."

"They will be."

"He's truly sick, Derek. He killed the proprietor of that house, the one who auctioned me."

"He admitted it?"

"Yes. He killed his mother, too, and God knows who else." She trembled again.

"Don't think about it, luv. You won't ever see him again, I promise you."

It was much later when Anthony and James came upstairs. Both of their expressions were still grim, after what they'd witnessed in that prison under the cellar. James had hoped to find one of Ashford's victims. He'd had men searching the wharf taverns and brothels all week. He had *not* hoped to find what they did, four women so terrorized and tortured that it was doubtful they'd ever fully recover.

Amazingly, they were in much better condition than would have been expected — aside from the scars they had been given. Raw wounds had been regularly tended before they were reopened. They'd been fed. Their cells weren't warm, but they weren't unduly cold, either, which had possibly kept down infections and the growth of germs. The stench they lived with and were accustomed to came from old congealed blood merely washed under the floorboards, and buckets for bodily wastes that were emptied only infrequently.

Only one of the women, a pretty young blonde, still had raw wounds and was the most terrorized. The others were covered in scars from their waists down, but they were fully healed and less fearful, since Ashford had stopped paying them visits long before. And what the caretaker did with them, well, it was nothing that they hadn't already experienced.

It could have been much, much worse, their minds as damaged as their bodies, if they hadn't already been accustomed to the brutality of men before Ashford found them — and used to selling their favors for a living. Fully clothed, there would be nothing to show for their ordeal there. But they would know, and they would never forget.

And James was giving them their revenge.

Anthony had fetched clothes for them from that room upstairs, old to be sure, but serviceable for the time being. They had declined wearing them — yet.

The oldest among them explained, "He always stripped down before the whippin's. Blood splatters, ye know."

An excellent point, since James and An-

371

thony had strapped Ashford to that same bed that Kelsey had occupied before they woke him. The whips were there. The knife was there. And they left the women there with him.

"They may kill him," Anthony pointed out as he closed the cellar door to block out the screams that were already coming from below.

James nodded. "If they do, then we'll give him a nice burial."

Anthony chuckled. "You don't think they will?"

"I think they'll want to pay him back in kind, and *that,* dear boy, is what the chap deserves. I expect he'll be ready for Bedlam when they're done with him. If not, I'll have to take care of him myself, to keep Derek from doing it."

"Hmmm, I agree, the lad's too young to go around killing chaps. Wouldn't want anyone to say he's taking after his uncles."

"Put a lid on it, puppy."

43

After her ordeal with Lord Ashford, Kelsey almost forgot that her Aunt Elizabeth and sister were in town and expecting to see her the next morning. She sent an excuse to postpone their visit until later in the week.

That visit was going to be a trying, emotional meeting as it was, endeavoring to keep the lies straight, undoubtedly having to come up with new ones — and missing them both as much as she did. She couldn't face that after the trial she had just gone through. Besides, Derek refused to leave her side, and she'd have a hard time visiting her relatives, whom he didn't know existed, with him tagging along.

In fact, it took nearly all week, and a great number of assurances that she was all right, to get him to relax his guard and go about his normal business. And even then, he wouldn't stop pampering her and treating her nearly like an invalid, until she agreed to speak about the incident. She supposed he felt that if she couldn't talk about it openly she would never really get over it.

There might be something to that, because it wasn't easy to begin telling him everything that had happened to her that day, but it grew easier. Afterward she did actually feel better. And he'd had other things to relate to her as well, things that she hadn't been aware of.

She hadn't known the caretaker had broken his neck, hadn't seen his body lying there in the cellar, because Derek had kept her head turned away from him when they'd passed him. The other man who had been bludgeoned and left in the stable with Henry had been her driver, who was going to be all right. He'd tried to help her, and for that Derek had added a huge bonus to his salary. The man would probably be devoted to Kelsey for life.

As for those poor women who hadn't been as fortunate, Derek's uncles had settled enough money on them so they wouldn't have to return to their previous occupations, wouldn't have to work again at all if they didn't want to. The Malory brothers didn't have to do that. It had been very nice of them that they did.

And Lord Ashford, well, she wasn't a bit surprised to hear that he was totally insane, since he'd already been very close to it. But what had pushed him beyond the brink did surprise her.

"He's been admitted to Bedlam, where he won't be leaving, now that his mind is completely gone," Derek had told her several days later. "My Uncle James turned those women loose on him, you see, and well, they gave him back what he'd given them — and then some."

Kelsey didn't mention that she'd probably have turned him into a eunuch as well, if she'd been one of those women. Derek didn't mention that one of the women had thought of that.

And then the morning came when she couldn't delay visiting her aunt and sister any longer. And it was as emotionally exhausting and upsetting as she had suspected it would be. The hardest part, which she hadn't expected at all, had been keeping Derek out of her conversation. Amazingly, his name kept coming to the tip of her tongue quite naturally, and she kept having to bite it back each time.

She got through the visit without making any mistakes. However, she went home quite upset over the whole affair and stayed upset all day. And unfortunately, that night was when Derek asked her to marry him.

They were having dinner. She had just taken a sip of red wine. It was fortunate the tablecloth was dark blue. It wouldn't show the stain too much.

"Sorry." Derek grinned sheepishly. "Didn't mean to startle you like that."

Startle her? Shock was more like it.

"That isn't something to jest about," she admonished, frowning at him.

"That isn't something I *would* jest about."

"But you can't be serious!"

"Why not?"

"Don't be obtuse, Derek. You know why. I'm your mistress. A lord in your position doesn't marry his mistress. It simply isn't done."

"It'll be done if I want it to be done."

That was such a ridiculously . . . *stubborn* statement, she almost rolled her eyes. But she was too upset by the subject to find anything amusing about it.

Of course, she'd love to marry him. She couldn't think of anything she'd like to do more. But she knew as well as he did that it was impossible. And that he'd brought it up to begin with made her angry. How dare he tempt her?

It didn't matter that she was a quite suitable match for him, or at least she had been before she'd sold herself in a house of ill repute in a room full of London lords. Selling herself had made her utterly unsuitable for marriage, even if he was the one who'd bought her.

"I won't marry you, Derek," she said in a stiff voice. "And I won't thank you for asking me."

"You don't *want* to marry me?"

"I didn't say that, I said I *won't* marry you. I won't cause you and your family yet another scandal."

"Kelsey, let me worry about my fam—"

"My answer is no, Derek, and it won't change. And I would appreciate it if you don't stay tonight. I would like to be alone."

He stared after her incredulously. She'd walked out on him. And she was furious. He recognized the signs. She contained it well, but she was bloody furious with him — because he'd asked her to marry him. And here he'd thought she'd be pleased by the notion, delighted even — he'd at least thought she'd say yes.

Derek sighed. He hadn't even gotten used to the idea himself yet, had only just figured out that he wanted to marry her, and that after a long week of fretting over some very strange feelings. What had started it was when it had occurred to him that with Lonny dead, and Kelsey aware of it, there was nothing keeping her with him other than her own honor. There would be no fear now that Lonny would enforce the bargain she had made. And she had to know Derek well enough by then to know that he wouldn't hold that bill of sale against her. She could leave at any time, just like a normal mistress. That he'd paid a lot of money for her no longer mattered.

And that put him into a bit of a panic. When he'd realized that he *was* panicked, he'd tried to figure out why. And the answer had come to him readily enough. He'd gone and fallen in love with his mistress.

It was a bloody stupid thing to do. Even he knew that. But he'd done it anyway. And he knew he didn't *have* to marry her. They could go on perfectly well just as they were — as long as she was willing to stay with him. But he didn't like that "as long as." He wanted permanence. He wanted to move her into his own house. He wanted her to bear his children. He didn't want to hide her anymore.

But she'd said no. And she'd said her answer wouldn't change.

By God, it *would* change — maybe not that night, though.

44

Derek stayed away for three days. Wisely, as it happened. It had taken that long for Kelsey to calm down. She finally determined that his marriage proposal had possibly come as a result of the Ashford incident, because of how extremely worried he'd been over her during it. The proposal had probably been impulsive, too. And now that he'd had more time to think about it, he'd realized what a fool notion it had been.

He didn't mention the proposal again when he showed up three days later, so Kelsey decided to leave the subject alone as well. Besides, after her anger over it had subsided, she'd actually taken it as a good sign, or at least as a sign that he was growing fonder of her than she'd realized. When a man didn't tell you how he felt, it was nice to get clues that gave some indication, and a proposal of marriage was a pretty strong clue.

They made up, as it were, though they hadn't actually had a fight. And making love with him that night was a little more heated than normal, was quite explosive actually, and so prolonged that they both overslept the next morning.

Kelsey arose first. Dressing quickly, she

went down to see what Alicia had prepared for breakfast, with the thought of bringing a tray up to Derek.

She didn't have a butler as that was one servant she didn't feel she needed in her small household, especially since she didn't receive any callers. And her footman usually saw to those duties. But when he wasn't around, whoever was downstairs and nearest the door answered it if someone knocked on it.

This morning that was Kelsey, since someone was knocking on the door just as she came downstairs. The surprise she received upon opening it, though, was quite unpleasant for that early in the morning.

"I make quite a good detective, don't I?" Regina Eden said, beaming at her.

Kelsey drew a total blank as far as any responses were concerned. Situations like this were *not* supposed to occur. Hadn't Derek promised her she wouldn't have to deal with his family anymore? And Reggie walked right in, as if she didn't doubt for a moment that she would be welcome. And she wouldn't doubt it. They were fast friends, after all — at least as far as Reggie was concerned.

Kelsey groaned inwardly. And all she could think to finally say was, "How did you find me?"

"Well, I went by Percy's house first, of

course. Not this morning. This was last week."

"Why?"

"To see if you were still in town, since I was. Nicholas had some business that came up, so we've ended up staying longer than I thought we would. Anyway, I went by Percy's and the dear wasn't in, but his butler said he had no cousin staying there with him, nor had he had one any time recently. I left a message for him to come by and see me, but he never did. And I'm not known for my patience. So then I checked the hotels nearby, and I don't mind telling you, I made a complete ass of myself, showing up at one hotel that had a Langton registered. It wasn't you, of course, but some lady and her niece. And she even had another niece named Kelsey, too."

"Imagine that," Kelsey croaked out.

"My sentiments exactly. But they'd never even heard of Percy, so, of course, her Kelsey couldn't have been you. And after I exhausted the hotels, I checked with the better rental agencies, and they had no record of dealing with you or Percy. But then — and I don't know why I thought of it, except that Derek has frequently at-tended to business matters for Percy in the past — I mentioned his name, and sure enough, he had just leased this house re-cently. So here I am."

Yes, here she was, and Kelsey didn't know what the devil to do. She couldn't very well ask Reggie to stay for tea when Derek might come downstairs at any moment. She had left him sleeping, but he tended to wake up pretty quickly once she was gone, as if he could sense her absence even in sleep.

And damned if a door didn't open upstairs and Derek's voice could be heard calling out, "Where did you go, luv? You could have at least wakened me. Kelsey?"

He must have assumed she was in the back of the house and couldn't hear him, because the door closed again. Kelsey was about ready to expire on the spot.

Reggie had looked up, of course, at the sound of his voice, had no trouble recognizing it, and said now, "What's *he* doing here — and up there?"

Kelsey was blushing furiously by then, and when Reggie glanced at her and saw it, she said "Oh" and started blushing herself. But then the whole picture must have formed in her mind, at least a picture resulting from her own conclusions, because she added indignantly, "Why, that bounder! How dare he take advantage of you like this?"

Kelsey groaned again, quite loudly this time. "It's not what you think — I mean, it is — but the circumstances aren't . . . please, Reggie, just go, before he comes down. I'll explain later."

"When later? This isn't something that I can just ignore, you know."

Kelsey didn't know why it wasn't, but she could see she wasn't going to get out of explaining. "I'll come by your house this afternoon."

"You promise?"

"Yes."

"Very well," Reggie allowed, though she was still bristling somewhat. "But I certainly hope there *is* a good explanation for this, because it would be my duty to inform my Uncle Jason about it otherwise. Derek knows better than to go around seducing innocent girls of good breeding. Even our rakehell uncles drew the line at that."

45

A dilemma — no, *another* dilemma — that Kelsey was not looking forward to facing. Horrid lies. Once started they escalated, one leading to another, and she was so tangled in them she could barely keep track of them. And this particular dilemma she couldn't forestall. She'd promised Regina an explanation.

But which explanation to give her? The real truth? Or the truth as Derek knew it, which was just another set of lies? And she was so sick of the lies . . .

She arrived at the house on Park Lane at around three o'clock that afternoon. She was expected, and was shown directly to a sitting room upstairs. A maid brought in tea. Reggie showed up right behind her.

"I want to apologize for how snippy I sounded earlier," Reggie said right off, as soon as the maid left. "It was just such a surprise and — well, I'm sure you understand. And I'm sure there is a perfectly good explanation. Why, I wouldn't even be surprised if Derek's asked you to marry him. That *would* put a whole different face on it, now, wouldn't it? I mean, Nicholas and I — well, goodness, listen to me go on, not giving you a chance to say anything. By the by, we won't be disturbed here — or overheard."

Kelsey smiled at that last. She did have to worry about being overheard — that is, if she made a clean breast of it. And that is what she wanted to do, more than anything, at least with this particular Malory. But she wouldn't do that, not without assurances.

Reggie sat down across from Kelsey, now that she'd fallen silent, and poured them each tea. She was waiting for Kelsey to begin, patiently, too. Kelsey was still searching for the right words. But there were none — at least, none to make this any easier.

"Actually," Kelsey finally began, "Derek *has* asked me to marry him."

Reggie beamed happily. "I knew —"

"But I won't, and I told him so."

Reggie blinked. "Why not?"

"Because of how he acquired me. You see, what you were told about me, it was all a lie. But he didn't know what else to tell you at the time. He didn't know you and I had already met previously."

"What was a lie?"

"I'm not Percy's cousin," Kelsey admitted. "I'm Derek's mistress."

Reggie rolled her eyes and said dryly, "I've already gathered *that*."

"No, what I mean is, I was already his

mistress when I first met you. He bought me at an auction in a house of ill repute, one frequented by many lords of his acquaintance. That's why I won't marry him. The scandal of such a marriage would be horrendous."

Reggie took a moment to absorb that, but then said, "Scandal is nothing new to my family — but what the devil were you doing in a place like that? And if you try to tell me you aren't a lady, that you belonged there, I'll toss you out of my house on your ear."

Kelsey's eye's widened, but then she burst out laughing. It felt very good indeed, certainly wasn't what she had gone there expecting to do.

She was still smiling when she said, "No, I wouldn't try to tell you that. Actually, I would like to tell you the truth, but I can't — that is, not unless you promise it won't go any further. Not even your husband can know, Reggie. And certainly not Derek. If he does, he would insist on marrying me, and I care too much for him to bring that kind of scandal down on him."

"But you and Derek are — what I mean is, well, why doesn't *he* at least know?"

"Because I haven't told him, nor will I. He doesn't know anything about me, really, other than the few lies I've told him. When I made the decision to do what I did, I had to come up with a new background for myself to protect my own family from the scandal that would evolve if it was ever discovered who I really am. Derek thinks my mother was a governess, that I benefited from the fine tutors that her charges had, and that's why my speech is refined."

"The gullible lout." Reggie snorted. "He actually believed that?"

"Why wouldn't he, considering where he found me?" Kelsey said in Derek's defense.

"Hmmm, I suppose," Reggie allowed. "But what is the truth, then?"

"Your promise?"

"I can't even tell my husband?" Reggie wheedled. "I could get him to swear —"

"Not even him."

Reggie sighed. "Yes, I promise."

Kelsey nodded, but took a sip of her tea, wondering where to begin. Perhaps with her parents . . .

"My father was David Phillip Langton, the fourth Earl of Lanscastle from Kettering."

"Good God, wasn't he the earl who was shot earlier this year by — er . . ." Reggie fell silent with a cough, blushing profusely.

Kelsey leaned forward to pat her hand. "It's all right, and quite common knowledge, apparently. Yes, my mother shot him. She didn't mean to kill him, though. She was just so furious with him because of his gambling. He had just lost the rest of his inheritance, you see, even our home, over a stupid game of cards."

"So *that's* why?"

"Yes. And my mother was so shocked that she'd killed him, rather than just wounding him to punish him as she'd intended, that she backed away from him in horror and backed right out the window that was behind her. I still think I could have prevented their deaths if I'd just got upstairs sooner when the shouting began."

Reggie did some patting now. "It's almost impossible to interrupt a volatile argument. The participants tend to ignore anything around them."

"I know." Kelsey sighed. "My parents *never* argued in front of the servants, yet there were at least seven of ours standing right outside their open door, avidly listening to everything and blocking me from getting inside, one even holding me back, warning me that that was no time to disturb them. And then the shot was fired . . ."

"That is so tragic — oh, dear, it *was* called The Tragedy, wasn't it?"

"Yes," Kelsey said, wincing at that word. "And everything really had been lost of my parents' wealth. That bastard who won that card game even came to evict my sister and me from our home only a few days after the funerals."

"Bastard is right," Reggie said, angry on

her friend's behalf. "Who was he? I'd like to introduce him to my Uncle James."

Kelsey smiled weakly. "I wish I knew. But I was too shocked at that time to remember his name."

"You poor dear," Reggie sympathized. "It's no wonder you did what you did."

"It wasn't because of that, Reggie," Kelsey corrected. "We still had one relative to turn to, my mother's sister, Elizabeth. She's a dear, sweet woman — whom you've met."

"Oh, good Lord," Reggie said as it dawned on her. "That was *your* aunt in that hotel?"

"Yes, she and my sister are in town for some holiday shopping — and they don't know what I've done. I've had to lie to them, too. They think I'm staying with a sick friend here in London."

Reggie sat back, frowning. "Now you have completely confused me."

"Sorry, I shouldn't have digressed. After my parents' deaths, my sister, Jean, and I went to live with our aunt, and she was very glad to have us. Everything would have been fine, should have been, if my aunt's husband, Elliott, had had a bit more fortitude."

"A scoundrel?"

"Not really, just weak of character, apparently. You should know that he comes from good family, but not from wealth. Even the house they lived in had belonged to my family. My mother never understood why Elizabeth married him, but she did, and I might add that she has lived very happily with him all these years — and she doesn't know what happened. We were able to keep that from her."

"Another gambler?"

"That's what I thought at first when I found Elliott sitting over a bottle of strong spirits, contemplating killing himself. He's always worked to support them, you see, and he had a very good job for many years. But he lost it. And he'd been so distraught over losing it that he hadn't been able to keep another job since. If he had just put that failure behind him and gone on — but I suppose he had lost confidence in himself."

"No fortitude, as you said." Reggie snorted.

"Apparently. Yet they continued to live as if nothing had changed. They even took in my sister and me when they couldn't afford it. The debts kept mounting. There was no money coming in, no money saved up to fall back on, and no one else to borrow from. All that had been done already. And it had reached a point where the creditors were going to take my aunt's house away in just three days if Elliott didn't settle his accounts immediately."

Reggie sighed. "I suppose you talked him

out of killing himself? Don't know if I would have."

"When it would only have made matters worse — for my aunt, anyway? She didn't know how bad it was and that she was about to lose her house. We were all going to end up on the streets, with nowhere to go and no one to turn to — and in just three days. If only Elliott had said something sooner, there might have been time for me to find a rich husband. But three days wasn't enough time."

"No, a bit more time than that is needed," Reggie agreed. "Unless you're in the process of being courted. I suppose you weren't?"

"No," Kelsey replied. "I was still in mourning, and in a new town. I hadn't met any eligible men there yet. And Elliott didn't hobnob with the gentry. He didn't know anyone to approach either. There wasn't even enough time for me to find a job, if I could have found one that would have paid well enough to support us. And I had my sister to consider. She's only twelve, and my responsibility."

"So you came up with the idea of auctioning yourself?" Reggie concluded.

Kelsey chuckled at that point. "Me? I had no idea such things could be done."

Reggie grinned. "No, I suppose you wouldn't. Then it was actually your uncle's suggestion?"

Reggie shook her head. "Not really. He was so foxed that night that he was rambling a bit. He mentioned a friend of his who'd faced the same situation, but whose daughter had saved the family by selling herself to an old lecher who prized virgins. Then he mentioned that some men would pay for a new mistress if she was 'fresh,' as in not having been discovered by his friends yet."

"I cannot *believe* he would speak of such things to his innocent niece," Reggie said, appalled.

"I'm sure he wouldn't have if he'd been sober, but he certainly wasn't. And it was a solution, when I hadn't thought there was any. But then, I was so shocked over the entire situation that I don't think I was thinking any clearer than he was. At any rate, I asked him if he knew of anyone who would pay to acquire a new mistress. He didn't, but he said he knew of a place that rich lords frequented where I could be presented to receive an offer."

Reggie frowned. "That doesn't sound like an auction to me."

"It didn't to me either," Kelsey admitted. "I had no idea that's what it would be, or that the 'place' was a house of ill repute. But I had already agreed, had already been left at that house. And it did still seem to be the only way to get Elliott's debts paid off in the short time allowed.

"Elliott certainly had no way to come up with that large a sum. He'd already exhausted all his options. His solution had been to kill himself so he wouldn't have to face telling my aunt that they were about to lose everything. And I still had my sister to consider. I didn't want her to lose her chance for a decent marriage someday. None of this was her fault."

"It wasn't your fault either."

"No, but I was the only one who could do something about it. And so I did what I had to do. But it hasn't worked out so badly, Reggie. I'm very happy with Derek."

"You love him, don't you?"

"Yes."

"Then marry him."

"No. I gave up my chance for ever marrying when I was put up on a table in a room full of lords and auctioned to the highest bidder."

"Derek must not think so if he asked you to marry him," Reggie pointed out.

"Derek was conveniently forgetting how he met me. But I'll never forget it. And he's had more time to consider and come to his senses. He hasn't asked me again."

"Stupid society rules," Reggie almost growled. "They've got no business governing our lives the way they do."

Kelsey grinned. "Are you forgetting that

you wouldn't be married to your Nicholas right now if those rules hadn't governed you at the time?"

Reggie coughed. "Quite right."

46

It was traditional for the Malory clan to gather at Haverston for the Christmas holidays. Derek usually stayed a week or two, as did most of the family. He had no plans to do otherwise that year. But because he was going to be gone that long, he took Kelsey with him. Not to Haverston, of course, though he bloody well wished he could.

He would have liked to show her the ancestral estate where he grew up, to introduce her to the rest of the family, to kiss her under the mistletoe that was hung over the entrance of the parlor each yuletide. None of that was possible, though — at least it wasn't until she agreed to marry him, and he certainly hadn't given up on that notion. He was simply biding his time, waiting for an ideal opportunity to broach the subject again. One where, he hoped, she wouldn't fly off the handle.

So he put her up in a nice inn nearby where he could still slip away to see her each day. But he didn't like it. And his mood was somewhat dampened because of it. He wondered if that was why Reggie had kicked him in the shin the first thing when she arrived. No, she hadn't had time yet to notice that he was brooding. Besides, it was just like her to kick him for no good reason, the minx — and to not tell him why.

Amy and Warren showed up, having returned from their wedding trip. The newly wedded couple were looking radiantly happy. That only added to Derek's misery.

To get his mind off his own problems, Derek tried to figure out who his father's longtime mistress was. But it was an impossible task. There were just too many people at Haverston, as big as it was, who had been there for as long as he could remember. The only thing to do was to simply ask his father. But it was hard to find him alone, with the entire family in the house.

He managed it, though, on his third day there. Jason had risen early, and Derek was just returning from spending the night with Kelsey. They met on the stairs. Derek, tired — the time he spent with Kelsey he didn't spend sleeping — almost blurted his question right out, but that would have been a bit tactless. He asked for a private word instead, and followed his father to his study.

It was so early that the drapes hadn't yet been drawn. Jason did this while Derek slumped down in one of the chairs by his desk.

He ended up blurting it out anyway. "Who's the mistress you've been keeping here all these years?"

Jason paused on his way to his desk. "I beg your pardon?"

Derek grinned. "Might as well fess up. I have it on good authority that your mistress lives right here at Haverston with you. Who is she?"

"None of your business," Jason said stiffly. "And on what good authority?"

"Frances."

"Damn that woman!" Jason exploded. "She swore she wouldn't tell you."

Derek was too tired to grasp the significance of his father's remark. "Don't think she meant to," he allowed. "I ran into her with her lover, you see. And I was about to throttle him."

At that, Jason blinked, then burst out laughing. After a moment, though, he coughed, assumed a bland expression, and asked, "Did he walk away?"

"Oh, yes. Wouldn't have been sporting to lay into a chap that tiny. Wasn't thinking of that, though. But Frances stopped me when she started yelling at me about your mistress. I think she felt it necessary to defend her position with that little tidbit, putting the blame for her unfaithfulness on your shoulders. She claimed you never even consummated the marriage. Gad, that was a bloody surprise."

Jason was blushing by then. "I thought

I'd made that clear when I told the family I was divorcing."

"You said she'd never had a true marriage with you, but I didn't think it was *that* unconventional. I mean, all those years, and not even once? But Frances pointed out that *you* never slept alone from the very start. And that's what's been driving me mad with curiosity: you've had a mistress all this time, and apparently the *same* one. That's an incredibly long time to have a relationship with one woman, at least one who ain't your wife. Who is she?"

"I repeat, none of your business."

Derek sighed. Jason was right, of course, it really wasn't anyone's business but his own. Derek wished his father felt the same way about his son's private life, but unfortunately, Jason did concern himself with Derek's personal activities to a degree — at least when Derek didn't keep them completely private. And he did that right now.

"Speaking of mistresses, what the deuce could you have been thinking of, to bring yours to your cousin's house for dinner?" Jason demanded.

Derek shot out of his chair, infuriated. Bloody hell, he hadn't expected to get the tables turned on him there. He felt betrayed.

"Who told you? Uncle James? Uncle Tony?"

"Calm down. You ought to know my brothers never tell me *anything* that I ought to know about. I have spoken to James, though. He was concerned that you're getting too attached to this girl, but he wouldn't tell me why he was concerned. And he didn't mention the dinner."

"Then how — ?"

"I heard about it from my valet, who is sweet on Georgina's maid, who overheard James and his wife talking about it. And James didn't even tell his wife that she'd been dining with your mistress. She still don't know, far as I know. It was the girl's name that was mentioned, which you yourself gave me, if you'll recall. So is she, or is she not, Percival Alden's cousin?"

Derek winced. His father had obviously already assumed that she was, and that accounted for more than half of his present displeasure.

"She's not," Derek assured him. "Jeremy came up with that idea, when Reggie found us with Kelsey at the races, to put a nice face on it. You see, Reggie had already met her previously and had decided they were going to be fast friends. Jeremy was just trying to save Reggie — all of us, actually — some unpleasant embarrassment."

"Why the deuce would Reggie want to be friends with a woman like that?"

Derek immediately took offense. "Maybe

because she's not *like that*."

Jason sighed and sat down behind his desk. "Blister it, unruffle those feathers, you know what I meant," he mumbled.

Derek sighed as well. He did know. But he was a bit touchy where Kelsey was concerned just then. Love, and the emotions it evoked, were new to him. So far, he was finding it not the least bit pleasant.

He wished he could share *that* with his father. But he didn't want to alarm Jason more than he already was by telling him he'd found the woman he wanted to marry. That wouldn't go over too well right then.

So he tried to explain, saying, "The trouble is, Kelsey looks like a lady, she acts like a lady, she even sounds like a lady. Most of the time, it's devilish hard to remember that she's not gentry."

"You're sure she's not?"

That wasn't the first time he'd been asked that. And it gave him pause just as it had before. What, after all, did he really know about Kelsey other than what she'd told him herself? But she wouldn't lie to him, would she? No, she wouldn't. He was positive — well, almost positive — about that.

But that small kernel of doubt made him admit, "I know only what she's told me, which isn't much, but she has no reason to lie to me. And considering how I acquired her —"

"Yes, yes, I suppose you're right. But you still haven't explained why you brought her with you to your cousin's for dinner. That was going outside the bounds, m'boy."

"I know, but Reggie bloody well insisted, and well, as long as she thought Kelsey was Percy's cousin, I didn't think it would hurt. And we told Reggie that Kelsey was returning to the country, so she wouldn't look to continue the friendship. That should have been the end of it, and no harm done. And, in fact, it was the end of it. Reggie hasn't seen her again, nor will she." *At least not until I marry her.*

But he didn't add that. And his father wasn't completely mollified. He didn't have to wait to find out why.

"*Are* you getting too attached to this girl?"

Derek almost laughed. "You're asking me that when you've kept a mistress — what? More'n twenty years?"

Jason flushed with heat. "Point taken. Just don't do anything foolish where the girl's concerned."

Anything foolish? Like fall in love with her and want to marry her? Too late.

47

It was Christmas Eve when Derek again asked Kelsey to marry him. He left the family gathering early to join her. He plied her with wine. He softened her mood with dozens of little gifts, silly things that made her laugh, like an oversized thimble, a hat with three foot-long feathers attached, bells for her toes. He was saving the engagement ring for last.

The opportunity couldn't have been more perfect. And the question — "Kelsey, will you please marry me?" — didn't send her into a froth. She turned to him and hugged him. She kissed him deeply. But then she took his cheeks in her hands and said, "No."

All things considered, he really hadn't been expecting that answer this time, any more than he had the first time. So he hadn't prepared any counterarguments.

In fact, all that came out was "Why? And if you mention a scandal again, I just may throttle you."

She smiled at him. "But you know there would be one, a very big one."

"Hasn't it occurred to you yet that I don't give a bloody damn if there is?"

"You say that now, Derek, but what about later, when it actually happens? And what about your family, who would also be affected? They'd have something to say about being dragged into that kind of scandal, I'm sure."

Which gave him the idea to put it to his family ahead of time. His father had just made a monumental announcement about his divorce. Derek could make one about his plans to marry — and find out just which way the wind blew.

He decided that Christmas dinner was the perfect time to announce his plans, with everyone gathered in the same room. The mood was festive. There was a great deal of laughter. But Derek couldn't do it, not when it would spoil the day for at least a few of them.

But the very next day he didn't hesitate. It was again at dinner. And not quite everyone was present this time. Diana and Clare had returned home that morning with their husbands. Their brother Marshall had left for the day to visit a friend in the next shire and hadn't returned yet. And Aunt Roslynn was upstairs attending to a very fussy Judith, who had come down with a cold. But that was all right. A few missing people wouldn't make much difference.

The rest of the family were gathered, and again the general mood was excellent. The women were discussing holiday recipes, babies, and fashions. James had sent a few digs at Warren, but his brother-in-law had laughed them off, and James didn't seem unduly annoyed. Nicholas and Jeremy were having a good-natured argument about Nick's stallion, which had lost that day at the races.

Edward and Jason were discussing one of Edward's new investments. They'd apparently made peace over the divorce issue — which Derek took as a good sign. The one nice thing about his family was they didn't carry grudges, at least within the family. There had been one exception, when James had been disowned for a good ten years, but even that had ended amicably.

So before dessert arrived, Derek stood up and said, "If I may have your attention for a few moments, I have some good news to impart, or at least what I consider good news. Some of you may not agree, but" — he shrugged, though he glanced down at the end of the table to his father when he added — "I've decided to marry Kelsey Langton."

Jason just stared at him, too incredulous for words. Anthony coughed. James rolled his eyes. Jeremy covered his.

Into the silence of that statement, Georgina said, "That's wonderful, Derek. She seems like a very nice girl."

And Aunt Charlotte asked, "When do we get to meet her, Derek?"

Edward, sitting a few seats down from Derek, leaned over and clapped him on the back. "That's splendid, m'boy. Know Jason's been gnashing his teeth over when you'd be settling down."

Amy, beaming at him from across the table, said, "Why didn't you decide a bit sooner? We could have had a double wedding."

Jeremy was chuckling and shaking his head at the same time. "Wouldn't want to be in your boots just now, cousin."

Nicholas nodded in complete agreement with that. "He does know how to dig a deep hole, don't he?"

Reggie poked her elbow into her husband's side and hissed at him, "You should have been this romantic when we met."

Nicholas frowned at her, then burst out with the realization, "Good God, how did you find out?" drawing several curious looks their way.

"Never mind," Reggie whispered. "But I think it's very brave of him to ignore convention and let his heart lead him in this matter."

"You would." Nicholas smiled at his wife.

Derek didn't hear any of that, and he said nothing more. He was still staring at his father, braced for the expected explosion. It didn't come.

Jason looked furious, no doubt of that,

but his tone was quite calm when he said simply, "I forbid it." And that started an uproar.

"Goodness, Jason, why ever would you do that?" came from Charlotte.

"Sounds like he knows who the wench is, don't it?" James said to Anthony.

"That would be my guess," Anthony replied.

But Edward had heard that and repeated, " 'Who she is'? Why, who is she?"

"Kelsey is Percival Alden's cousin," Georgina put in helpfully.

"Actually, George, she's no relation to Percy a'tall," James told his wife.

"I say, can someone tell me what's going on here?" Travis asked in confusion.

"Like to know that myself," his father said gruffly, looking toward Jason now.

"Might be appropriate, puppy, if you add a bit to your announcement," Anthony said to Derek. "You've gone this far, might as well spit the rest out."

Derek nodded curtly. "It's true that Kelsey isn't Percy's cousin, as some of you supposed. She's my mistress."

"Oh, dear," Charlotte said, and took a quick sip of her wine.

"Egads, have you flipped your gourd, cousin?" Travis asked incredulously.

And Amy said to her brother, "Men have been known to marry their mistresses, especially when the lady is otherwise suitable for marriage."

"But that ain't the case here, squirt," Jeremy told his cousin.

At which point Amy mimicked her mother's response. "Oh, dear."

"I don't see how that makes a bit of difference," Georgina said. "If he wants to make an honest woman of her, I say good for him."

James rolled his eyes at that. "You're thinking like an American again, George."

"I should hope so," Warren said in defense of his sister, giving her a wink.

"That might not raise any brows where you come from, Yank," Anthony remarked. "But here it just ain't done."

Warren shrugged. "So he marries her and moves to America, where it *is* done. He might just enjoy kicking off the shackles of convention."

"It's a thought," Derek agreed, grinning. Not that he would consider it, but . . .

"I forbid that, too," Jason said.

"Well, that settles that, don't it?" James said dryly, because, in fact, it settled nothing.

Edward pointed that out in case anyone had missed the sarcasm. "He's old enough, Jason, that you can't *just* forbid it, much as you'd like to. Why don't you try talking some sense into him instead?"

Tight-lipped, Jason nodded curtly, stood up, and left the room. Derek sighed. This was the part he hadn't been looking forward to.

48

Jason had gone to his study. Derek entered it and closed the door, fully anticipating that this would be one of their louder discussions. And Jason did look like thunderclouds about to burst, standing behind his desk with his hands braced against it. He had restrained himself in the dining room. He wouldn't there.

Derek made an attempt to forestall the diatribe. "There's nothing you can say that will change my mind. If Kelsey will have me, I'm going to marry her."

That changed Jason's expression quite a bit. "If?" he asked hopefully.

Derek's own expression turned chagrined as he admitted, "She's refused me."

"Well, thank God for small favors. At least one of you has some sense."

"You're saying I have no sense because I love her?" Derek said stiffly.

Jason shook his head. "It's all right to love your mistress. Lord knows I do. It's even all right to share your life with her, if you can manage it circumspectly —"

"As you have?"

"Yes," Jason said, then stressed, "but it is *not* all right to marry her when you have a responsibility to marry within your class

— and you *do* have that responsibility, Derek, as the future Marquis of Haverston."

"I know my responsibilities. I also know that it won't be easy, the path I'm choosing. But a scandal is not the end of the world, Father. I *am* a scandal, have been one since the day I was born. I survived that; I'll survive this."

Jason sighed. "Why didn't you tell me of this foolishness when we last spoke?"

"Because I knew this would be your reaction. But I'm going to follow my heart. I have to. I love her too much not to. So I will ask her again, and again, until she agrees."

Jason shook his head. "You're not thinking clearly in this, Derek, but at least she is. And I can hope she will continue to —"

"Jason!" Molly burst into the room all aflutter. "I just heard that Derek wants to marry . . . his . . ." She fell silent, blushing furiously as she noticed Derek there. "Oh, forgive me, I thought you were alone."

It was the blushes that gave them away, because Jason was now wearing one, too. "Good God, *she's* your mistress?" Derek guessed.

They both said "No!" at the same time, and with too much emphasis.

Derek just chuckled, not fooled in the least. "Damn me," he said. "Never would've figured it was you, Molly." And then he glanced toward his father, grinning. "You should have married her. I wouldn't have minded calling Molly m'mum, indeed I wouldn't. In fact, she's been more of a mother to me than Frances ever was."

At which point Molly burst into tears and ran back out of the room, slamming the door behind her.

Derek blinked. What had he said?

"Bloody hell," he mumbled to himself. "Didn't mean to make her cry." And he looked to Jason for an explanation.

"She — er — gets rather emotional during the holidays. Happens every year."

"That's too bad. But assure her that I'm not shocked or anything — well, I *am* shocked. Never would have suspected it was Molly. But I *am* fond of the old girl. It will just take some getting used to, I suppose."

"Why don't you *not* get used to the idea?" Jason suggested, he thought reasonably. "I would as soon you forget about it entirely."

Derek grinned, shaking his head. "Can't do that. Puts you in the same boat with the rest of us imperfect males who just can't resist the fairer sex. I rather like that, damn me if I don't."

"Bloody hell."

The discussion hadn't ended in the dining

room after Derek and Jason left. If anything, it got more heated after Jeremy let it slip that Derek had bought Kelsey in an auction and explained where that auction had been held.

Reggie had a devil of a time keeping her promise to Kelsey, but keep it she did. However, knowing the truth, she was in full support of Derek's decision and made no bones about it. Her Uncle Edward was the loudest against it, but that wasn't a bit surprising, conservative as he was.

That her two youngest uncles were also against it was annoying, though. She knew damn well that if they were faced with the same decision as Derek, they would have done exactly the same thing, and to hell with public opinion.

"She could be the sweetest, nicest gel this side of creation, and it still wouldn't work," Edward said. "It would be different if no one but the family was aware of the facts, but that ain't the case."

"She was also quite innocent *before* Derek got his hands on her," Reggie pointed out, perhaps a little too bluntly. "I suppose that makes no difference, either?"

Edward went red-faced. James chuckled. Jeremy sat up, blinking.

"Hell's bells, cousin," the lad said. "The elders are present."

Reggie was already blushing herself by

then, but Anthony further admonished her, "You're too much the romantic, puss. You know Eddie boy is right on the mark. That room full of gents who watched Derek buy her weren't around later to hear if the chit was innocent or not, nor would they bloody well care. But they sure as hell ain't going to forget her. And if Derek ends up marrying her, you think the story of how he got her won't spread even wider?"

"That was certainly a mouthful, old chap," James said. "Could have just summed it up with the simple fact that the wench will never be accepted by the *ton.*"

Reggie snorted. "This family has weathered many a scandal, most of which can be laid at the door of just two of its members." She looked pointedly at Anthony and James as she said this, before adding, "I hardly think that one more is going to break us."

"Won't hurt us a'tall, Regan," James agreed, and for once his brothers didn't jump immediately down his throat for using the pet name he had for Regina. "Kelsey is the one who won't be able to overcome that sort of scandal, and neither will Derek. Society will shun them both. In my case — and Tony's, for that matter — we did the shunning, so it didn't bloody well matter to us whether we were accepted or not. But Derek don't feel that way. He's a social creature, always has been. And if Kelsey cares anything at all for the lad, she won't take that away from him."

"Quite a mouthful there yourself, brother." Anthony chuckled, to which James merely shrugged.

But Reggie sighed. Derek hadn't mentioned that Kelsey had refused him, so she couldn't introduce that fact either. And the whole argument was pointless anyway, since Kelsey *wasn't* going to marry him.

So she defused the subject by pointing out, "I believe Derek said he *wanted* to marry Kelsey, not that she had agreed to marry him. She could well refuse him, and that would be the end of that."

"Refuse Derek, prime catch that he is?" Edward snorted. "Don't see that happening, 'deed I don't."

"It's possible, Uncle Edward," Reggie replied. "You haven't met her, but she strikes me as a very sensitive sort, and not at all grasping. I'd wager that she'd rather leave Derek than cause him any harm. And she'd consider his social ruin as harm."

49

When Kelsey opened the door to her room at the inn, she was expecting Derek, not his father. And it was definitely his father. Jason Malory introduced himself immediately, leaving no doubt who he was, not that she'd had any. He also marched right into the room without an invite. But he so intimidated Kelsey with his formidable size and his harsh expression that she wasn't about to point that out.

She was quick to say, "Derek isn't here," hoping that would send him on his way.

It didn't. And she was so flustered by his presence that she only realized after the fact that she shouldn't have volunteered that information. But obviously he knew.

"Yes, I just left him at Haverston," he said. "Figured you'd be nearby, with him as smitten as he is and this the closest inn."

She was already blushing as she asked, "Then it's me you wish to see?"

"Indeed," he said. "I want to hear what you think of this nonsense."

"Ah, which nonsense would that be?"

"Derek wanting to marry you."

Kelsey gasped. "He *told* you that?"

"He told the whole family that."

Kelsey grasped the nearest chair and

worked her way into the seat. Could she expire of shame? It certainly felt as if she could.

"He shouldn't have done that," she said in almost a whisper.

"I agree — but why do you think so?"

"Because, as you say, it is nonsense. I have no intention of marrying him. I told him so."

"Yes, he mentioned that, too. My concern is, how serious are you in your refusal? Because he isn't going to give up the notion."

"If that is all that worries you, Lord Malory, you needn't let it. I am aware of the scandal that marriage would cause, and it's not only Derek I wish to protect from that but my family as well."

"Your family?" He frowned. "I wasn't aware that you had any family. Who are they?"

"That isn't important," Kelsey told him. "It is enough for you to know that my family means everything to me. I am in this position because — well, that isn't important either, but I knew when I did what I did that I would never be able to marry. Suffice it to say, a scandal of this sort would harm my family as much as it would yours, and I have no intention of letting that happen."

Jason's expression relaxed considerably.

He even looked somewhat embarrassed himself.

"I begin to understand," he said gruffly. "I'm sorry there is no solution to this matter. I have a feeling you would have made Derek an excellent wife, if it were possible for him to marry you."

"Thank you. But I will endeavor to make him happy — without marriage."

Jason sighed. "I never would have wished my own situation on my son — but I'm glad he has you."

That was the nicest compliment she could have had from him. He didn't stay to embarrass either of them with further sentiments. He rushed off, actually, probably because he didn't want to run into Derek. But she figured that Derek already knew, that he must have seen his father in the hall, when another knock came only minutes after Jason had left.

But again, it wasn't Derek standing there, nor had Jason decided he had more to say to her. This time it was Derek's mother. But Kelsey didn't realize that at first, not until she had a chance to note how identical a few of their expressions were, how they had the same smile, and how worried the woman was.

"I'm sorry to disturb you at this late hour, Miss Langton," the woman began.

"Do I know you?"

"No, there's no reason why you should." The woman smiled. "I'm Molly Fletcher, the housekeeper at Haverston. I've only just found out about you, and Derek's just found out about his father and me — and, well, I need to talk to him."

Kelsey was blushing again, furiously. Derek's damned announcement had obviously traveled through the servants' quarters already, but . . .

"You and his father?" The answer came to Kelsey before she got the question out. "Oh! I'm sorry. No need to explain. But Derek isn't here."

"He's not? I saw him leave Haverston. I thought surely he was coming to you."

"And you assumed I was nearby."

"Why, yes, I did."

Kelsey shook her head in amazement. Did all men travel with their mistresses? Or was that just standard practice for the Malorys?

"Well, if he's not at Haverston, I have no idea where he is."

"Then he's gone off to be alone," Molly said, wringing her hands. "I was afraid of this. It's what he always did as a child when he was upset. He'd go off alone to brood."

"But why would he be upset?" Kelsey asked. "He's been mad with curiosity lately to find out who you were, that is to say, who his father's — well, I would imagine he's relieved to finally know."

"He wasn't supposed to know, Miss Langton. He wasn't supposed to ever find out. But since he has, well, I don't want him to think badly of me."

Kelsey frowned, not quite understanding the woman's concern. "That would be a bit hypocritical of him, don't you think?"

"Not necessarily," Molly replied. "There are other factors — but it's not important. I'll wait and speak to him another day." Then she too left.

When the next knock came at the door, Kelsey no longer assumed it would be Derek. It was, though, and he had one arm hidden behind his back. He brought it around to hand her some very exquisite roses.

She smiled in pleasure. "Goodness, where did you find these at this time of year?"

"I raided m'father's conservatory."

"Oh, Derek, you shouldn't have."

He grinned, pulling her into his arms for a tight squeeze. "He won't miss them, with the hundreds of different varieties that he has. But I certainly missed you today."

Kelsey stiffened, recalling her other visitors. "I'm surprised you had time to, seeing as the day has been so eventful for you."

He looked down at her warily. "How would you know it's been eventful?"

"Your father was here."

He let go of her to rake a hand through

his hair. "Bloody hell. He didn't upset you, did he?"

"No, why would the fact that you told your *whole* family about us upset me? As for your father, he just needed some reassurances that I wouldn't be marrying you."

"Bloody hell," Derek said again, looking quite exasperated.

And before he had fully digested that, she added, "Your mother was here, too."

"My *mother!*"

"Yes, she was worried that you were upset over what you found out tonight."

"Found out? Oh, you're talking about Molly? But she's not . . . my . . . No! She can't be. He told me my mother was dead!"

Kelsey blanched, hearing that. "Oh, Derek, I'm so sorry. I assumed that you knew who your mother was, just that you didn't know that she was still your father's mistress. But please, I was only guessing — and obviously, incorrectly. She didn't say she was your mother."

"No, she wouldn't. I was never to know, apparently. But I see it clearly now. She's my mother, all right. And damn them both for keeping that from me."

50

Derek was absolutely furious. His mother was alive — and not just alive; she'd been living all those years right there in Haverston. And they hadn't seen fit to tell him. They'd let him think that Molly was no more than a servant. They'd let him think his mother was dead.

That couldn't be forgiven. Jason could have told him anything else, that she had run off, that she was too ashamed to have her identity known, that she wanted nothing to do with the son she'd borne. Anything else would have been easier to stomach than that she had been there all along and he had been unaware.

He went looking for his father. He supposed he should have given himself time to calm down first. Kelsey had suggested that, had tried to stop him from returning to Haverston that night.

But he was too livid to listen to reason. And the more he thought about it, the angrier he became. There would be no calming down, at least not until he had some answers.

He didn't find his father in his room, nor anywhere else in the main part of the house. He either wasn't there — or he was with Molly. Derek suspected the latter and went down to the servants' wing to find out. He didn't need to ask which room was hers. He'd been there many times as a child, when he'd fallen into the habit of taking his woes to Molly. And how natural it had been to do so, now that he thought of it.

And he was correct. He could hear their voices in the room before he knocked. Then the silence afterward, which was even more telling.

Molly answered the door, and her surprise was evident. "Derek! Did Kelsey tell you I wished to speak with you?"

He stepped into the room. There was no sign of Jason, and no place in the room to hide a man that large. Yet he *had* heard his father's voice. He hadn't just imagined it.

He looked at Molly. "No, was she supposed to tell me that?"

"Well, no," she said, finally noticing that his expression was too tightly contained, that something was definitely wrong. Warily, she added, "But, then, what are you doing here this late, Derek?"

He didn't answer that. He instead called out to the room at large, "You might as well come out, Father. I know you're here."

Molly gasped. Several long moments passed while Jason decided whether or not to reveal himself. And then a section of the wall opened, reminding Derek of that hidden door in Ashford's house of horrors.

"How convenient," Derek sneered. "I suppose it leads directly to your room?" he asked his father and got a curt nod. "Well, that explains how you've managed to keep this affair secret for so long."

"I suppose you're angry that I went to speak with the girl?" Jason asked.

"No. I would have preferred that you not bother her, but it didn't surprise me that you felt the need to."

"Then you're angry because I went there to see you?" Molly asked.

"Not a'tall."

"Derek, it's bloody well obvious that you *are* angry," Jason pointed out.

"Oh, yes, I am that," Derek said in a cold, tightly controlled voice. "Can't remember ever being this angry, actually. But then it's not everyday that you find out the mother you were told was dead — isn't!"

Jason sighed, a sadly defeated sound. Molly turned quite pale.

"How did you find out?" she asked in a whisper.

"Kelsey noticed a resemblance when you spoke with her tonight, and she'd never been told that my mother was supposed to be dead. I suppose an outsider, who hasn't known either of us previously, might see similarities that those who've known us many years wouldn't." And then he glared at his father. "Why didn't you ever tell me?"

It was Molly who answered, "I wouldn't let him."

"Don't delude yourself, Molly — or should I call you Mother? No one stops Jason Malory from doing what he feels is the right thing to do."

"You're thinking in generalities, Derek, when there were many factors involved. Your father wanted to tell you the truth, believe me he did. Even recently, when Frances threatened to reveal the truth to you unless he permitted the divorce, he wanted to tell you."

"Frances knew?"

"Apparently, though Lord knows how or when she figured it out. But I convinced him that it was too late to change the story now."

"*That's* why you permitted the divorce?" Derek asked his father. "Because Frances was blackmailing you? And here I thought you were being generous in giving the old girl her freedom."

Jason winced at the derision in Derek's tone. Molly, on the other hand, lost her temper.

"How dare you speak to your father that way?" she demanded. "You have no conception of the hell I put him through to get him to keep my identity a secret from you. You have no idea of the hell I went through in deciding that that would be the best thing — for you."

"The best thing?" Derek said incredulously. "You denied me a mother. How in the bloody hell do you see that as *the best thing* for me?"

"Do you think I wanted to give up being a mother to you? You were everything to me. I loved you from the moment I knew you were conceived."

"Then *why?*"

"Derek, this was twenty-five years ago. I was young and illiterate. I spoke like a London chimney sweep. I had no idea then that I could improve myself. I was too ignorant to even know that was possible. And from the day your father decided to make you his official heir, I was horrified that the future Marquis of Haverston would be embarrassed if he knew, if everyone knew, that his mother was a mere parlor maid who couldn't even read and write. My son was going to be a *lord,* a member of the peerage. I didn't want him to be ashamed of me, and you surely would have been."

"So you took it upon yourself to predict my feelings as well?" Derek said, shaking his head, then he threw his father an accusing look. "And you let her sway you with assumptions like that?"

Molly spoke up before Jason could. "I can

be very persuasive, and I was adamant that you not know. But mostly, your father gave in to my insistence because he loves me. And, Derek, you already had your illegitimacy to deal with. I knew that wouldn't be easy for you, and it wasn't. But at least it had been assumed that you have noble blood on both sides. It would have been much worse if it was known who your mother really was."

"You still could have told me. You could have kept it from the rest of the world if you felt the need to, but you could have told *me*. I had a right to know. And the fact is, Molly, that I feel absolutely no shame in knowing you're my mother. Your assumption was just that, an assumption. What I do feel, however, is rage that you have never *been* my mother, that you have dealt with me all these years, knowing I was your son, but you didn't give me the same knowledge. You let me think you were no one to me. You let me think my mother was dead!"

He couldn't go on. He got too choked up on his emotions, especially when he saw the tears forming in her eyes. He walked out of the room before he gave in to tears himself.

Jason gathered Molly in his arms, hearing her wail, "Oh, God, what have I done?" as she began to cry in earnest.

He asked himself the same question, but all he could say to her was, "Everyone makes mistakes when they're young, Molly. This was one of ours. Give him some time to get used to the truth. Once he thinks about it, really thinks about it, he'll realize that you *have* always been a mother to him, that you've been there to share all the aches and pains of his growing years, that you helped to raise him into the fine man he has become."

51

"I wish I had been there to hear it," Roslynn told her husband as she handed Judith to him with an added, "Here, it's your turn to walk her."

"Hullo, sweetheart," Tony said to his daughter as he gave her a loud kiss on the cheek. "Not feeling too good, are we?" Then he said to his wife, "Be glad you weren't there. It was bloody embarrassing."

"Embarrassing? Among family?" She snorted.

He raised a black brow at her. "And just what could you have added to it?"

He'd already recounted the entire discussion to her, but she still found it difficult to believe that Kelsey Langton wasn't the lady she had appeared to be.

"I would have told your brother how old-fashioned his forbidding it was."

Anthony grinned. "I hate to mention this, Ros, but Jason *is* old-fashioned."

"So don't mention it," she retorted. "But what's more important here, love or public opinion?"

"Is that a trick question?"

"This isn't funny, Tony," she admonished. "Love is more important and you know it. Or are you telling me that you wouldn't have married me if I didn't have a few earls and lairds in my family tree?"

"Do I have to answer that?"

"I'm going to be hitting you, mon, if you canna be serious," she said, slipping into her Scots brogue.

He chuckled. "Not while I'm holding Judith you won't — now, now," he added when she started toward him. Then, in a grumble, he said, "Oh, very well, yes, I would have married you anyway, but, *fortunately,* I didn't need to worry about your suitability. And besides, you're forgetting that the girl was bought in a whorehouse auction. *That,* m'dear, goes a bit beyond mere public opinion."

"Only a few people know about that," she pointed out reasonably.

"You must be joking," he replied. "As juicy a tidbit as that is? It's probably made the complete rounds by now."

Several rooms away, James and his wife were discussing the same subject as they lay curled together in bed. At least Georgina was trying to discuss it. James had other things on his mind just then, and his wandering hands left little doubt as to what.

"I don't see what her lower-class upbringing has to do with anything. You married me, didn't you?" Georgina reminded him.

"And I certainly don't have a silly title attached to my name — well, at least I didn't before I married you."

"You're an American, George. Makes a big bloody difference if you come from another country, which she don't. She talks like a duchess, giving her nationality away with every word that comes out of her mouth. Besides, I'm not the one who has to produce the next generation or two of marquises. That, m'dear, falls on Derek's shoulders. There was no need for me to ever marry, which as you know, I had no intention of doing — until you crawled into my bed."

"I did no such thing," she retorted. "As I recall, you *yanked* me into your bed."

He chuckled, nuzzling her ear. "Is that what I did? Smart of me, if I do say so m'self."

"Hmmm, yes — now, stop that! I'm having a serious discussion here."

He sighed. "Yes, I noticed, more's the pity."

"Well, I want you to do something about this matter," she insisted.

"Excellent idea, George," he said, and positioned her for a very deep kiss.

She came up sputtering. "Not *that* matter — at least not yet," she amended. "I'm talking about Jason's attitude. It wouldn't hurt for you to talk to him, to point out how unreasonable he is being."

"Me? Give advice to one of the elders?" And he started laughing.

"It's not funny."

"Indeed it is. The elders are too set in their ways. They don't take advice, they give it. And Jason knows he has the right of it in this case. For that matter, so does the girl. She ain't going to marry the lad, George, so this whole discussion is moot."

"And what if her refusal is because she knows how his father feels about it?"

"Then she's smart enough to know they wouldn't have a happy marriage if they go against Jason's wishes. Either way, there is no solution for them. So give it a rest. There ain't a thing we can do for those two short of giving the chit a new identity, and even that can't be done. That auction was too bloody public. If it were other than that, something might be worked out, but that ain't the case."

Georgina mumbled something under her breath. James grinned.

"You can't solve everyone's problems, dear girl. Some just ain't solvable."

"Why don't you endeavor to make me forget that?" she suggested.

"Now, that I can do," he said, and got back to the deep kissing.

And in the next wing over, Nicholas Eden was saying to his wife, "You know more about this than you're letting on, don't you?"

"A little," Reggie admitted.

"And you're not going to enlighten me as to what that is, are you?"

She shook her head at him. "I can't. I had to promise I wouldn't."

"I hope you know this is very aggravating, Reggie," he complained.

She nodded in complete agreement. "It's more than that, it's tragic. They *should* be allowed to marry. They love each other. And it's going to drive me crazy if nothing can be done about this."

He put his arms around her. "It's not your problem, sweetheart."

"Derek is more like a brother to me than a cousin. We were raised together, Nicholas."

"I know, but there really isn't anything you can do to help."

"Well, you don't think *that* is going to stop me from trying, do you?"

52

Most of the family gathered in the parlor for afternoon tea the next day. The newlyweds were the only two so engrossed in each other that they barely noticed the strained atmosphere in the room. For the others, the conversation was stilted at best, everyone taking pains to not bring up Kelsey's and Derek's hopeless situation.

Derek and his father were very obviously not speaking to each other. This was assumed to be because of Jason's stand on his son's marriage. No one asked how their talk had gone after they left the dining room together the night before but it was pretty apparent that they still didn't see eye to eye. In fact, Derek appeared angrier than he had then.

And then the butler showed up at the door with a visitor who didn't wait to be announced, who pushed right past him, in fact. The woman was in her early forties and very handsome for her age, hinting that she had once been quite a beauty. And although she wasn't very tall, she was quite sturdy in build, and at the moment, her expression, her very stance, made her appear downright formidable. A dragon came to mind, one about to breathe a bit of fire.

"I'm looking for Derek Malory."

Derek stood up and gave the woman a slight bow, though because of her sharp tone, he was a bit wary in admitting, "That would be me, madam."

She turned to him and demanded, "Where have you got my niece hidden? And don't lie to me. I know you've got her. My husband, that bounder, has made a complete confession to me. He got your name from that scoundrel who sold her to you when he picked up his blood money."

Not a word was heard after that statement. Absolute silence.

And then Reggie chimed in, "Do sit down, my good woman. I'm sure Derek isn't hiding your niece. In fact, I wouldn't doubt that she's not far from here."

Elizabeth narrowed one eye on Regina. "Don't I know you, young lady?"

"Yes, we met recently at your hotel. I was looking for Kelsey myself, and although you said you did have a niece by that name, I determined that the Kelsey I was looking for couldn't possibly be related to you." And then Reggie grinned, delighted that Kelsey's aunt had finally learned the truth, which just might make a huge difference. "Looks like I was quite wrong, doesn't it?"

"Indeed," Elizabeth huffed.

Derek finally spoke up, frowning in confusion. "Just a minute. Am I to understand that you're Kelsey Langton's aunt?"

"Your understanding is perfect," Elizabeth replied, scowling at him again.

"But I wasn't aware that she had any relatives still living."

"She doesn't have many, but it's quite irrelevant whether you knew or not."

"Most of us here have met your niece, madam. And like Derek, we were unaware that she had any family to speak of. It might help if you introduce yourself," Jason said.

"And just who might you be, sir?" Elizabeth asked him stiffly.

"I'm Derek's father, Jason Malory."

"Ah, good. You can ensure that your son cooperates in this matter. And I am Elizabeth Perry. That will mean nothing to you, of course, since I married down, means even less to me at the moment. However, my grandfather was the Duke of Wrighton, a title that has laid unclaimed and will continue to be unclaimed until Kelsey produces a son."

"Good God!" That came from Anthony.

"She told me her mother was a governess!" Derek said incredulously.

"Hardly," Elizabeth all but snorted. "Her mother, who was my only sister, died early this year of an unfortunate accident — after she shot her husband. You might have heard of that incident? Kelsey's father was David Langton, the fourth Earl of Lanscastle."

James started laughing. "Explains why she looked, acted, and spoke like a lady, don't it?"

His wife replied. "But this is delightful. She's now quite suitable —"

"Not quite, George," James cut in.

Roslynn added, "But much closer to being —"

"Not *even* close, sweetheart," Anthony cut in.

Both wives frowned darkly at their respective husbands but were silent. They would, of course, have plenty to say later, when they had those respective husbands alone.

Reggie mused at that point, "I wonder why Kelsey didn't mention this duke great-grandfather of hers when she told me all — well, most of this."

"D'you mean to say that you were aware that she was the daughter of *that* Langton?" Derek frowned at his cousin. "And you didn't bother to tell me?"

Regina squirmed uncomfortably, but tried to explain. "She made me promise, Derek. You don't think I *liked* keeping such a big secret, do you? It was driving me mad, knowing the truth and not being able to add it to the, ah — discussion we had last night."

Elizabeth looked at Regina a bit more

kindly. If Kelsey had confided in her, when she hadn't told her lover the truth, then she must like the girl.

So she explained to her, "Kelsey doesn't know who her great-grandfather was, so she couldn't have mentioned him to you. He died long before she was born, and my sister and I decided not to burden her with the knowledge. The burden to produce the next Wrighton heir put too much of a strain on our mother, who only had daughters, and then on my sister and I when it was our turns. But now it is up to Kelsey, because I never had any children of my own, and my sister only had the two girls before she died."

"Has it not occurred to you, Lady Elizabeth, that what your niece has done has damaged her chances for a good marriage?" Jason asked carefully.

"Certainly it has," Elizabeth replied. "Which is why I would have shot my fool of a husband if I'd had a weapon handy when he confessed what he'd done."

"What does he have to do with this?"

"Kelsey and her younger sister, Jean, came to live with my husband and me after the funeral, and that fool convinced her that we were going to be paupers, that the creditors were going to take my house away, that the only way to keep us off the streets was if she became some lord's mistress, who would pay off Elliott's debts."

"Are you saying that wasn't the case?"

"Certainly not — although my husband did actually believe it, and he *had* got himself deeply in debt without telling me. But when I married him — against my parents' wishes, I might add — my mother settled a rather large sum of money on me, with the advice that I never let Elliott know about it, and to this day I never have. And speaking of which —" She pulled a fat stack of money out of her reticule and approached Derek. "I believe this is the sum you —"

Derek cut her off, "I don't want your money."

"But you *will* take it." And she tossed the money onto the sofa behind him. "Kelsey's obligation to you is at an end. She is coming home with me."

"No."

"I beg your pardon?"

Derek cleared his throat, saying, "Perhaps that was a bit too blunt."

"A bit?" Anthony chuckled.

"Do stay out of this, old chap, and let the lad muddle through on his own," James suggested. "It's only just getting interesting."

Elizabeth had glanced at both men when they spoke. Jason mumbled something under his breath before he enlightened her, indicating James and Anthony. "My younger brothers — who rarely treat anything seriously."

"Beg to differ there, Jason," James replied. "If you want a serious opinion —"

"I don't," Jason cut in.

"Have to disagree myself, Jason — good Lord, does that mean I agree with James?" Anthony asked with a feigned look of disgust. "Ros, quick, feel my forehead. I must be coming down with Judith's fever."

James snorted. Jason started to growl. Edward, who had been silent so far, joined the fray.

"Really, Tony, that was uncalled for."

And Reggie exclaimed at that point, "Famous! You four are having a row at a time like this?"

"Not a'tall, puss," Anthony replied, giving her one of his roguish smiles. "Just giving the youngun time to crawl out of the hole he's digging for himself."

"Oh — well, in that case, do continue."

"Thank you, Uncle Tony, but that isn't necessary." Derek faced the woman in front of him. "Lady Elizabeth, I can't say that I'm sorry that you weren't apprised of your husband's difficulties sooner, or I might never have met your niece. But —"

"That is rather selfish of you, young man," she interrupted stiffly.

"So it is, but I love her, you see. And I want to marry her."

Elizabeth blinked. She hadn't been expecting that. But she hadn't been expecting Derek Malory to be such a handsome young man, either. She had gone there in high dudgeon, prepared to do whatever was necessary to get Kelsey out of this appalling dilemma. She hadn't considered that her niece might not want out of it.

"Does Kelsey know that you want to marry her?" she asked Derek.

"Yes."

"And how does she feel about that?"

"She refuses to marry me."

"Why?"

"Because of the scandal."

"Ah, yes, the scandal that can't possibly be avoided. Did I mention that the title that will pass through her to her son comes with a fabulous fortune and estate? Despite whatever scandal will follow the girl, she really won't have much difficulty in finding a husband."

"This family has had too much scandal attached to our name already," Edward put in huffily. "And we certainly have no need of any more fortunes."

"So that's the way the wind blows here?" Elizabeth asked with an indignant sniff.

"No, it is *not*," Derek answered emphatically, frowning at his uncle.

"My son is correct. He will have my support if he marries the girl."

Every eye in the room turned toward Jason, most of them wide with disbelief. And silence prevailed again.

Georgina broke it first. "Goodness, James, I didn't know you were *that* persuasive."

James snorted. "Don't look at me, George. His change of heart was none of *my* doing."

And Anthony added, "James persuasive? Only with his fists, dear girl, and if you'll notice, there ain't a mark on the elder there."

But Edward complained loudly, "This is absurd, Jason. You're letting the fact that she now has fine credentials sway you? Hasn't it occurred to you that that will make the scandal even worse?"

"It likely will," Jason agreed. "But I had already changed my opinion, and I won't change it again now just because she's turned out to be a lady. I've decided that I owe Derek my support in this, so that he doesn't make one of the same mistakes that I did."

"What mistake?" Edward asked.

"That is between Derek and me. If the girl will have him, then he'll have my blessings."

Derek didn't thank his father for his surprising support. But it did put a few dents in the anger he was still harboring. And then there was that silly lump in his throat again, all but choking him.

He had to clear his throat, several times, before he could say to Elizabeth, "If you'll come with me, I'll take you to Kelsey. Perhaps you can manage to change her mind about marrying me."

Elizabeth humphed. "That's if I agree that she ought to. But after listening to your divided family, young man, I'm not at all sure that is the case."

53

Kelsey sat stiffly on the sofa in her room. Derek was there, pacing back and forth, his expression inscrutable. Elizabeth was there, too, sitting beside Kelsey. And that was why Kelsey's face was flaming. They both knew the truth now, everything. And she was so embarrassed, she had nearly run from the room — a number of times.

"You should have come to me, Kelsey," Elizabeth was saying. "I had more than enough money to cover Elliott's debts. None of this need have happened."

"That didn't seem an option at the time," Kelsey replied. "Neither Elliott nor I had any idea that you had money of your own."

Elizabeth sighed. "I know. And I realize the sacrifice you made to protect us all. It just makes me so damn mad that this happened at all. I swear, I really would have shot Elliott if I'd had a pistol handy."

"I didn't expect him to confess."

"The guilt was eating him up, I suppose. He knows he went beyond the bounds of decency. And he deliberately put the idea into your head, my dear. He admitted that, too. That he was desperate is absolutely no excuse."

"Where is he now?"

"I don't know, nor do I care," Elizabeth said stiffly. "I kicked him out of my house. Nor can I ever forgive him for this atrocity."

"It was still my choice, Aunt Elizabeth. He didn't force me to sell myself."

"Do *not* defend him —"

"Then let me," Derek cut in. "I'm bloody well glad he did what he did, for whatever reason."

"Derek!" Kelsey exclaimed.

"I am," he insisted. "I'm sorry for the anxiety you went through, but I'm not sorry I met you, Kelsey, and I wouldn't have met you otherwise."

His expression wasn't at all inscrutable now, it was impassioned. He was quite serious. And actually it thrilled her that he was — and started her blushes all over again.

"Selfish," Elizabeth mumbled. "And beside the point, Kelsey is coming home with me. After a year or two, when this mess is forgotten, she will be launched properly."

"No," Derek said adamantly. "If you wish me to begin a proper courtship, I will agree to that. But I won't agree to waiting a year or two —"

"Young man," Elizabeth interrupted sternly, "this is *not* your decision to make, and I don't believe I mentioned anything about my niece marrying *you*."

Kelsey gasped when he actually glared at her aunt. "Madam, you know very well that due to my relationship with Kelsey, I have compromised her beyond redemption. Why the deuce aren't you *insisting* that I marry her?"

"Because I will not insist that she marry anyone. The choice is hers to make as to whom she marries, and when, and I haven't heard yet that she wants to marry you."

Kelsey had to cover her mouth to hide her smile. Seeing these two butt heads was . . . surprising, to say the least. And she knew her aunt. Elizabeth was being arbitrary just to give Derek a hard time. She probably thought he was an ideal match for Kelsey. She just wouldn't admit that.

And then she sighed, because Derek was now looking at her for an answer, and her answer was still the same. "Nothing has changed as to that, Derek. I am not as confident as my aunt that this matter will be forgotten. Men know you were there that night, they spoke to you by name, and they know I became your mistress. They would be appalled if you married me. Nor would they keep silent about it."

"How many times must I say it, Kelsey? I don't give a bloody damn about any scandal that would attach to us."

"That isn't true and you know it," she replied. "You were extremely careful about creating any scandals because your father so abhors them."

"My father is now in support of our marrying," he said stiffly.

She blinked. "He changed his mind because I actually have a 'Lady' attached to my name?"

"No, because of my mother. I believe he wanted to marry her long ago, but he let convention guide him, and he now regrets that."

"But your father's support isn't going to stop —"

A knock at the door cut her off, and Regina Eden didn't wait for a "Come in" but poked her head inside, and with a big grin. "Oh, good, I'm not interrupting anything," she said, and walked right in.

"Reggie, we are having a rather private discussion here," Derek told her.

"Are you?" She feigned surprise. "Oh, dear — well, this won't take long. I just thought you ought to be apprised of the scandal that's going to break tomorrow."

"Another scandal?" He sighed. "What now?"

"Well, I have it on very good authority that a rumor is going to begin making the rounds tomorrow in London that Derek Malory's longtime fiancée —" She paused to glance at Kelsey. "Did you know that they'd been engaged since she was born?

Well, anyway, this young lady was so worried that he wasn't really keen on marrying her that she decided to force his hand, as it were, to see where his sentiments lay."

"Reggie, what *are* you talking about?" Derek asked incredulously. "I've never been engaged in my life!"

"Of course you have, cousin, and do let me finish. This *ondit* gets much better."

"She's lost her mind," Derek assured Kelsey. "I swear I don't have a fiancée —"

"Oh, hush, cousin, you do now," Reggie cut in with a grin. "Now, as I was saying, this young lady is a bit of a hoyden, and is fond of practical jokes — was myself when I was younger — and she decided that the only way to determine how Lord Malory actually felt about her was to force him to buy her, and at an auction, no less. Imagine that. Outrageous, I know, but the poor girl is so in love with him that she wasn't thinking clearly on the matter. And he did pay to get her out of that silly auction, an exorbitant sum, I might add. So romantic, don't you think? Of course, he took her straight back to her aunt, and he's moved up the wedding date, to ensure that she doesn't do anything else so foolish."

Derek was flabbergasted. "Good God, Reggie, you've actually solved it, and brilliantly!"

She beamed at him, though with a bit of

a smirk. "Didn't I though. And by the by, even Uncle Edward agrees that this scandal is so silly that it will cause only a few chuckles among the *ton,* at least among the gentlemen. The ladies, now, are going to think it's quite romantic, just as I do."

"That's likely true," Elizabeth agreed. "It does have a certain appeal, with the young man forced to rescue the lady from her folly."

"Kelsey?" Derek said. "This scandal is nothing compared with the truth, which no one will ever know about."

She knew what he was asking her. And she didn't answer immediately. It took a few moments for it to sink in that the reason she had given for not marrying him was gone. And the reason she hadn't given him was now her only obstacle to happiness.

She blurted it out. "You expect me to marry a man who has never once said he loves me?"

Derek stared at her incredulously. Regina rolled her eyes. Elizabeth actually chuckled, saying, "Men are so remiss when it comes to that. They'll tell everyone else, except the one who needs to hear it."

"So are women," Derek pointed out, and raised a brow at Kelsey. "Or have I heard that sentiment from you?"

Kelsey blushed now. "I suppose I have been remiss as well."

"This is possibly our cue to leave," Reggie said to Elizabeth.

"Quite right."

Kelsey was still staring at Derek, didn't even hear the door close upon her friend and aunt. And he took her hand and pulled her off the sofa, then kissed her hand gently.

"Say it, m'dear. Say you love me."

"I do," she admitted. "Very, very much."

He grinned at her. "I knew that. And you knew that I love you. You've known it since I first asked you to marry me. Why else would I want you for my wife?"

She sighed and leaned into him. "Who knows what motivates a man? I certainly don't. I needed to hear it, Derek."

He hugged her close. "Silly girl, you'll never stop hearing it now."

54

Derek entered the parlor at Haverston with Kelsey at his side, her hand firmly clasped in his. "I have another announcement to make," he said proudly to his family, gathered there.

"Not necessary, dear boy," James replied, smiling at him. "The look on your face says it all."

"Let him say it anyway, old man," Anthony told his brother. "Ain't often a Malory willingly puts the shackles on."

Derek grinned. "Lady Kelsey has agreed to marry me, thanks to Reggie's rumor-spreading capabilities. By the by, where is the minx? I owe her a bloody big hug."

"I'd say she's off gloating with that bounder she married," James answered dryly. "The little darling is just too pleased with herself just now."

"And rightly so," Amy put in. "I'm so happy for you, Derek."

"Still say moving to America was the better option," Warren added.

"Bite your tongue, Yank," James said. "My nephew happens to be *civilized*. He wouldn't have liked living amongst you hot-headed barbarians."

Warren just chuckled. "You married one

of those Americans, or has that slipped your notice?"

"My George is an exception, I'll have you know," James insisted.

"Thank you — I think," Georgina said with a grin.

But Anthony complained, "You know, he's *no* fun to goad anymore, indeed he ain't. But at least old Nick still takes the bait — very dependably, too, I might add."

"Don't he though?" James grinned. "But, then, the English *are* much more dependable."

Warren just snorted at that added dig, but Edward said, "Give it a rest, you two. This is a time for well-wishing," and then he added gruffly, smiling at Kelsey, "A pleasure to meet you, m'dear. I'm sure you'll make a fine addition to the Malory fold."

"Yes, she will," Jason said quietly.

Derek glanced at his father, in his usual spot by the fireplace. Jason's expression was guarded, but Derek couldn't blame him for that. Their last words hadn't been at all pleasant.

"Might I have a word with you, Father?"

Jason nodded and led the way to his study. Derek brought Kelsey with him. And they came upon Molly coming down the hall, which saved him having to fetch her.

"Would you join us, please?" Derek asked

her, indicating the study, which Jason had already entered.

Molly nodded stiffly and preceded him, moving to stand beside Jason. Derek felt guilty for causing her wariness. She was his mother — but he still hadn't quite gotten used to that fact.

"I was angry, I'll admit," Derek began. "But there's no room for that with the happiness I'm feeling now." He brought Kelsey's hand up to his lips, in case there was any doubt about what had caused his happiness. "But with those hot emotions no longer clouding my thinking, I've realized a few things."

He had to pause to clear his throat. That damn lump was starting to rise again. And Molly's expression had softened. She had smiled at Kelsey. She was now smiling at Derek.

"Oh, hell," he said, and crossed the room to gather Molly into his arms. "I'm sorry. I didn't mean to cause you any distress. I was just so shocked, and felt so — deprived." He leaned back to look at her. "I *know* you've always been there when I needed a mother. I just wish I could have called you Mother. But I think I understand why you felt that wasn't necessary."

"Not unnecessary, Derek," she replied gently. "Just better for you — but I'll admit now that I might have been wrong to make that decision. I missed so much because of it. And now, knowing how you feel, I'll probably always regret it —"

"Don't," he cut in. "There have been too many regrets already. And at least I know now. I'll understand, though, if you still don't want me to call you Mother."

She burst into tears then, and hugged him tight. "Oh, Derek, I've always loved you so! You can call me any bloody thing you like."

He laughed at that. Jason chuckled as well. Derek looked over her head at his father, and saw something he never had before. Jason really and truly loved Molly Fletcher. It was there in his eyes as he looked at her.

"I don't suppose you two have thought about getting married yourselves?" he asked.

Jason gave a long-suffering sigh. "She still won't have me."

Molly humphed as she wiped her eyes. "*That* isn't necessary," she said. To Derek she added, "Your father and I live very happily as we are, I'll have you know. There's no need to stir up a hornet's nest just for a silly piece of paper, no need a'tall."

"I plan to work on it," Jason said, winking at Derek.

Derek grinned. "Sort of figured you would."

"But I won't be changing my mind," Molly said, then smiled at Jason. "Although I won't mind your efforts to try."

Later that night, when Derek took Kelsey back to the inn to pack her things — she would be moving into Haverston until the wedding — he said, "You know, my Uncle Anthony had a good point tonight at dinner. I really don't dare risk getting you angry with me — ever."

Kelsey grinned. "Your uncle was being silly. Shooting husbands doesn't *really* run in my family. Now, tossing them into fire-places is another matter."

Derek laughed, pulling her into his arms. "I'll remember that, luv. But I don't plan to ever make you angry with me. Madly in love with me is how I'll be keeping you."

"Hmmm, that sounds nice," she said, kissing his cheek, then his neck. "Can I have a little demonstration, d'you think?"

He groaned and sought her lips for a very heated kiss. "Your wish is my command," he said huskily a few minutes later. "And that's one request that I'll never get tired of hearing."

She looked up at him with love gleaming in her gray eyes. "Then show me, Derek. Show me now."

He did, with the greatest pleasure.